Secret Island

Secret Island

Jane Aiken Hodge

G. P. PUTNAM'S SONS / NEW YORK

G. P. Putnam's Sons
Publishers Since 1838
200 Madison Avenue
New York, NY 10016
First American Edition 1985
Copyright © 1985 by Jane Aiken Hodge

Library of Congress Cataloging in Publication Data

Hodge, Jane Aiken.
Secret island.

I. Title.
PS3558.O342S4   1985   813'.54   85-12118
ISBN 0-399-13038-1

Printed in the United States of America

1 2 3 4 5 6 7 8 9 10

1

'You nearly didn't make it.' The girl with the purple hair sat down again and refastened her seat belt. 'I was hoping I'd get your window seat.'

'Sorry to disappoint you.' Daphne Vernon shoved her bag under the seat in front and fastened her own belt. 'I near as hell missed it. Trouble on the line.' She was still breathless from the swift dash through the Gatwick terminal buildings. 'We've been sitting outside the station for half an hour. Signal failure or something.' She ran her hand through naturally curling short, dark hair. 'I thought I'd go round the bend; start to scream or something.'

'Much good that would have done.' Heavy eye make-up and the purple hair in spikes.

'I don't think.' If she had started, would she have been able to stop? 'They nearly didn't let me through at check-in. Said they were closed, and not very nice with it.' Was it when they saw the red label that had come with her ticket that they changed their minds? 'Lucky I'm travelling light.'

'You mean that's all you've got?' She looked down in amazement at the small case under the seat, and Daphne thought she was perhaps older than her way-out appearance suggested. Older than herself? Nearer thirty than twenty?

'I hate a lot of baggage. Just as well this time.' She fastened her seat belt. 'Bring as little as possible,' Cousin Sophia had said in her letter, 'we live differently, here on Temi.' What would she have done if she had missed the plane? It did not bear thinking of.

'We're moving already! You did run it fine, and no mistake. Mind if I hold your hand? I don't much fancy take-off. And on my own, too. My girl friend let me down

5

at the last moment. 'Flu, she said. I reckon it's a new man myself. How mean can you get? What am I going to do on Kos, all by myself? You on your own?' An unmistakable note of hope as her cold hand found and gripped Daphne's.

'Not exactly. I'm going to relations . . . a cousin.' The instructions in the letter had been explicit. 'I value my privacy. Please tell no one where you are going.'

Cousin Sophia. If she had gone ahead and killed herself that night, as she had planned, she would never have had the letter. And she had meant to do it. She had most certainly meant to. After the disaster of her marriage, the teaching job in Brighton had been a miracle, life-saving. Losing that had been bad; the long unavailing search for another had been soul destroying. And the battle with the Social Security people had not helped. Gradually, trudging the summer Brighton streets, watching her hoarded savings dwindle away, she had felt the old, grey tide of depression drift in and swallow her. Worse, much worse than at school, or after the parting with Mark. The doctor, back in Oxford, had given her enough pills then to dispose of an army, but she had stopped taking them, hating what they did to her mind. So she still had them when she made her decision, spent her last fiver on the half bottle of whisky and been handed it in the plastic bag you were supposed to put over your head to finish the business. The plastic bag had saved her life. Too sordid . . . too ridiculous. To be found like that. She had drunk the whisky, thrown away the pills, and Sophia's letter had come next day.

'Fancy having a cousin on Kos.' The girl in the next seat was squeezing her hand to regain her attention. 'Is she our age? What does she do? Do you know her well?'

'I've never met her. Hardly even heard of her. Just an old family story. She's lived in Greece always, I think. Since way back.'

'Old then.' Disappointed. 'But there'll be young cousins maybe? Everyone says Greek boys are smashing. Masterful. You have to watch your step, mind. You going to stay long?'

'I don't really know.' The ticket, enclosed with cheque,

labels and hotel voucher in Cousin Sophia's letter had been an open return. But what was there to go back to? She had given up the dreary bed-sitter in Brighton. Oxford was full of Mark, and memories. Her mother was probably off somewhere with a new man. She did not much want to think about her mother. 'What do you do?' Questions of her own might ward off what was beginning to feel a little like an inquisition.

'As little as I can. Temping mostly; a bit of modelling when I can get it. I strip well, though I do say so. No porn, mind you, just good, clean sales stuff. What about you? Idle rich, I suppose, if you can stay away as long as you like.'

'Good God, no.' It actually made Daphne laugh. 'I lost my job,' she explained. 'I teach – used to teach.' That was wrong, too. 'Taught for a year in Brighton. Language to foreign students. I thought they got a raw deal; made the mistake of saying so. So – no job.'

'Tough. How did you get on with the sharks at the Labour Exchange?'

'Badly. I was born in the States, you see. My father was working there. They didn't do their paperwork right. My mother's no good at it, and father was always busy. I began to think it wasn't so much that I'd get no money from the Social Security people as that I'd be deported. And they kept losing the papers and making me start all over again.'

'I know; devils. Thanks for the hand.' She pressed and released it. 'Pam Slaughter.'

'Daphne Vernon.'

'Hi. And here comes the drinks trolley, and about time, too. Got to keep an eye on them.' She leaned forward. 'Or they pass you by. Just a woman. Like in pubs. It makes me mad.'

'Me, too.' Daphne suddenly found herself in sympathy with her harshly glittering neighbour. 'D'you know what they said when they fired me? Of course, they weren't admitting to the real reason. Times were bad. Had to cut down, they said; couldn't let the men go, they had families to support.'

'Had they?'

'Like hell. A couple of gays; they lived together.' She paused to order her drink, suddenly aware of how badly she needed it. She had only flown once before since she was little and that had been with Mark, the time they went to Rhodes. Brimful of happiness, she had just been aware of her old enemy, claustrophobia, had grabbed for Mark's hand and fought it off, without even telling him about it. Today was going to be different.

With the serving of drinks, the noise level in the crowded cabin was rising steadily. The trolleys effectively blocked the aisle. She licked dry lips and tried to make herself breathe slowly, steadily.

'You all right?' Pam Slaughter handed on her gin and tonic. 'You look kind of rough.'

'I don't like planes much either.' Swallowing and speaking were both getting harder, her throat tight with panic. The grey walls of the cabin pressed in on her. A hammer beat in her head; sweat seeped on to her forehead and the palms of her hands. I am not going to faint. It is all in the mind. That was what the doctor had said the one time her mother took her to him. It had not helped then; it did not now. With an effort that hurt she switched her thoughts to Cousin Sophia's letter. 'Dear Kinswoman,' it had begun. Was Sophia her father's cousin, or a generation earlier? This was helping. Breathe and think. Think and breathe. Maybe Sophia would have news of father.

Eleven years old, was she? Twelve? That last time he came to see them. He would not even come into the house, but took her out for a walk round the little town, saying little, and left her at last for a while outside the men's room by the museum. It had made her realise more than anything else just how completely he had left them, but when he came back and found her in tears she could not explain.

'Food at last.' Pam Slaughter passed her the sealed tray of packaged, hygienic, unappetising food. 'And am I ever ready for it.' She had bought two bottles of sparkling white wine and pressed one of them on Daphne. 'You look as if you could do with it. Been having a bad time, then?'

'Kind of.' Depressing that it showed so clearly. But of course it did. Loved by Mark, she had known herself beautiful, male heads turning when she passed. Losing him, she had given up, felt herself returning to anonymity.

'You could do a lot with yourself, you know.' Pam Slaughter poured wine for them both. 'Your hair's O.K. All you need's a bit of colour; eye make-up, a little trouble taken.'

'Why?'

'How do you mean, why?'

'Why should I bother?' She had had this conversation so often that it came easily, and, meanwhile, the waves of giddiness were slackening, the pounding in her head had eased.

'You really are in a low.' Pam Slaughter refilled her glass. 'If it's a man, I can tell you, he's not worth it. And if you're trying to tell me women only make the best of themselves for men, I won't believe you. We do it for each other, love, and don't you forget it.'

'Competing,' said Daphne. 'I don't want any part of it.'

'You poor thing.' Tolerance verged on disdain in her tone and she rather ostentatiously dug out a Greek phrase book from her capacious bag and began to study it. Daphne knew she should be doing the same thing, but closed her eyes instead, trying to blot out the looming walls, the babble of talk. Cousin Sophia. Father used to talk about her sometimes. The wonderful cousin, he called her. Why? Memory closed down there. Something mother had said? Probably. Was it that phrase of father's that had made it possible to accept Sophia's amazing invitation? No. She would have anyway. It had been so strange, so vivid, to wake up that morning and find herself alive after all. Intended suicide concentrates the mind wonderfully. Besides, there had been something curiously heart-warming about the tone of the letter that began, 'Dear Kinswoman'. Not to mention the powerful argument of the cheque it contained. Cousin Sophia . . . Her breathing eased gently into sleep.

'We're almost down.' She was waked by a nudge in the ribs. 'Had a good sleep?'

'Marvellous.' Looking out and down, she saw parched, golden earth, a great dark sweep of sea, a white church on a hill.

'Greece.' Pam leaned across her again. 'Looks like the back side of nowhere to me. Ooh, there's the seat belt sign. My ears feel funny.' She clutched Daphne's hand. 'I wish we were down. You being met?'

'A taxi.' The plane touched, bounced a little, steadied on the short runway.

'Lucky you. There are dozens on my tour; all different hotels; we'll be hours . . .' She let it trail off hopefully, but Daphne remembered Sophia's letter and hardened her heart.

'Nice to be with a tour,' she said. 'They'll look after you.'

'I hope.' She stood up as the plane came to a standstill. 'I feel a wreck, but what the hell.' In fact, she had redone her elaborate face while Daphne was asleep, and Daphne, quickly applying a token gesture of lipstick, felt the usual mixture of distaste and inadequacy. The man across the aisle stood back to let her follow Pam. Surely she had seen him somewhere before? Imagination, probably. Since the long misery of the parting from Mark, her memory had tended to play her up. Names and faces . . . faces and names . . .

Outside, the air was warm and smelt of herbs. She paused for a moment to savour it, and the feel of the sun on her back, and the man from across the aisle bumped into her and begged her pardon.

'That's O.K.' She joined Pam Slaughter for the walk to the small terminal building. Inside, a tired official flicked an impatient finger as she fumbled for her passport. 'Not very civil.' Pam followed her through the channel.

'No. I suppose he's been at it all day. That looks like your man.'

'So it is.' The man with the big tour placard was already surrounded by a labelled group. 'Good luck, then, Daph. Maybe I'll drop in on you at the Zephyros some time and see how you're getting on.' She raised a friendly hand and moved off to join the group.

Left alone, Daphne puzzled for a moment, then looked down at the label on her bag. Pam Slaughter had sharp eyes. An odd creature. What really went on behind the elaborate exterior? It was not only that she was older than she behaved; there was surely something phoney, too, about all that feminist talk. Anyway, she was gone, and it was a surprisingly great relief to be free of her too-instant friendliness.

No need to wait for the luggage to come up, and there seemed to be no customs examination, nothing to stop her walking out into the brilliant sunlight, one of the first to do so. Outside, she stood for a moment, blinking, dazzled, wishing she had not packed her dark glasses. Buses, a few taxis, a couple of mini-vans; it was like an airport anywhere in the world, only less of it. People were beginning to crowd out now, pushing past her, making for the buses, talking in the high, excited tones of recent arrival. What would she do if nobody met her?

'Hotel Zephyros?' The little man in the shabby brown suit pointed to her red luggage label.

'Yes, thank you. I hope you haven't had long to wait.'

'Is O.K.' He shrugged, picked up her case and led the way to a taxi parked by itself.

She would have liked to sit in front, but got meekly into the back when he opened the door for her. The wine had brought out ingrained fatigue and the drive was a blur of random impressions. The airport, high up on a plateau, deep gulleys falling away from it, a glimpse of sea, deep blue in evening light, sunshine golden on the walls of the crusaders' castle she had read about, and everywhere the brown, bleak feeling of a sun-parched land. She had expected a green island, like Rhodes, but this was bone-hard, thirsty country.

She grabbed an ancient strap as the taxi swooped down a zig-zag hill, with dizzying views of plain and sea. A woman sat side-saddle on a donkey, heels frivolously kicking in the air; a valley showed the brilliant pink of oleander and the first touch of green. But the watercourse, doubtless a torrent in spring, was dry now, like the rest of the landscape. Small, dusty villages gave glimpses of men sitting in pavement tavernas, their day's work done, their women no doubt at home cooking.

The road got suddenly better; a picture of an old-fashioned box camera with a line across it must forbid photographs and was explained by an army barracks, set back from the road among evergreens. The taxi driver said something under his breath, and she saw a slogan, daubed in red on a wall across the road. KKE and the hammer and sickle. There had been elections the year she and Mark were in Rhodes, and the socialist party had surprised the world by getting in. What had happened since?

I don't know, she thought, ashamed, I just don't know. And leaned forward to get a better view of a huge sow and her piglets rootling in a dry river bed. There were goats, too, tethered by their feet, and cows, by their horns. What did they find to eat in this dry, dusty country?

It was getting a little greener. Cedars marched precisely up the sloping hill to the right of the road. Behind it, mountains loomed, brown and grey. The driver muttered again and swerved to avoid a group of tourist bicyclists, homeward bound from the beach in various stages of sunburn: some mahogany, some dangerous scarlet. The traffic was heavier now and he used his horn with abandon. They passed a glum-looking building that proclaimed itself the Scorpio Disco; an outbreak of what looked like light industry; then he swung his car suddenly across the traffic and into a quieter, tree-lined road. 'Old Kos,' he said, over his shoulder, and waved an arm to the right. She had already seen a tumble of grey ruins to her left, now looked where he pointed, down an alley of cedars to what must be the Roman theatre she had read about. But they had passed it already. 'Kos,' he said again, pointing to the left now, where a greener group of ruins straggled uphill towards modern houses. If she had time before the summons came from Cousin Sophia, she must come back here.

More ruins on the right. She tried in vain to read the

notice as they swung left, then right, into a wide, suburban street. They passed a stall loaded with water-melons, swung sharp left towards a sudden view of the sea, and stopped outside a featureless, concrete hotel. The driver pulled her door open and she climbed out a little muzzily and stood looking from the hotel's modern terrace to tamarisks and the sea, while he got out her case.

'Come.' He picked up the case and she followed him meekly up the steps and into the hotel lobby.

There was no one at the desk, but a neat, dark, firm-featured woman rose from a seat and spoke fast and unintelligibly to the driver. They talked for a few moments that seemed long to Daphne, then the woman smiled at her. 'Welcome,' she said. 'The Kyria's guest.'

'Thank you.' Daphne opened her bag and reached for her purse to pay the driver, but the woman put out a restraining hand. 'No, no,' she said. 'All is paid. The Kyria has given her orders. You are guest of Kos.'

'Thank you,' Daphne said again, glad of the phrase-book work that had reminded her 'kyria' meant 'lady'.

'The Kyria says you stay here until she send.' She picked up a key and moved over to summon the lift.

Daphne was looking round her. A couple of men sat on high stools at a bar at the far end of the lobby. The other way, glass doors opened into a small dining-room apparently laid for breakfast. 'You have a restaurant?' She was hungry already after the inadequate lunch.

'For breakfast only. You will find many tavernas in Kos. It is no distance, but for tonight you go across the road to my cousin who runs the Olympia. There you can eat good food and look at the sea.' The lift had stopped at the second floor and she led the way down the corridor, threw open a door and said, 'Here you will rest.'

'Thank you.' A small, plain room with two beds and a balcony looking out to sea. How long would she be staying here, she wondered, opening her case to get out soap and toothbrush and spare an amused thought for the battery of cosmetic aids Pam Slaughter would expect. But just the same, facing the colourless image in the glass, she took Pam's point.

Not worth a second glance, she thought, and remembered, with painful illogic, the publishers' party for the launching of Mark's book, and how he had dragged her away early, consumed, she had realised even then, with jealousy because she was having too good a time, being too successful.

He had laughed about it afterwards, admitting the jealousy, and she had walked into his arms and told him her success was his. 'Don't you see? I shine, if I shine, because of you, because I'm happy. You're my life, Mark. Don't ever be jealous again. Don't you know what you've done for me? Saved me from? I was half-alive when I met you. Shadow without substance. Now, I exist; I'm real.'

Had it frightened him? She had often wondered. But she had found how right she had been when they parted. When the grey fog tide of depression seeped back; when she became invisible again. Don't think about Mark. Not now, alone like this. It's not safe. Above all, don't remember depression; don't think of it. Don't . . . She had expected another letter; some kind of welcome. Unreasonable. Madame had welcomed her; the driver had refused to be paid; she was expected. Stop brooding; it's not safe. Do something. She washed her face, combed the curl back into her hair and went out to lean her elbows on balcony railings and look across dark sea to bare mountains that must be Turkey, formidably near. She did not know a great deal about the Greeks, but she knew how they felt about Turkey. Bouzouki music, obviously from a loudspeaker, drew her attention back to the Olympia which was indeed just across the road. A scattering of tables in a courtyard with a few trees. Glassed-in booths sheltered it from the sea on one side and the traffic on the other. A few people were already sitting here and there and she remembered the time difference and reset her watch from five to seven o'clock. She had travelled in the brilliant patchwork skirt Mark had made her buy for that party, now picked up a black shawl against the breeze that flickered around the balcony. Just as well Cousin Sophia had wanted her to bring as little as possible. She had nothing to bring. But at least, thanks to her cheque, she had been able to buy the fourteen pounds' worth of drachmae that were all one was allowed. How long would it last?

In the lobby, the dark-haired proprietress came forward to meet her. 'You go to the Olympia? If you do, I will make you known to my cousin, who is also a friend of the Kyria. Then for your first night all will be easy.'

'Thank you. You are very kind.'

'For the Kyria, we are all kind. She is a very great lady. That is how you say it in English?'

'Yes. I wish I could speak Greek the way you do English.'

'You should learn, though here in Kos you will not need it, since English is still taught in our schools. It is only the old who do not always understand. And one must be patient with the old, must one not?' Talking, she weaved her way expertly across the wide road, through a flock of bicyclists. 'You ride?' she asked, dodging one. 'It is the best way to go, here in Kos, where everything is small and nothing is far. If you want to hire, I have a cousin, there,' she pointed to a grove of trees beyond the Olympia, 'who will see you have good bicycle.'

'If it doesn't cost too much.'

'Oh, cost!' She shrugged expressively. 'If need be, the Kyria will pay. But for you, my cousin will make a good price. Just a few drachmae. You will see. Everything here on Kos is cheap, specially for you. Alex,' she hailed an anxious-looking young man with long, black, greasy curls, who was lolling on the steps of the café building. 'Here is the Kyria's kyria, come to have her first Greek meal with you.' And then, disconcertingly, burst into a volley of staccato Greek. At last, she smiled at Daphne. 'I have told him to take good care of you, and to tell our cousin you must have a bicycle tomorrow.'

'Thank you! Would you have a drink with me, madame?' She should have said kyria.

'I thank you, but no. I must get back to the hotel.' She had seated Daphne at a table that looked through tamarisks to the sea. 'Here you will be well.' She spoke, again in Greek, to the dark-haired waiter who had brought a menu from another table, and left.

15

'Thank you.' A quick glance at the menu reassured Daphne that it was in English, French and German as well as Greek. 'And may I have an ouzo, please?'

'Ah.' Alex had a rather engaging lop-sided smile. 'You know Greece then, kyria?'

'Not well, but I was on Rhodes, once. I like your ouzo and your retsina.'

'Good,' he said. 'Then I bring you an ouzo and a half-bottle of retsina, and you think what you will eat. There is swordfish tonight, and shrimps.' He ran lightly up the steps into the café building.

Daphne was reading the menu and doing sums. Call it a hundred and fifty drachmae to the pound. Shrimps were expensive, at three hundred, but moussaka was cheap at eighty. Should she have told him she didn't want the half-bottle of retsina? But she did. Tonight I need it, she thought. Tomorrow will be time enough to worry. And tomorrow she might hear from Cousin Sophia.

Alex came back almost at once with her ouzo, cloudy already on its ice, and a squat little bottle of retsina.

'Thank you.' She smiled up at him. 'And I'll have the moussaka and a Greek salad, please.'

'Not the moussaka. That is for the tourists. Not good. We cannot cook it here, you understand. We only grill here. You should have fish, or the souvlaki. *Mama mia*, but my cousin's souvlaki is good.'

'Then I'll have that, thank you.' It was one hundred and ten drachmae, but it was also her first night.

'And I bring you tsatsiki for while you wait,' he told her. 'How do you say, gift of the boss?'

'On the house. That's very kind of you.' More and more she found herself wondering about Cousin Sophia, whose name seemed so powerful here on Kos.

She took a second enlivening sip of ouzo, added a little water to make it last and took the letter out of her bag.

Dear Kinswoman,
    I am the cousin of your father's mother. Perhaps you know nothing about her. Her husband was American

Dutch and thought nothing of her Greek kin, but we had been girls together, she and I, and kept in touch until they moved to England, and my father brought us home to Greece, so many years ago, in 1912, when the islands became free at last of Turkey. Then came the war that was to end all wars, and I never heard from her again.

Now, though I do not feel it, I know I am an old lady. I have friends but no kin here in Greece. You will find that as one gets older, family grows more and more important. I am a rich old lady, luckily for me, so (I hope you will not mind) I have had enquiries made in order to find you. I learned that you have been married, and are now parted, and am sorry for it. I am not, in fact, convinced that marriage is always the best lot for a woman, but I do believe in the importance of contracts. But at least I hope that this may leave you free to pay me a long visit here on my island of Temi so that we can get to know each other.

And then followed the precise instructions about the journey. She skimmed to the last paragraph:

I shall make arrangements for you to be brought over from the Hotel Zephyros as soon as I can. My island is a very private place, and I wish it to remain so. You will understand this, when you come. So, bear with me, and make sure you are always back at the Hotel Zephyros by ten o'clock at night. My guests come to me in the dark hours. Bring as little as possible. We live differently here. I hope you will like it.

The waiter set down the plate of tsatsiki in front of her, and she was glad to see that it was the highly flavoured yogurt dish she had thought she remembered from Rhodes. Onion, cucumber, and perhaps a touch of garlic? It was just the thing for a stomach queasy with hunger and long stress. The bread was tough and good, and Alex had taken the metal cap off the bottle of retsina and poured her a full glass. She raised it and drank, silently, to Cousin Sophia.

17

2

It was velvet dark but still warm when Daphne paid her remarkably small bill. Alex would not take a tip. 'No, no.' He put the coins firmly back into her hand. 'Here on Kos, it is all included. You tip nowhere. The tourists we permit. Well, tourists . . .' An expressive shrug. 'But you are not a tourist. You are the Kyria's friend.'

'I'm her cousin,' said Daphne.

'*Mama mia*, a cousin of the Kyria! She has family, then? We always said she was like the mother of heaven, risen from the sea. But, for this, there must be a toast. Hey, Carlo!' He turned and shouted towards the interior of the café. 'Bring the brandy bottle, and glasses!'

'Carlo?' she asked, pleased that he had paid her the courtesy of giving the order in English. 'But that's an Italian name, surely?'

He smiled the lop-sided smile. 'Remember your history, kyria. Here in these islands we only escaped from Turkish rule in 1912,' he spat, 'to fall into the hands of the Italians. You will see, when you go to the ruins tomorrow, as no doubt you will, that their Mussolini did much work here, as he did on Rhodes. It is not all bad, and the Italians were not all bad either. So – Carlo has an Italian grandfather and an Italian name.'

'And you say, "*Mama mia*".'

'We all say that. We are – what would you say? – international here. Your Kyria would approve, I think.'

The brandy – 'Not for the tourists,' said Carlo, pouring – was delicious.

'Now you will sleep.' Alex escorted her to the Olympia's entrance. 'Much noise but you will sleep.' It felt almost like an order.

She had meant to walk a little by the sea, savouring the mild Mediterranean night, but a glance at her watch showed her that the leisurely meal had taken longer than she expected. It was half past nine. Be back at the hotel by ten, Cousin Sophia had said. Suppose the summons came tonight. In a way, she longed for it, but on the other hand, warmed by this friendly evening, she also felt it would be pleasant to spend some time on Kos. To rest here.

The bed was flat, the pillow hard, but the brandy did its work and she slept deeply and woke at last to the knowledge that the night had indeed been noisy – traffic? voices? – but she had slept through it all. Pulling back the curtains, she looked out on a scene awash with sunshine. The Turkish mountains looked more distant today, wreathed in mist; the Olympia was quiet; a huge tourist bus drew away from the hotel and she recognised its noise as part of what she had half-heard through her sleep.

Downstairs, breakfast was almost over, but the rather surly-looking waiter had a smile for her, and a steaming cup of coffee. Rolls and butter and sweet Greek cake and the extraordinary feeling of a whole sun-drenched day ahead of her. Why was it so different? There had been too many empty days in Brighton. There, they had been a burden, something to be got through; here, it was good to know that her heaviest responsibility was to decide whether she explored first, or swam, and where she was to have her lunch.

At nine thirty the waiter closed the dining-room door and she took the hint and rose to leave. The proprietress was standing at the open front entrance. 'Good morning,' she said. 'Here is my cousin, who has a bicycle for you.' And, when she saw Daphne hesitate, 'You will need it for the beach. Here is O.K. but Tingaki is much better. And also for the Asklepion. The Kyria would be sad if you did not go there.'

'Oh, I want to. But it's not far, is it? I thought I'd walk.'

'Not in this heat, so tired as you look. The Kyria said I must look after you. It is not looking after to let you get a stroke from the sun. So, my cousin will give you a good price by the day and, when you finish, if it is too much, I add it to the Kyria's bill and she is pleased with me. Look,' she produced a map. 'For the Asklepion, you go this way. Entrance there is twenty-five drachmae. After that, you go on, like this, through Lipari, then you turn, here, and find the good beach of Tingaki where there are umbrellas for shade, and good tavernas for your lunch.'

'It sounds lovely.' How long had it been since anyone planned a day for her? 'But I want to explore the town.'

'Today you should rest. There are shadows in your face that would make the Kyria sad. The sun and sea will take them away and you go to her like new.'

Daphne could not help laughing. 'I'll do my best.' She had recognised the way to the Asklepion as the road by which the taxi had brought her. She would let Kos itself wait until the cool of the evening. If madame thought she ought to see the Asklepion she had best do so.

Half an hour later she was wobbling a little uncertainly down the right-hand side of the road along which she had come the night before. Cousin Spiro's bicycle was a remarkable bright green affair with more gears than she had ever used, but she was relieved to see that bicycles were in the kind of majority on Kos that they had been in Oxford. There should be safety in numbers, she hoped, as a three-wheeled truck loaded down with water-melons sounded its horn and swept too close by her.

She resisted the temptation to stop and explore the little theatre and the ruins across the road from it, passed a cypress-lined avenue madame had told her led to the grave-yard, and turned left at a rather industrial-looking corner. Kos was beginning to strike her as a prosperous island, with light industry as well as agriculture and tourism.

She forgot these practical thoughts as she bicycled up the long, cypress-shaded road and through the modern gate that led into the lowest level of the Asklepion. It was early still, but the sun was hot and even with all her gears it had been a hard, uphill ride. But here was quietness. She put her bicycle in the shade of a tree near the entrance kiosk and was about to lock it when the custodian approached her, smiling. 'No need,' he said. 'Here all is safe.'

'Thank you.' It would be rude to insist on locking it. She paid her twenty-five drachs and got her invaluable *Travellers' Guide* out of her bag. She had bought it for the trip to Rhodes and it had been an effort to make herself get it out when Cousin Sophia's letter came, but it had supplied all she knew about Kos. Now, holding it, she had a bitter-sweet, overwhelming memory of the day she and Mark had driven to Kamiros. They had found the site closed, but a bribable official had let them in, to wander there alone, and make love at last, passionate, devouring love among the ruins of Athena's temple. Through all the ecstasy of Mark's love-making, it had troubled her at the time, and he had laughed at her.

With the memory, black depression swept back, filling her to the bitter brim. The sun still shone; cicadas chirped their hymn to it; a lizard, motionless on grey rock, pretended she did not see it. In a way, she did not. She was back in the cold darkness. Worse than at school. As bad as the night when she nearly killed herself. With sun hot on her back, she was coldly thinking that she could get back on the green bicycle, ride to madame's beautiful beach, and swim out, far, far out to sea. So easy. An accident. A strange beach. Madame had said she looked tired. Cousin Sophia would mind, a little, and not for long, not for an accident to a stranger, an unknown cousin.

'Dear Kinswoman,' the letter had begun. It had been, somehow, more than an invitation. I am not quite alone, Daphne thought. For the first time since Mark, I am not alone. She opened Jean Currie's good book and made herself read about Kos, and concentrate on what she read:

Asklepios — who was he? There are several legends describing the birth of the god of healing. One says that Apollo saved him from the pyre on which his mother met her death and took him to Mt. Pelion . . . his association with Apollo also invested him with powers of light and fire, probably a metaphoric 'warming back to life'.

How strange. She stopped reading. She herself was being warmed back to life. Only a few seconds had passed; the lizard was still on its rock, but she could feel the black tide ebb away. Free at last, almost light-headed with the relief of it, she checked the map and climbed the flight of restored steps that led to the hospital level of the sanctuary. There should be a spring to her left, and, yes, there it was bubbling out of the rock wall, its sound a blessing in the quiet place.

'Careful.' A man's voice. 'It's alive with wasps.'

'Goodness, so it is. Thanks.' She stopped clear of the cloud of insects that buzzed over the little stream and smiled at the man who had warned her. Harmless, was her first thought, one of those pale, sandy, undistinguished Englishmen who stay the same age between twenty-five and fifty. This one was probably in his late twenties, and she noticed with amusement that his eager gaze was directed not at her but at the book in her hand.

'I'd been hoping for an excuse to speak to you.' His smile warmed the pale face and showed the blue eyes as strikingly intelligent. 'Could I possibly have a look at your guide book? I came away without mine, and the local one's full of high-flown phrases, some very interesting grammar and not a great deal of information.'

'Of course.' She handed him the book, open at the map of the Asklepion. 'We're here.' She pointed.

'The hospital level? Yes, that figures. Check-in point and the pubs down at the bottom there, where the Roman baths are, and then you came up here to begin your actual treatment. But I expect a lot of them had been cured already by the journey, don't you? They came from all over, you know. Nothing like a sea voyage.'

'Better than the plane.'

'Just so. And the landfall better too. Were you as discouraged as I was when you saw that flat brown plateau yesterday?' He smiled at her look of surprise. 'You didn't notice me; why should you? But I noticed you all right. You sure did catch that plane by a whisker.'

'Yes.' It had hardly been a compliment.

'Furies after you again today?' he asked. 'I thought you looked a bit glum down there, if you don't mind my saying so.'

She did, very much. 'Furies?'

'The kindly ones. Euphemism,' he explained, irritating her still more. 'Like the Cape of Good Hope. Say they're kind and maybe they will be. You ought to shake them here, though, bit of luck. Plenty of women have before you.'

'Women? Don't tell me they made the journey? Surely they stayed behind, good little Penelopes, and kept the home fires burning, while the great man went and chased his subconscious through five volumes, folio?'

'Don't like us much, do you?' There really was something very engaging about his smile. 'And I'm not sure you're right about this place. Don't bite me, please, but just because modern women have a raw deal, and I'm with you there, it doesn't follow it's always been the case.'

'No? You think Daphne liked turning into a laurel? And Danae being taken by a shower of gold? Or Europa and that damned bull . . .' She paused, running out of instances.

'Well, it might have been more fun than the *Kinder, Kirche, Küche* bit, if you think about it. And, anyway, I was thinking of earlier still. Very powerful, I think women were, in the original Greek set-up. Look!' He had been, rather disconcertingly, looking not at but beyond her as he spoke. 'Come and see this. Case in point, I think, and not in my guide book, or yours. Which maybe says something about the modern world.' He took her arm and guided her away from the spring, to step across the little stream where the wasps were less thick. 'Just look at her.' He pointed at a huge, headless statue of a woman leaning against the retaining wall at the back of the plateau. 'The Christians chopped off their heads,' he explained. 'All the statues. Or flattened their noses. Pity. They should have domesticated them, the way they did the sacred places. But maybe they thought they were too tough stuff, and maybe they were right. She's not exactly a ringer for the Virgin Mary, is she?'

'No. She's splendid.' Daphne was admiring the flowing line of draperies.

'Yes. And powerful. There's another, see.' He pointed along the wall. 'And more in the Museum. I was there when it opened this morning,' he explained. 'Pity to waste a minute.'

'You're not here for long?'

'I don't know. I'm waiting for a very special invitation. If it comes, I'm off. If not . . . oh well, I'll cross that bridge when I have to. But I hope it won't come to that. Everyone says she's a friend of learning, the Kyria.'

'Kyria?' She turned to him in surprise.

'Ha! I was right.' He looked like a chess player aware of a brilliant move. 'Red labels. Always uses them, they say. Stroke of luck when I spotted yours, and then when I saw you this morning. Well!'

'I don't understand.'

'You're here by her invitation, I take it. Lucky you. She'll chase your furies for you, if half what I've heard is true. I'm . . . just hoping to be asked. Maybe you'll put in a word for me when you get there? I'd take it kindly. Tell her I'm harmless. I really am; no kidding. Jacob Braun. A. M. Harvard. Failed D.Phil., Oxford. Address Boston or Oxford depending on the time of year. Book in progress, of course. You can have the whole c.v., if you like. I can do it by heart.'

'Boston?'

'Good. I have surprised you. You thought me a typical, mild Englishman, and all the time I am a Sephardic Jewish redhead from the States. You think me a mad archaeologist, and I am merely a failed D.Phil. It does you good to be surprised,' he concluded, with pleasure.

'I hadn't thought that much about you,' she said crossly, because she had. 'You don't seem to know much more than I do. And no guide book, either.'

'But I know that I do not know,' he said. 'That's what counts. And how to set about finding out.'

'Like borrowing my guide book?'

'Right. A double gambit. Your guide book and your

influence with the Kyria Sophia. I do badly want to meet her. She's quite a lady, from the little one can find out. But you don't want to talk about her?' He was quick, this Jacob Braun. 'So – let's make the most of this useful guide book of yours.' And he proceeded to take her on what she found an almost too capable tour of the site, pausing at last at the very top, where a rough flight of steps led to a path up through the pine woods. 'Shall we follow the example of Asklepios' patients, and go for a walk in these sweet-scented woods, doubtless the sacred grove?'

'No,' she said. And then, aware that it had come out more abruptly than she intended, 'Thank you. But I'd really rather like to have another look round by myself. If I might have my guide book back?' Absurd to be so out-of-reason disappointed not to have had this magical place to herself. There had been something so strange, so strong about that first sense of healing warmth; she had wanted to explore it further in her mind, not to be lectured about Greek myth by this opportunist stranger.

'I'm sorry. I've bored you.' He looked so dashed as he handed back the guide book that she felt a wave of mixed irritation and sympathy. 'Forgive me, and dine with me tonight? I do want to persuade you that I'm harmless.'

'So I'll speak to the Kyria?' But after all, why not?

'Among other reasons.' He produced a street map from the top pocket of his shirt. 'I found a pleasant restaurant last night, here, under trees on the edge of the Agora. It's called the Coral; anyone will direct you. I'll get there early and get a table; say seven thirty? Please?'

'Right.' Once again she knew she sounded ungracious. 'Thank you.' She took the guide book and walked away from him across the top terrace, half-aware of the wide view, miserably certain that the place had lost its magic for her. She turned when she reached the top of the triple flight of steps, meaning to wave a friendly goodbye and make up a little for what she felt to have been her churlishness, but all she could see was his back, disappearing into the pine woods.

So much for that. She paused at what Jacob Braun had

told her was the altar of Asklepios, trying to will herself back into the mood he had broken. No use. It was gone. She went on down the next flight of steps and stopped to listen to the voice of the fountain and the little stream it fed. But a German couple were arguing furiously about the best place for him to photograph her. She sighed, and shrugged and went on down the last flight of steps to collect her bicycle. I'll come back, she thought. Alone.

The ride to the beach was hot and harassing and longer than madame at the hotel had made it sound. The jeans and loose shirt that had seemed cool in England were sticking to her unpleasantly when she finally turned down the side road that was signposted for Tingaki, and the beach, when she got there at last, was more crowded than she had expected. She walked along it through cheerful parties under striped umbrellas to a place where tamarisks provided some free shade. Madame had told her that umbrellas and the beach recliners that went with them cost fifty drachs, which she could ill afford, even if she was going to have her dinner bought.

Was that why she had accepted Jacob Braun's invitation? Not entirely. She wanted to know more about this man who knew so surprisingly much about her Cousin Sophia. If he was taking her out to pump her, she would play the same game. Besides, just now, any company was better than none. The depression was creeping back. She tore off jeans and shirt, revealing the bright bikini underneath, and plunged into the sea. It struck ice-cool after the hot sun and she did about fifty yards of her swift efficient crawl before pausing at last, well out, to catch her breath and look back at beach, green tamarisks and grey-brown mountains behind. Treading water, she heard a shout, looked around and saw a windsurfer scudding towards her.

What happened exactly? She struck out fast to avoid him, he swerved at the same time and the sail came surging down on top of her. Its metal support struck her a glancing blow on the head, she saw stars, sank, took a breathful of water, made herself strike out strongly for the surface. As she reached it, dizzily, choking and gasping, she felt hands

26

close over her ears, recognised the life-saving technique she practised herself and relaxed to be towed, still fighting for breath.

She had been quite far out and their slow shoreward progress gave her seething head time to steady, but she knew better than to struggle, and lay passively, letting herself be pulled through the water by what she recognised as a very powerful swimmer indeed.

'I am so sorry!' The strong hands let her go, her feet found bottom, and she stood up, waist deep in the water, a hand to her head, where the blood was beginning to flow. 'I am so *sorry*,' he said again, taking her hand to lead her inshore. 'Are you all right?'

'Well . . .' Her hand had come away covered in blood, and she let it trail in the cleansing water. 'I think so.' But it was hard work, walking through deep water, and she was glad when he put a firm arm round her to help her towards the shore where a little crowd was waiting.

'Michael will fix you up,' he said. 'He's done first aid. I am most terribly sorry, but it is our bit of beach, you know.'

'I didn't.' She took a deep, steadying breath. 'It's my first day. I didn't see any signs.'

'There aren't any. That's why I feel so bad. You weren't unconscious, were you?'

'I don't think so.' She thought about it. 'No, I'm sure I wasn't. So, no concussion.'

'And head wounds do bleed.' His voice was anxious, as if he was reassuring himself as much as her.

'They certainly seem to.' She could feel warm blood flow down her shoulder and wondered whether it was imagination or if she was going to faint. They were climbing the bluff. It felt like a mountain. The crowd closed jabbering around her; she swayed against his arm, let go . . .

When she came to herself, she was lying on three chairs, with her head on what felt like somebody's rucksack. 'That's better,' said a voice. 'Sit her up a little. She's coming round.'

She looked about her dizzily, glad of a firm arm round her. Chairs, tables, a rudimentary bar at the end of the room, crates of Coca-Cola and beer. 'I'm so sorry.' She started to put her hand to her head but it was firmly restrained.

'Not yet,' said the voice that had spoken before. 'I've dressed it as tight as I dare, but don't touch. It's nothing serious, I promise you. Does it hurt much?'

'No,' she said, surprised. 'Not a great deal.'

'You didn't feel me bandaging it.' He sounded pleased with himself.

'You're a doctor?'

'On holiday in the hotel here. Dr. Manson. Busman's holiday. You'll be all right. No reason why you shouldn't go swimming again in a few days, healthy girl like you, but keep off the windsurfers' patch. Poor young Chris feels terrible. Christopher Maitland,' he added.

'I certainly do.' She recognised this voice, and lifted heavy eyes to the man who had both hit and rescued her. A Greek god, she thought muzzily, memories of Jacob Braun's lecture echoing in her mind. Apollo of the hyacinthine locks? 'Do you really feel better?' he asked eagerly, shifting the arm that held her to help her sit up a little.

'Much.' The room swayed and settled.

'You lost quite a bit of blood.' The doctor was taking her pulse. 'But you'll do. Take it quietly today. You might have a bit of a headache. Leave the dressing on a couple of days. No need for another doctor, unless it acts up. I'm afraid I'm leaving tomorrow or I'd take another look.'

'I do thank you,' she said.

'For nothing. Glad it was no worse. I was afraid at first it was going to mean stitches, but you'll do, a healthy young thing like you.'

Healthy? Suddenly, she was fighting hysterical laughter. She had thought of suicide, of swimming out to sea and letting herself drown. How very nearly her wish had been granted. And how instinctively, when it happened, she had struck out to save herself. That was something to remember.

'Steady,' said the doctor. 'I think you should get her a glass of something, Chris. What do you fancy? I don't know your name, Miss Mermaid.'

28

'Daphne. Daphne Vernon.' She smiled at the white-haired doctor as he repacked a neat, efficient-looking case. 'Could I have an ouzo, do you think, with a lot of water? Would that be all right?'

'Just the thing, I'd say. You get it, Chris, and I'll take Miss Vernon outside. You'll be better in the air,' he told her. 'If you feel you can make it.'

'Yes, thanks.' She let him help her to her feet and guide her out to a shady table under trees. 'You know each other?' It had been puzzling her.

'Beach friends,' said Dr. Manson. 'Chris has been teaching me to windsurf. He's good, damned good. It was the worst of bad luck he lost the wind as he tried to dodge you. Chance in a million.'

'Stupid of me,' she said. 'Not to have looked the beach over for hazards before I plunged in. But it all seemed so safe.'

'Nothing's really safe,' said Dr. Manson.

'No.' Her spine tingled, a strange atavistic feeling.

'You were damned lucky,' he said. 'An inch or so, and it would have been your temple. Not the place to be hit with a blunt instrument.'

All my problems solved, she thought. And was revolted. Life, suddenly, seemed full of rich possibility. And here was Christopher Apollo with her ouzo, and drinks for himself and the doctor. Evenly tanned all over, he might have been a Greek or even an Arab if it had not been for his closely curling, platinum blond hair. Hyacinthine was wrong, she thought, and laughed at herself and thanked him for the ouzo.

It tasted delicious, and made her realise that she was hungry. 'My things?' For the first time, horrified, she remembered her purse with its few, precious drachmae, still presumably under the trees where she had left it.

'Don't worry.' Christopher's voice was reassuring. 'They're safe enough on the beach. Kos is an honest island. But tell me where they are and I'll get them for you.'

'Under the trees,' she said. 'Beyond where the umbrellas stop. A blue towel and a Marks & Spencer bag.' And, looking that way, saw an unmistakable head of purple-dyed hair. Pam Slaughter had found the way to Tingaki too.

'You must have been just behind us.' As he moved to the door, light from outside made a halo of the golden curls. 'I'm surprised you didn't notice.'

'I wanted to get into the sea.' She felt suddenly on the defensive, and was furious to hear her voice shake a little.

'I'm sorry. It's just — you gave me such a fright. Drink up your ouzo, and when I get back I'll get us some lunch. Old Luke has the best fish on the island. Will you keep an eye on her, Doc?'

'A pleasure.' But when Christopher returned with the blue towel and the Marks & Spencer bag, Dr. Manson got up. 'And now, if you'll excuse me,' he said. 'It's back to the sea. My last day. If you're sure you're all right?'

'Absolutely. And more than grateful.'

'For nothing. You'll see she gets back to town all right, Chris? She'll need to take it easy for the rest of the day.'

'Sure.' He turned to Daphne. 'Did you bike out?'

'Yes.' Her head was beginning to throb and she did not much like the idea of the hot ride.

'It's O.K.' He read her thoughts. 'I'll borrow Michael's jeep. He hires out the windsurfers and I've been working for him this summer. No problem. Just relax, and let's think about lunch and a bottle of wine to put some blood back into you. My pleasure,' he forestalled her protest. 'And Luke's swordfish is out of this world. I trust you like retsina as well as ouzo.'

'Love it. But not too much right now.' Shock waves were still running through her.

'I'm sorry. You've been so damned brave I keep forgetting how nearly I killed you. But I'll get you home in one piece, cross my heart. Where are you staying?'

'At the Zephyros.'

'No restaurant.' Once again he had read her thoughts. 'And the doctor says rest. Tell you what, I'll get Luke to put you together a picnic supper; it may be a bit odd; the Greeks don't go much for picnics; but it will be a lot better than having to go out again. And I don't reckon that old gorgon of a madame would do much for you.'

'You know her?' She was both surprised and pleased by his thought for her.

'I know Kos pretty well by now. Been here all summer, and of course working with Michael one gets to hear things.'

'All summer,' she said. 'Lucky you.'

'Well, yes and no.' The wine had come and he poured for them both and toasted her silently. 'I just decided I'd like being unemployed better here on Kos than back home in Birmingham. I'm an architect,' he explained. 'Want to be. Couldn't find anywhere to do my year's practical, got a chance of a job bringing a yacht out, thought, what the hell, do some practical study of a Greek ruin or two, and see where that gets me. So here I am,' he concluded, 'keeping body and soul together by helping Michael teach fat Dutch girls how to windsurf.'

'I bet they love it.'

'Well, yes they do.' He met her eyes with a kind of rueful frankness. 'One of them's taking me out to dinner tonight, or I'd ask to share your picnic. May I phone in the morning and make sure you're O.K.? If you should need to go to the doctor again, Michael would know the ropes.'

'I think madame would fix it,' she told him. 'She's been very kind to me.'

'Has she so?' He looked as if he was going to say more, then, 'Here's our swordfish, hot from the grill. You dare tell me it's not the best thing you ever tasted.'

3

They finished the wine with Turkish coffee and flaky, delicious baklava, and Daphne hardly noticed the bumpy ride back in the jeep with her bicycle rattling behind them. Her head throbbed more than ever and she dipped in and out of sleep and was grateful, once, waking as he braked sharply, to feel the strength of Christopher's right arm around her. At the Zephyros, he handed her a lumpy plastic bag. 'Your picnic supper. I just wish I could share it. Sweet dreams, and I'll give you a ring in the morning.'

The hotel lobby was empty and the lift waiting. No note in her pigeonhole. She took her key, glad not to have to explain her bandaged head, found her room cool and half-dark, window shut and curtains drawn, fell on to the bed, and slept.

She was waked, what felt like hours later, by bouzouki music from the Olympia. Rolling over, she reached out to pull back the curtain and look at her watch. Half past six. For the first time, she remembered Jacob Braun and the table he was going to get at the restaurant by the Agora. She sat up quickly, and regretted it as the throb in her head became a sledge-hammer. No use. If she went, she would pass out. And no way could she let him know what had happened to her. He would think her a rude brute, but what could she do?

Telephone him? She looked at the instrument by the bed with loathing. Even if she managed to get through, she could not expect much joy from the restaurant, certainly busy if one had to get there early to get a table. How long would he wait? How angry would he be? Now she knew she could not go, she wanted to, passionately. Ridiculous. A man who was merely cultivating her because of her

Cousin Sophia. So, serve him right if she stood him up? That was bound to be what he would think, and she found she did not like it at all. But at least it suggested to her how she could make amends. When she got to Sophia's island, if she ever did, she would try to get him the invitation he wanted.

Time had ebbed away. It was eight o'clock. He would have given her up by now. Slow tears seeped under her eyelids. What a bore this accident was, what a maddening bore. But crying made her head worse. She could not be ill, alone here in a strange hotel. Lie still; relax; stop feeling sorry for yourself. Think about Chris for a change. He had wanted to take her out, and not because of Cousin Sophia. Beautiful Chris, doubtless now smiling at his fat Dutch girl as he had smiled at her. Thinking about her, perhaps? Brave, he had called her. Easy to be brave, if one would just as soon be dead. But she had fought for her life. For dear life? How very strange. And, thinking this, she recognised hunger, climbed shakily out of bed and looked for the picnic Chris had bought for her.

Black olives, a lump of cheese, a rather stringy bit of chicken that tasted of a herb she had never encountered, and, bless Chris, a can of Coca-Cola. It was warm, of course, and fizzed all over her when she opened it, but it still seemed the best drink she had ever tasted. There were small, sweet grapes, too, tasting of honey, and she ate it all, watching the last light ebb from the sky. Tomorrow was time enough for minding about Jacob Braun. She crept into bed and slept for twelve hours.

She woke with a clear head, the throbbing gone. She had been more afraid than she had admitted to herself. Facing that, she also faced her reflection in the glass and saw that comment was inevitable. The blow had caught her on the side of her head, and the doctor had had to cut away some hair to apply his neat bit of strapping. To make matters worse, she had a black eye on that side, which gave her a deplorably rakish appearance.

But it was after nine o'clock. She put on clean shirt and jeans and hurried downstairs to the crowded breakfast room, grateful that today she could hurry without ill-effects.

'Good morning.' The waiter pulled back a chair for her, then looked again. 'What happened?'

'I got hit by a windsurfer. It's nothing. I was lucky.'

'Devils,' he said. 'They and the water skiers. They think of no one but themselves. One day, there will be a bad accident and everyone will be sorry. But, till then . . . I am glad it is no worse, kyria. You will have coffee?'

'Yes, please.' She ate quickly, aware of curious glances and the approach of nine thirty. In the lobby, madame was lying in wait.

'This happened at Tingaki?' she asked. 'I am so sorry. I should have told you. You must tell the Kyria how very sorry I am. You are O.K. now? You saw a doctor?'

'Yes. There was an English one at the beach. I'm quite all right, thank you. I shall be a little quiet today, but that's all.'

The telephone rang behind the desk and madame moved round to answer it. 'For you, kyria.' She looked surprised as she handed the receiver across the desk.

Chris, of course. 'How are you today? I'm glad to know you must be up.'

'I'm fine, thanks. That was a marvellous picnic. I'm just going to have a quiet day . . .' Did she hope that he would come and pick her up in the jeep?

If so, she was to be disappointed. 'I'm so glad.' His voice was hearty. 'I'm on duty here at the beach today, but *not* running down any mermaidens. Dine with me tonight, and tell me I'm forgiven.'

'I'd like to, thanks.'

'There's a restaurant beside the Agora,' he told her. 'Called the Coral. Could you find that, do you think? About seven thirty? I'll be there, with a table.'

'Lovely,' she said, and heard him put down the receiver. He had been very sure she would come. 'It's the man who hit me.' Why did she feel it necessary to explain to madame? 'He wants me to dine with him at a restaurant by the Agora.'

34

'The Coral,' said madame. 'You will like it. But for the day you will stay very quiet? Not even swim, perhaps?'

'No. I thought I'd go and take a look at the Museum.' And just when had she decided that?

'Good. It is cool at the Museum, and never crowded, and the Kyria will be pleased.' She looked at her watch. 'In half an hour I must drive into town. Come with me, and I will leave you outside the Museum. For half an hour? An hour? When I have finished what I have to do, I'll pick you up and bring you back, if you want to come.'

'Thanks. That sounds splendid.'

Driving along the front, madame pointed out to sea. 'Look, the jetfoil from Rhodes. It comes in every morning at half past ten. The main harbour is ahead there, beyond the castle. You should look at that, too, some time when you are feeling better, but, today, it would be too hot.' She swung the car to the left. 'Hippocrates Street. It leads into Eleftherios Square, where the Museum is. There are good cafés there, if you get tired of statues. I will not be able to park, but I will look for you at the Museum steps in about an hour. Maybe more? If I do not see you, I'll wait as long as the traffic lets me, then go on. There are always taxis down by the harbour.'

'Yes, if I'm not there please don't wait. I might even walk back.' Daphne got out of the car. 'Thank you so much.' She felt oddly liberated, standing alone on the steps of the Museum, looking across the busy square, which was not square at all, to Turkish buildings that were an old mosque and the market. *Eleftherios* meant 'liberty' she remembered, and wondered when the square had got its name. Freedom from the Turks? The Italians?

Depressingly modern outside, the Museum was built in a colonnaded square around a courtyard displaying what her *Travellers' Guide* called a fine mosaic pavement. She studied it rather dubiously, remembering what she thought had been better ones in the Rhodes museum, and suspecting the heavy hand of one of Mussolini's restorers, then turned to look at the statues placed around it so that they could be seen from both front and back.

35

'Ooh, snakes,' said a familiar voice behind her. 'I hate them. What's she doing to it anyway?'

'Hullo.' Daphne turned to greet Pam Slaughter with more surprise than enthusiasm. What in the world was she doing in a museum? 'I think she's feeding it an egg,' she explained. 'My guide book says she's Hygeia, Aesculapius' daughter.'

'Funny hairdo,' said Pam, and then, 'What the hell happened to you? Somebody beat you up?'

'I got hit by a windsurfer.' Daphne's hand went up to touch the strapping.

'Rotten luck. Tingaki's a dead loss if you ask me. How's your hotel? Mine's a dump. Nothing but couples, and most of them Dutch. Tell you what, how about you and me having a bite together tonight down by the harbour, and giving the local talent a look over? They're all out on the prowl then, someone told me. Or we might find ourselves someone off one of the yachts. That would be smashing. I just fancy a cruise. Be a devil; say you'll come. I'll stand you a drink first. I wish I could say supper too, but I'm broke. Couldn't find anyone to share my room, see, blast my girl friend, so I'm stuck with paying for two.'

'I'm sorry.' A strident note in Pam's voice was making her head throb. 'I'm afraid I've got a date.'

'Wasted no time,' said Pam, without rancour. 'Tomorrow then?'

'I'm not sure I'll be here tomorrow.' Daphne stretched the truth. 'I've not heard from my cousin yet.'

'Tough. Funny if they'd forgotten all about you. You'd be kind of stuck, wouldn't you, with no flight back? Someone was telling me the planes are booked solid, that way. End of the season, see. The natives seem to think it's winter already. Oh well,' she hitched a strong-smelling, brand-new leather bag a little higher on her shoulder. 'I reckon that's about enough of this dump. If you're still here tomorrow night, look for me at the first café this side of the castle, O.K.? It's kind of a failed English pub. I'll be there sevenish. Do come if you can. Bye-bye for now and watch out for windsurfers.'

The Museum seemed blessedly quiet after she had gone, and Daphne sat for a while on a bench, dutifully admiring the rather solid statue of Hippocrates in its place of honour, and wondering why Pam Slaughter was so eager to be friends. I'm not her type at all, she thought. But what was she really like, behind that elaborate exterior? She got up at last and moved on, to pause with pleased surprise by a group of huge women's figures, many of them headless, all amazingly alive, vigorous. They must be the ones Jacob Braun had spoken of. There was one towards the end of the last gallery whose half-turned head and alert expression caught her eye and held her for a long time. A totally modern face. The efficient principal of a women's college? An eminent politician? The contented mother of a huge family? She thought of her own mother, sighed and turned away. She must buy some postcards.

She found the Hygeia at the desk, and the Hippocrates, but when she asked for her favourite nameless woman, the custodian shrugged and said in his admirable English that it was the end of the season . . . He only had the picture in the Greek guide to the Museum, and that was an extravagance she could not afford. Anyway, her mother would much prefer a view of the town, maybe with 'x' marking the Zephyros. And who else was there to write to? Her college friends had never seemed to dislike Mark, had just somehow ebbed away during the three years she had been with him. She had minded it at the time, minded it even more after they parted, when, looking around to try and pick up the pieces of her life, there had seemed none to pick.

On the steps of the Museum, hot sun beating down, she looked at her watch. A quarter of an hour still before there was any chance of madame arriving, and instinct told her that madame would be later than she had said. She hesitated, looking across at the crowded café on the other side of the square. Its shade was provided by a mixture of rather skimpy trees and umbrellas, and she felt sure that the moment she sat down the sun would shift (the earth would shift?), nothing is stable . . . and she would have it hot on the back of her neck.

'Nothing is safe,' the doctor had said. Damn, she thought, I'm tired. I shouldn't have come. Down to the harbour for a taxi? Back into the Museum, to pay another twenty-five drachs for cool shade?

'Good morning.' Jacob Braun took the steps at a long stride. 'You've not been abducted at least.'

'Abducted?' And then, 'Oh dear, I am so sorry. I felt awful standing you up like that, only, you see . . .' As she turned towards him she saw him focus on her bandaged head.

'What in the world happened to you?' He sounded somewhere between irritation and sympathy, and she could not blame him.

'I got hit by a windsurfer.'

'Good God. Badly?'

'Badly enough. I . . . I was scared.' It was comfortable to tell him this.

'I don't wonder. You look pretty rugged.' And then, smiling at her. 'Sorry! Tact's never been my long suit. Come on; let's find you a place in the shade.' He took her arm to guide her down the steps. 'It's all crowded, but down by the harbour the trees are thicker. Don't talk; just come.'

She was glad to. The world was beginning to shimmer around her; she closed her eyes and let his thin, muscular arm be her guide. Cars hooted, people brushed against her, she did not care. She was, for a curious moment, safe.

'There we are. Steps up.' He must have seen that her eyes were shut. 'And a quiet corner.' He sat her at a table in deep shade.

'Lovely.' She was looking past him to the busy tree-lined street and beyond it to masts, the feel of the sea, the golden wall of what must be the castle. 'Thank you.' She smiled up at him, suddenly a grateful child.

'Just sit,' he told her. 'Coffee, perhaps?'

'Could I have a Coke?'

'The very thing. Get some sugar into you. Poison normally; what you need right now.' He caught a waiter's eye

38

and ordered Coke for her and coffee for himself. 'Feeling better?'

'Yes, thanks.'

'I'm sorry I bored you yesterday.' Oddly he had taken a thought out of her mind. She had been wondering if it was because she was hot and cross that she had broken all her own rules and plunged so rashly into the sea. 'Trying to make a good impression,' he went on. 'Always fatal. Let's start again, shall we?' He took off his dark glasses and polished them absent-mindedly, considering her with deep-set, far-seeing blue eyes. 'What did you think of the Museum?'

'I liked it. Just the right size.'

'You mean, small. Like everything else on Kos. Yes, it's a virtue in a way, though I can't help regretting the mosaics Mussolini had sent to Rhodes.'

'Did he really? I was thinking the ones there were better.'

'Clever of you. You know Rhodes then?'

'I went there once.' She would not speak of Mark, knew it sounded abrupt, ungracious, felt herself colouring and was irritated again, both at herself and him. Luckily, the arrival of their drinks made a little pause in the conversation and gave her time to recover. What was it about this inoffensive man that so brought out the worst in her? She made an effort: 'I see just what you mean about the women's statues in the Museum. There's something very strong about them, isn't there? There's one marvellous one in the last room. She could be anybody's head mistress.'

'"The efficient principal of a women's college."' It was the quotation she had thought of herself. 'I'm glad you liked them. You see, they are partly why I so badly want to visit the Kyria's island.'

'Oh?'

'I've got a theory about Temi. The name, and the island. I've written to the Kyria Sophia a couple of times and got the brush-off courteous. So you can imagine what hopes I build on you.'

She could not help a wry smile. 'Not my *beaux yeux*.'

He coloured under the new sunburn. 'Sorry! My mama

39

says my tongue's my worst enemy. But, honestly, today, with one of them black and all that strapping. Are you sure you ought to be out and about? Where are you staying, by the way? I was mad as hell last night when you didn't turn up and I realised I hadn't found that out. I'd never make a private detective.'

'I'm at the Zephyros. And I really am sorry about standing you up last night.'

'Think nothing of it. I'm just sorry for the reason. How did you come to get hit?'

'Like a fool. I plunged into the sea without looking around first. Something I don't usually do.' A death wish? 'It was right slap in the windsurfers' patch. And then we both dodged the same way. One of those bad luck things.' She smiled. 'He rescued me most gallantly.'

'I'm glad to hear it. You weren't concussed, I hope?'

'I don't think so. I remember it all. An English doctor patched me up.'

'Lucky. But from the looks of you, the sooner you get to Temi, the better. It's the place for you now. You know about the Kyria's island?'

'Not much. I hardly know anything about her, to tell you the truth.' She must not discuss Cousin Sophia, who valued her privacy, with this too-interested stranger. 'Do tell about your theory. If I'm going to persuade my cousin to invite you, I need to know why you want to come.'

'I was hoping you'd ask that. But the last thing I want to do is start boring you all over again.'

'Was I dreadfully rude yesterday? I'm sorry ... It was something about the place. I wanted to have it to myself.'

'And I came crashing in. I do apologise. And I'm ashamed, because I know just what you mean. Have you been to Epidaurus?'

'No. Why?'

'It's like that, only more so. A really quiet place. If anyone had come gabbling at me, the first time I went there, I'd have been really rude. But, don't you see, that's why I want to get to Temi.'

'Am I being very dumb? I don't see the connection.' She was fighting irritation with him again.

'I'm sorry. You really don't know much about the Kyria's island, do you? Well, it's not what you could call widely publicised, but you can pick it up in the footnotes if you keep your eyes open. There's something on that island that goes way back, far, far beyond all the pleasant hellenistic stuff here. Are you a feminist?' he asked, surprising her.

'Not very active, I'm afraid. Of course it's in the air, isn't it, and about time too, but when I was at Oxford there was so much else . . .' Amazingly, she had nearly told him about Mark, who had loathed what he insisted on calling Women's Lib.

'You were at Oxford, too? That's nice. I wonder if you were there when I was flunking my doctorate.'

'Seventy-six to seventy-nine, but I stayed on afterwards.' Once again Mark, the reason she stayed, dominated her thoughts.

'Pity,' he said. 'We could so easily have met. But I was kind of chained to the grindstone. Can you be chained to a grindstone?'

'It sounds uncomfortable.'

'It is. Have another Coke.'

'I'd love one.' Amazing to feel so much better. 'Funny you should ask about women's rights. I lost my job back in June. A straight case of discrimination and not a hope in hell of doing anything about it. And you could say it served me right, couldn't you, for being so inactive.'

'I suppose you could. Not even a trade union?'

'My own fault again. It all seemed so temporary. But then, they don't actually seem to want to go to the barricades for women, do they? The trade unions, I mean.'

'I suppose their power corrupts just like any other kind. What did you do when you lost the job? Home to the bosom of the family?'

'No bosom to go home to. My mother . . . Oh well, she and I don't get on. And she was away anyway. I actually wrote her.' It was painful to remember this. 'No answer.'

'Tough.' She felt him understanding just how tough it had been. 'No father?'

'He vanished years ago. When I was a child. At least –' Why did this quiet listener make her feel she must be strictly fair about her father? 'I suppose really my mother left him. He wanted to live in the States, you see, and she couldn't stand it there. Went back to England when my grandmother was dying and just stayed on. Father came once.' She had never told anyone about this. 'I don't know just what he wanted, but he didn't get it. I minded horribly at the time.'

'I should think so. I never had a father, he died before I was born. In Poland, that was. After he died my mama got out – managed to get to the States for me to be born there. She's quite a gal, my mama; you'd like her. She always comes up fighting. Like you.'

'Me?'

'Well, look at you. Of course I don't know what was the matter on the plane, but it wasn't funny, was it? Black depression, like yesterday? And then you get hit on the head by the largest possible blunt instrument, and are you swooning in your chamber? Like hell. You're out studying mother goddesses in the Museum and being picked up by strange men. Coming back to your father, do you ever hear from him?'

'Not for years. I wrote to him actually when I got my Oxford scholarship. I was so pleased; so surprised. My letter came back marked, "Return to Sender". He'd gone away and left no address. Horrid. Mind you,' once again she felt impelled to explain, 'he'd settled everything he had in England on my mother ages before.' No need to tell him how soon it had all been spent. 'You were telling about the island.' She changed the subject. 'About Temi, and we got off on to women's rights. Why?'

'Because that's what it's all about.' He rubbed his nose thoughtfully, a gesture she was beginning to recognise. 'It's a fascinating set-up on Temi, always was, and is again, by what I've managed to pick up. It goes way back, you see, to some basic, original form of female worship, female government if you like.'

'The Great Mother? Lilith? Ge? All that?'

'Yes and no.' He looked pleased, as with an apt pupil. 'Artemis rather than Demeter. Well, look at the name.'

'Temi?'

'From Artemis, I rather think. Of course that's probably fairly recent; fourth century B.C. Something like that.'

'Not my idea of fairly recent.'

He laughed. 'Sorry. But you know what I mean.'

'I suppose so. "A thousand ages in thy sight . . ."'

'"Are like an evening gone." Just so. And leaving not many wracks behind either. But there's the name, and a good deal of spin-off here on Kos. Females do keep cropping up. In the Museum; in the history. There was a lady called Artemisia reigned over there.' He pointed towards the castle wall which masked the inevitable Turkish mountains from their sight.

'Mightn't the name Temi come from her?'

'Clever, but no. It's earlier than that. The other way round I'd think. There's no mention of Kos in Homer, but there's a line I think refers to Temi; it's a bit corrupt.' He broke into sonorous Greek.

'Yes?'

'Sorry. It means — I think it means, "Temi of the secrets and the strong winds." You wait until the strong wind gets up here on Kos and you'll understand. Your hotel's not called the Zephyros for nothing.'

'And the secrets?'

'Are what I long to learn about. You are going to put in a good word for me, aren't you?'

'I expect so. But I ought to warn you that my cousin was very firm in her letter. She says she values her privacy. I ought not really to be talking about her at all.'

'But how can you help it, with a pushing character like me? I'm sorry. You'll have to explain to her that I was a circumstance beyond your control. When are you off, by the way?'

'I don't know. Cousin Sophia just said she'd send for me.' This was uncomfortable ground again. She looked at her watch. 'I think I ought to be getting back to the hotel.

Thank you very much for the Coke. It was just what I needed.'

'You look better. Are you up to the walk, or shall I call you a taxi?'

'Oh, I'll walk, thanks.' Was she relieved or disappointed that he had not suggested lunch?

'How about dining with me tonight?' he asked. 'Just to show there are no hard feelings.'

'I'm sorry. I'm afraid I can't.'

'Too bad.' He had paid the bill, now rose as she did. 'I'd like to give you another note for the Kyria Sophia. May I drop it round to the Zephyros? I'm at the Xenia, by the way. Pity I'm not going back there now,' he too looked at his watch, 'or I'd see you that far. You know your way?'

'I suppose I just keep along by the sea.'

'That's it. Take care of yourself.' He was suddenly in a suppressed but visible hurry.

Left alone, she stood for a moment in the shade, watching the busy harbour, angry with herself for having talked so freely. What had made her mention that Sophia was her cousin? Jacob Braun's tongue might be his enemy, but he was a dangerously easy man to talk to, just the same. She thought she was glad to be dining not with him but with Christopher Maitland.

4

Back at the hotel, Daphne found her pigeonhole empty and remembered what Pam Slaughter had said. She would indeed be in trouble if no word came from Cousin Sophia. But why imagine that? Was Temi connected to Kos by telephone? Almost certainly not. She wished madame had been there to be asked, but a smiling girl who spoke no English had handed over her key. Despite her friendly welcome at the Olympia and the good, if expensive, lunch of grilled swordfish, she felt very much alone.

Her head was throbbing again. She slept heavily and woke to the change of light that heralded evening. She added a baggy scarlet shirt to her newer pair of jeans and brushed her hair carefully round the strapping. Mark had liked her in scarlet. 'My scarlet woman.' Suddenly, overwhelmingly, she wanted him. His arms around her. His . . . Stop it. If you must think about him, think rationally, think it through at last. He had made it clear, right from the start, that theirs was to be only an affair. 'A happiness,' he had called it. And how was she, who had seen her mother flit from man to man throughout her childhood, to know that it would not be the same for her? That loving and leaving was not her line? The permissive society not her scene?

And then, miraculously, Mark himself had decided that they should get married after all. She had never understood why, and had been too busy and too happy at the time even to wonder much. With everything she had silently longed for suddenly falling into her lap she had even begun to think sly thoughts about a baby. Had Mark sensed it? Had that perhaps started the trouble? Or was it just that marriage, suiting her, did not suit him. Damn. She slashed

45

on lipstick to match the shirt. Her black eye was worse and she made a face at her reflection in the glass. Cold comfort that Christopher would know it his fault.

But when he rose from his table under the trees to greet her, she felt suddenly better. If he had been Apollo in bathing trunks, he was an adman's dream in jeans and a deep blue shirt that accentuated the contrast between tanned skin and golden curls. She saw female heads at neighbouring tables turn as he rose, knew herself envied, and could not help enjoying it.

'You came.' His welcoming hand was cool and firm. 'I was afraid . . . How are you? Does it hurt much? You've a black eye! I am so sorry.' He pulled out her chair for her in a gesture both practised and charming.

'Thanks.' She smiled up at him as she sat. 'No need to apologise. I look a wreck, but I feel fine now.'

'That's what matters. I am so glad. You'll have an ouzo?' He ordered it from a waiter who appeared miraculously at his elbow. 'What have you been doing with yourself all day?'

'Not much. I went to the Museum.'

'Such as it is.' Patronising. 'Of course most of the best finds from here are in Rhodes or Athens.' He handed her the huge menu. 'Let's think about food, and get it done with. Their kebabs are good, and so's their taramasalata.'

'Then that's what I'll have.' Tonight, it was restful to have her mind made up for her, as Mark used to do.

'And so will I.' The waiter was hovering again, and he ordered. He was the kind of man, she thought, for whom waiters would tend to hover.

And, to prove it, here was their ouzo already, cloudy on its ice, and Christopher was rising with a quick apology. 'Will you excuse me for a moment? There's a man over there I want a word with. It's a bore being out at the beach all day.'

'Yes, of course.' She watched idly as he rose and crossed the road to the lighted tourist shop on the opposite corner. She had noticed as they talked that there seemed to be a constant coming and going there, not so much of tourists as of locals. A man had picked up two children, loaded them into the sidecar of his motor bike and driven off with them. Another man had come in from a shop across the road to talk eagerly with someone just out of her line of vision, presumably sitting behind the counter. Now, she watched Chris greet this man and saw the two of them talk with the invisible third for a few moments before a woman joined them from the darker back of the shop. It was like watching a lighted stage, she thought, as the talk became eager, heads leaning closer together. Just for a moment, she caught a glimpse of spiky purple hair as the invisible speaker leaned forward across the counter, then the group broke up as a couple of tourists climbed the steps to enter the shop. The woman moved forward to serve them, the other man vanished behind the counter towards his invisible interlocutor, who could not possibly have been Pam Slaughter, and Chris came back down the steps. She looked away, not wishing to be caught watching, and bent to pat a gaunt tabby cat that had leapt down from the trees beside her.

'Don't.' Chris joined her. 'They're all mangy. Scavengers. Scat!' He aimed a blow at it and it vanished into the darkness under the trees.

'Poor thing,' she said. 'It looked so hungry.'

'Don't you believe it. Besides, feed one and you'll have the whole pack of them around us. Not my idea of a restful meal.'

'No; sorry.' Odd how he suddenly reminded her of Mark. 'What does KKE stand for?' she asked idly, to change the subject.

'Damned if I know. It's the communist party slogan, of course. Why?'

'I saw it scrawled outside what looked like a barracks on the drive in from the airport,' she told him. 'With a hammer and sickle, too, which figures. And it's written up on the top storey of that shop across the road.' She did not add that it was where he had just been.

'Oh?' He did not sound much interested. 'Greek politics! A mess, if you ask me. And a dead bore. Have some more wine.' As he refilled her glass, the lights went out, leaving

47

them in heavy, solid darkness amid a rising babble of voices. 'Don't worry.' His voice was reassuring. 'Power cut. They happen all the time. We'll have candles in a few minutes. I rather like it. Gives you a feeling of what it must have been like, here by the Agora, in the good old, bad old days. But I'm sorry there's not a moon for you.'

'Yes. Too bad.' In the thick darkness, a cat brushed against her legs and she quietly handed it a gristly bit of kebab. 'How long do they usually last?'

'The cuts? It varies. Maybe half an hour; maybe all night. Don't worry, I'll see you safe home. Look, here come the candles.'

'Oh, how pretty!' Waiters were bringing flickering candles in glass containers which indeed suggested that power cuts must happen quite often. She quickly passed the now feverishly purring cat another bit of kebab before the candle was put down on their table.

'Romantic.' He refilled her glass and dropped his hand lightly on hers. 'I do want to thank you, Daphne.'

'Thank me? Why?'

'For being such a heroine yesterday. You'd have lost me my job if you'd made a fuss. I got a proper tongue lashing from Michael as it was, but if you'd made a thing of it he just wouldn't have been able to keep me on. He told me so. And I need that job. I just got started on an article on Koan architecture. It might make all the difference if I could get it published in the *Architectural Review*.'

'I should think so.' She was impressed, but quietly removed her hand. 'Will it take you long?'

'There's a lot to do. I'm working all hours and saving like mad. And Michael has half-promised me a bit of work in the winter. It's difficult for him, of course; it all has to be pretty casual, that's why a public row like you might have made would have done for me. I really am most enormously grateful, Daphne.' He reached out, recaptured her hand and pressed it warmly. 'Now, tell about you. What are you doing, all by yourself, on a Greek island?'

'Having a holiday. Getting hit on the head by strange men. Being given a marvellous dinner – these are the best

48

kebabs I ever had.' Surreptitiously passing another bit to the cat, she steered the conversation back to architecture and the paper he was working on. 'I suppose you've been over to Rhodes and had a look at Lindos?'

'I started there, of course.' His tone suggested that he was not used to young women asking him constructive questions. 'Came over here for a day trip, liked it, met Michael, and settled down. Rhodes has been written up to exhaustion point, and, besides, what with Mussolini's restoration and the tourists, I can tell you, I was glad to get away.' He refilled their glasses from the litre bottle. 'The Agora here is much more interesting, but there's somewhere else I need to get to, an island with an odd name, out there towards Turkey. From the little I've managed to pick up it sounds like a must. All sorts of antiquities and some kind of model village. Funny thing, it's not in any of the books, and the locals here shut up like clams if you ask about it.'

'How did you happen to hear about it then?' She put the question casually, between a bite of kebab and a sip of wine. The island must surely be Temi and Cousin Sophia would want to know about this.

'Let me think: how did I first?' He took a thoughtful sip of wine. 'It was on Rhodes, one of those waterfront cafés, a group of us got talking, you know how it is, and someone – an American I think it was – said he'd heard of a fabulous island, somewhere round here, full of stuff. Trouble was, we were all pretty high at the time. When I asked more about it he sobered up and shut up.'

'Maddening for you. Have you managed to find out more here?'

'Not a thing. Even Michael won't talk about it. Temi! That's the name. He admits it exists, and says it's none of my business, blast him. You can see, if there really is something there, it would be the making of my paper.'

'But surely, wouldn't it be archaeology rather than architecture?'

'How naive can you get! A scoop's a scoop.' Perhaps aware that his tone had been sharper than he intended, he turned away to order baklava and Greek coffee without consulting her. 'You see, I know your tastes already.' His voice was warm again. 'Talking of which, what are you doing on Sunday? It's my day off. Michael's promised me the jeep, so I can take you on an architectural prowl, with a swim or two on the side. There's a sand beach down south I'd like to show you.'

'It sounds lovely.' What should she say? 'I'd like that.' If he had not sounded so certain she would come, she would have felt guilty that Sophia's invitation might make her stand him up.

'Fine.' He tilted the last drops of retsina into her glass. 'Now, how about a liqueur? There's a banana flavoured Koan speciality that you ought to try.'

'It sounds perfectly horrible.'

'It is. Have a brandy.'

'No, thanks. I've had quite enough already. Besides, I hate to let you spend so much, when you're trying to save.'

'Good God, don't give it a second thought. Anyway, it's dead cheap by English standards.' He was paying the bill. 'And a great pleasure. I'm beginning to be glad I was such a clot yesterday. Otherwise, I wouldn't have met you. I've not talked to an English girl for ages.'

'It's only Dutch ones who take you out, is it?'

'Oh, a German or two, and some Swedes. Michael likes it. I get them to bring me here, and his cousin who runs the place gives him a rake-off. It's the way things work in Greece, as I expect you know. Not the career my mamma would have chosen for her little boy, but if it gives me the chance to write my article . . . I'll be looking forward to Sunday, Daphne. I promise I'll try not to bore you with my theories, but I warn you I've been dying for an intelligent, English-speaking listener.'

'Thanks!' Daphne could not help the note of laughter in her voice, but resisted the temptation to say, 'You sound just like my husband.' Ex-husband? Shadows banished by wine and company gathered again. She shivered and pulled her shawl round her shoulders.

'I'll drive you home.' He rose and adjusted the shawl for

her, letting his hands linger a moment on her shoulders. 'Michael lent me the jeep when I said I was taking you out. The least he could do, he said. It's parked just round the corner.' He took her arm as they stepped out of the warm circle of the restaurant's candles, another of his agreeably old-fashioned gestures. 'The last thing you need is another fall.'

'I'll say.' But he was too tall for his arm to be anything but an inconvenience, and she was suddenly tired of being made to feel a helpless little thing. She glanced down at the illuminated dial of his watch and saw that it was a quarter past nine already. Meals were a slow observance here on Kos. But the welcome lift home would get her to the hotel in plenty of time for Cousin Sophia's ten o'clock deadline.

'Tell you what.' He was feeling for the jeep door in the darkness. 'How about dropping by at my place for that brandy on the way home? Or a soft drink if you'd rather. I've got a room above a book shop on Hippocrates Street. It's on the way. One of the ways. I won't keep you up late, but I'd like to show you what I've done so far on my Kos article. I've been longing to try it out on someone.'

'I'd love to see it ... But — Sunday, perhaps? I've had it, for tonight.' Did the Dutch girls all go meekly home with him the first time he asked them?

'And it's all my fault.' He crashed the car into gear and drove her swiftly home through the dark town, saying nothing. 'There you are.' He changed down noisily outside the Zephyros. 'Safe home, Goldilocks, and not a wolf in sight. But I'll see you in, just the same.'

'Don't bother.' She turned firmly in the doorway of the Zephyros and held out her hand. 'Thank you for a lovely evening, Chris, and please thank Michael for the use of the jeep.'

'I'll do that. And remind him about using it on Sunday. I'll be looking forward to that, Daphne.' If he had been irked by her rebuff, he had got over it.

'So shall I.' She thought it was true.

'Right, till Sunday then. I'll ring you about time. Good

night. Sweet dreams. I'll hang on here until you're safe inside.'

'Thanks.' He had parked so that the headlights lit the hotel steps for her. Standing at the top to wave goodbye, she could see candles flickering in the lobby beyond the glass doors. Pushing through them as the jeep's engine roared into life, she was relieved to see there was someone on duty at the desk.

'For you.' The smiling girl reached into her pigeonhole and handed her a note and her key. 'And this.' A candle in a Coca-Cola bottle.

Sealed. Cousin Sophia's unmistakable flowing hand. 'Miss Vernon.' She smiled at the girl, put her candle down beside the one on the desk and read the note quickly by their almost adequate light. No greeting:

> My friends will come for you tonight. Tell no one, but pack and be ready. Sit on your balcony until you see a car under the trees by the sea. It will flash its lights three times. That is your signal. Go down, leave the key, no message, Madame Costa will understand. My friend Andros will be waiting on the hotel terrace. He will say, 'For the Kyria?' and you will say, 'Yes, her cousin.' And he will bring you to me.

And then, a postscript: 'Dear Daphne, forgive the cloak-and-dagger element. I will explain it when we meet. I look forward to that.' If it had not been for that postscript she did not think she would have gone. And yet, what else could she do? Go back to England? To what? Even the bleak little room in Brighton was no longer hers. No. She had come this far: she would go on.

The lift was not working, and the candle flickered strangely in the draught from the staircase. She had trouble fitting her key in the lock, with the candle held in the other hand, which shook a little. It was hard work, too, packing in the dark, carrying the candle from bedroom to bathroom, terrified all the time that it would go out. She should have asked for matches, but the girl at the desk would never have understood. At last, it was done. She put her small bag in the lobby, left the candle on a table just inside the balcony door, and went out as she had been instructed. The air was warm; candlelight across the road at the Olympia showed people still eating there; beyond that was blackness, with far away a cluster of lights that must be on the shore of Turkey.

Time passed. The candles at the Olympia went out one by one, leaving the darkness absolute except when a car went by, or a group of bicyclists with cheerful voices and wavering lamps. A tourist bus drew up outside the Zephyros and she listened as its passengers climbed out, talking excitedly in one of the Scandinavian languages, all very merry, stirred up by the darkness. She could hear them making their cheerful way up through the hotel, with much banging of doors and loud good nights, and wondered how many couples would come together in the dark. It made her think of Mark again. She shivered ... with cold, with loneliness ... and went in to collect her shawl. The candle was burning low. If Cousin Sophia's messenger did not come soon, she would be helpless here, without a light.

She paused by the guttering candle to look at her watch. Almost two o'clock and the hotel quiet at last. Would there be time to get to Cousin Sophia's island before dawn? Or did that not matter? Maybe they were not coming at all. Maybe the power failure had affected their plans. Maybe it was all an elaborate practical joke at her expense.

Ridiculous. It would be a madly extravagant one. But perhaps Cousin Sophia was mad? Strange and a little frightening to think that no one knew about her letter. Except Jacob Braun, of course. No one in England even knew she was here on Kos. She had bought a postcard for her mother, but had not written it yet. She almost wished she had not been quite so instinctively cautious with Chris. He had heard about Temi already, it would surely have done no harm to tell him she was going there, make him promise not to talk about it. Then, taking off into the darkness like this, she would have known that he at least

53

knew where she was. What would he think when he rang to fix the time for Sunday and found her gone? Leave him a message? But Cousin Sophia's note seemed to forbid this. And here, at last, was a car coming quietly to a halt across the road, its sidelights illuminating tamarisks and the sea for an instant before they were switched off, on, off, on, off.

Three times. She picked up candle and bag, shut the door quietly behind her and felt her way down the stairs. As she reached the open door on to the terrace, the candle flickered and went out. But someone had come forward to meet her, flashlight pointed low to the ground. 'For the Kyria?' he said.

'Her cousin.'

'Good.' He took her bag. 'Come. Silently, please.' Holding the flashlight low to guide her across the road, he remained a shadowy figure, a disembodied voice with a surprising American accent. 'Quick, please.' He held the passenger's front door open for her, threw her bag into the back and moved swiftly round to get in himself and start the car, which he had left running. 'Good,' he said again as they slid away in the direction of the town. 'I am sorry to have kept you waiting so long.' His American-English was fluent. 'The Kyria will be getting impatient for her guest, and we must hurry if we are to arrive before dawn.' He had turned, as madame had that morning, up Hippocrates Street, now drove swiftly and surely through a tangle of narrow streets until she had totally lost her sense of direction. He was using sidelights only, and from time to time their beam would give her a swift vignette: the Agora, full of strange shadows; a pillared courtyard; white trumpet flowers on a tree by the roadside; and then what seemed almost a country road, unsurfaced.

'There,' he said at last. 'No one can follow. Not long now to where the boat waits.' The car swung to the right, on to tarmac again, and speeded up. Its lights showed the sea on their left, and she realised that they must have passed behind the Zephyros. 'Today, we leave from Therme,' he told her. 'It is not far, luckily.' He stopped the car. 'You should fasten your safety harness, kyria. The road down the hill to Therme is not good.'

'Thank you.' She was grateful when he helped her clip the harness into its lock. Her hands were shaking more than ever.

'No need to be afraid.' He must have recognised this. 'You are the Kyria's honoured guest. It is only ... what is the word? It is only gatecrashers she fears. You will understand why when you see Temi. Now, forgive me, I must think of my driving.' The car left the tarred road and inched its way slowly downhill on gravel, round a series of breathless hairpin bends, their steep corners swiftly illuminated and gone again as he swung the car round them.

'You drive well.' She was grateful for the safety harness.

'Yes.' The lights showed sharp rockface as he turned one last corner to reach the level, by the shimmering sea. 'If you work with the Kyria,' he told her, 'you do all things well.' He stopped the car, reached around to pick up her bag, got out and opened her door. 'It is all quiet,' he said. 'No one awaits us here except our friends.'

When he stopped speaking, she realised just how quiet it was. The soft slap-slap of the sea. The small sounds of the car cooling down. Nothing else. Just blackness and silence. She felt very small and enormously alone.

'Come,' he said. 'They are ready for us.' There was a noise now, the purr of an engine starting up. He took her arm, her bag slung over his shoulder, the flashlight held low in his other hand.

I am quite mad, she thought. What am I doing here, on a Greek beach, alone?

'The Kyria says, you must not worry.' Had he read her mind? 'She says, now, I say to you that you must trust her. It is the world's fault, not hers, that you must come to her, like this, so secretly. When you get there, you will understand.'

'I don't like it.' But she let him guide her across noisy shingle to the firm stone of a jetty.

'She does not either. She hates it. '

A light showed on the boat whose dark shape she could now just make out. Hands reached down to help her on board and guide her wordlessly down into the tiny cabin. As she settled on a hard bench with her back to the side of the boat, the engine roared into full life, making speech impossible.

She leaned back and closed her eyes. Somehow, without consciously doing so, she had decided to come. Here she was. It was settled. The boat was throbbing its way steadily out to sea, out into the dark.

Amazingly, she slept, tired by the long day, lulled by the rhythm of the engine. Waking, she knew that it had changed. The boat had slowed down, seemed to be moving erratically now, a sharp turn to the left threw her against the side of the boat. She hit her head and heard herself gasp with pain.

'I'm sorry.' Her guide must have heard her. 'I should have warned you. We are in the channel now. We are late and Niko took it too fast.'

'Channel?' An anxiously questing hand felt for blood on her strapping and found none.

'Between the cliffs. The only way to the island. The Kyria says that must be why Homer called it Temi of the secrets. Ulysses and his companions would have rowed, of course, slower and so less dangerous. Impossible in spring, when the current is running strong, or any time when the wind is up. We'll be there in ten minutes now, if Niko finds his way, which he always does. This is the most secret and most difficult part of the way. There's not a chart in the world shows the channels round Temi.' He left her, summoned by a shout from Niko.

She sat for a little while, pain ebbing, making herself breathe steady and deep, willing the sick dizziness to pass. Then, as the boat slowed still further she got unsteadily to her feet and felt her way to the cabin door which now showed as a lighter patch in the darkness. Leaning against it, she was aware of the black loom of cliffs rising high on either side of the boat. Were they beginning to close in above it? Yes, the pale strip of sky was narrowing. Clutching the side of the door, she made herself concentrate on the hint of light above, fighting for breath. 'It's all in your mind,' her mother used to quote the doctor. 'Control it, for God's sake.'

Control it? Breathe in . . . Slow. Breathe out . . . What had Jacob Braun said about his mother? She always comes up fighting. Another swift turn of the boat threw her against the side of the door and brought them into a great, blessed glow of light. A colonnaded quay. Light pouring out from behind tall pillars that vanished up into absolute darkness. Black figures, silhouetted against the light, were oddly shaped, somehow. A quick exchange of question and command between boat and quay and a rope snaked ashore.

'Come, kyria.' The boat made fast, Andros came back to join her. And then, seeing her for the first time in the light: 'But what is this? You are hurt?'

'My head; the other day.' Now her questing hand felt the bandage moist with new blood. 'I hit it again just now.' As the boat steadied, the world swayed.

'The Kyria will be angry.' He said something in swift Greek to his companion, picked her up as if she weighed nothing and carried her ashore.

Voices, anxious, questioning . . . He was carrying her up steps . . . She wanted to open her eyes but it was too hard work . . . Now a woman's voice, very deep; anxious; angry?

She opened her eyes with a great effort and looked up at the face that seemed somehow larger than life. 'Nobody's fault,' she managed. 'I am so sorry . . .' The blackness closed in.

5

Daylight, and a feeling of safety, of well-being. Something cool . . . Someone was bathing her head. Peace? Safety? She opened her eyes and looked up at the smiling face that had been part of her dreams. 'Cousin Sophia?'

'Yes, child. And glad to hear you ask it. You gave us a fright, but you're better now.' It was command, as much as question.

'Yes.'

'That's good. And by what I can learn, you never were concussed.'

'No. You know about it?'

'I do now. Why no one thought to tell me . . .' The smile Daphne found so beautiful vanished, leaving the handsome face severe under curling white hair.

'You remind me of someone . . .' She lay, searching her slow mind. 'I know. In the Museum. A woman with a lovely face.'

'Thank you.' The smile was back. 'I'm glad you went to the Museum, Daphne. Glad you came, come to that.' Grey eyes set among laughter lines seemed to sum her up, but . . . lovingly? 'Welcome to Temi, cousin. How does your head feel now? No, don't touch,' she gently restrained Daphne's questing hand. 'I took the bandage off. Not a bad job, but it will heal better without. An English doctor, I understand. Tell me about the young man who hit you.'

'Not his fault. Mine. I was upset, rather. I plunged into the sea without looking about me properly. Crazy thing to do. Right in the windsurfers' patch, and poor Chris ran me down.'

'Chris?'

'Christopher Maitland. He helps out at the windsurfing place. He wants to be an architect. He's writing an article about Koan architecture.'

'Interesting,' said Cousin Sophia. 'Did he tell you all this while the doctor was bandaging you up?'

'Oh, no. He gave me lunch and drove me back to the hotel.' She felt herself blushing. 'And I had dinner with him tonight . . . last night.'

'Doing his best to make amends,' said Cousin Sophia drily. 'Not last night, by the way, the night before. You've had a good sleep – and needed it.' She smiled. 'It's given me time to study you a little. I hope you don't mind. You've been having a bad time, haven't you? Not just the accident.' She reached out and took Daphne's pulse with a professional hand, warm with life. 'Better, but I think that's enough talk for now. I've a draught for you to drink, then you'll sleep again, and, I think, wake quite better.'

'A draught?' It sounded oddly old fashioned.

Cousin Sophia was smiling again. 'You don't know anything about me, do you? It makes me all the more grateful that you took the plunge and came. I run a very exclusive medical establishment.'

'Oh!' Daphne exclaimed. 'That's what he meant. "The right place," he said. For me.'

'This man Chris?'

'No.' Smiling now. 'Someone else. His name's Jacob Braun and he says he has written to you. He badly wants to come here.'

'He does, does he? Why, I wonder?'

'He said he'd written,' Daphne said again. 'He's . . .' She hesitated. 'I'm not sure. Sociologist? Archaeologist? He knows a lot about Temi, says he doesn't know whether it was more interesting in the old days, or now. He told me about the women's figures up at the Asklepion and the ones in the Museum. One of them really does look like you,' she digressed, feeling that she had done Jacob Braun's views less than justice. 'He knew who I was, by the way. That I was connected with you.'

'Did he so? I must think a little about Jacob Braun.' Cousin Sophia picked up a silver goblet. 'I'll look out his letters while you sleep. Drink this, Daphne, be welcome, and dream well.'

Could she have slept the clock round? She woke to a sense of broad daylight, even in the cool recess of this quiet room. For the first time since her accident, her head felt totally clear, and she lay savouring this and listening to the sound of water, quietly trickling, somewhere outside the curving windows. Peaceful ... peaceful. She dozed and waked again to the rattling of china. A dark slim girl in a saffron-coloured tunic was standing by the bed, tray in hand, smiling down at her.

'The Kyria said you would be awake, kyria, and hungry.' She put the tray down on the natural wood table by the bed, and helped Daphne pile pillows behind her. 'When you have eaten, ring and I will take the tray and tell the Kyria you are ready for her.'

'Thank you.' Grapes, brown rolls, honey, and the best coffee she had ever tasted. When she had finished, she sighed with simple pleasure and reached out to ring the bell beside the bed.

'That is good. You ate it all.' The girl appeared almost at once. 'The Kyria says, stay in bed until she comes. She will only be a few minutes.'

It was wonderfully pleasant to lie and do nothing. When had she lost the gift for this? She could hear music somewhere outside (piano and strings perhaps?) and was briefly tempted to get up and look out of the window, but inertia combined with an instinctive obedience to Sophia's commands and she stayed contentedly in bed, even dozing a little more.

'Good morning.' One of the windows was in fact a door and Cousin Sophia pushed it open, showing a glimpse of green courtyard outside. A kind of cloister, Daphne thought, smiling her greeting. 'Zoe says you are better,' Sophia went on.

'She told me I was. That you said I would be. And of course I am.'

'Thank you for the "of course". Do you want to get up or shall we talk first?' She pulled up a straight chair and sat down in one graceful movement by the bed. Like the girl, she was wearing a tunic that reminded Daphne of dancing class at school, but hers was a dark purple. 'We all wear them.' She had read Daphne's thought. 'Will you mind? You will find they are wonderfully comfortable once you get used to them. Our guests are sometimes a little ill at ease at first, but, do you know, many of them ask to take theirs home with them. They say it helps them to relax.'

'You have many guests?' Daphne thought of her strange, secret journey.

'Yes. You could say it is what we are about, here on Temi. We have made it, once again, into the place of healing it always was. Not just a hospital, you understand, a place for sickness of the mind, too. And other things. Most people find help here. I hope you will. You need some, I think?'

'Oh, yes. But how did you know?'

Sophia smiled. 'It shows, a little. But, also – I hope you will not mind it – I am a very rich woman. It gives one a remarkable degree of freedom, of power, if you like. I have used it to find out about you. But, of course, just knowing the facts of someone's life only tells one so much. I am hoping you will flesh out your facts for me. Will you mind doing that?'

'I think I'd like to. Mother never listened.' She stopped short, surprised at what she had said.

'Your poor mother. I am not sure there is a great deal of help possible, by now, but one must always try. I am ashamed, Daphne, that I did not think about my family sooner, but I have been very busy. An establishment such as this is not built in a day.'

'No. A place of healing, you said? I wish you would tell me about it.'

'I want to, but I wonder where to start. With the war, perhaps. I did something – it does not matter what – but something that made the Greek Government very grateful to me. Afterwards, they made all sorts of kind and flattering offers. Luckily, I knew what I wanted. I had found Temi. Nobody's island. It's not even on most maps. Temi of the secrets. I had discovered one of these; almost by accident; the way through the channel. It saved my life. Our lives. So, "Give me Temi," I said, and they thought me a fool, and did. A dear friend of mine, a lawyer, drew up the charter they signed.' She laughed a little. 'It went on for pages. I thought it absurd at the time, but I have been grateful to him since. I imagine he had mineral rights in mind. Anyway, it gives me a pretty free hand, here on Temi, and I've been glad of it. You see, we none of us had any idea of what was here. That was no time to be doing research, with the world still in ruins. I thought – we all thought Temi was just another of the scatter of tiny, unoccupied islands that dot the Aegean.'

'And it's not?' She longed to ask what Sophia had done to earn a whole island, but was aware of an unspoken prohibition. Curious to understand this unknown kins-woman so well so soon.

'Far from it. The channel was only the first of Temi's sur-prises. When we settled here, after the war, we began to dis-cover the others. You said you went to the Asklepion on Kos?'

'Yes. That's where I met Jacob Braun.'

'Ah, yes, Jacob Braun. I found the letters he wrote me . . . But we will talk of him later. Of course you would have met him at the Asklepion. Well, when we began to dig the foundations for a house, here on Temi, we came on the buried remains of another Asklepion, or something very like it.' She smiled an almost mischievous smile. 'I am afraid the Greek authorities rather regretted my all-inclusive charter when I told them about it, but they were gentlemen; they kept their word. You see, no one had found the channel, so no one had been to Temi, so far as one can tell, since the great earthquake of the second century A.D. It was all still here, buried, preserved: the buildings, the statues, the altars . . . and the offerings. They were down here on the lower levels, of course. We found them almost at once. Gold, Daphne. Do your eyes light up? Ours did. It gave us such power. Oh, we were fair to the Greeks. We gave them their share of it all, and let them handle it. Most of the treasures have been fed quietly into their museums. I insisted that there be no credit to Temi, or there would have been an end to our peace, and by then, you see, I had had my idea.' She paused, smiling. 'But, really, you should see as well as hear. Do you feel strong enough to get up and dress? I would very much like to show you my establishment.'

'Oh, yes, please.'

'Good. I'll be sitting in the cloister when you are ready. You'll find the chiton easy to put on.'

'It's a very luxurious establishment.' Daphne swung her legs out of bed.

'It has to be, for my clients. Don't hurry, there is all the time in the world. There always is, if you let there be.'

Daphne's tunic was dark blue and was indeed easy to put on. She rather liked herself in it, and was delighted to see how well the wound on her head was healing. Sophia's salve must have remarkable powers, she thought, carefully brushing her hair around the scar. A touch of lipstick to enliven that pale face? Perhaps not. Sophia's clear brown skin had had the glow of unadulterated health. Nor did she pick up her bag. Her passport and few drachmae were safe enough here.

Crossing her small courtyard, she stepped out into a sun-dappled cloister and took a quick breath of amazed delight. The cloister was circular, its twelve plain columns set like the figures of a clock. A stream came splashing and sparkling out from below the pillar to her left and cut clear across the centre circle, to vanish under the facing column. Bougainvillaea, climbing up several of the pillars, made a green and purple shade, but was clipped back to let the sun shine down on to the mosaic in the centre by the stream.

'Asklepios and his daughter Hygeia.' Sophia rose from a comfortable-looking modern canvas chair. 'Lovely, isn't it? We had to have it restored a bit, where it had cracked in the earthquake, but I really don't think you'd know.'

'The colours are so fresh! It's not a bit like the one in the Museum on Kos.'

'It's been protected, always. And always will be, now. We put a plastic coating on, when we had finished the restoration. Invented by a friend of mine. He's dead, I'm sorry to say. You'd have liked him. Of course this mosaic is centuries older than the one on Kos, which dates from after the earthquake that ended life here on Temi.'

'Goodness.' Daphne looked about her. 'How old is all this then?'

'I'm ashamed to have to tell you, but I don't know exactly. It was a question of conflicting interests, you see. I did not want to let in the archaeologists, which would have meant letting in the whole world. To use this place as it should be used, I had to preserve its quiet. Do you feel it?'

They were silent. The stream talked; a cricket chirped; the music Daphne had heard earlier began again, quietly, strings and piano in friendly conversation, from somewhere upstream. 'It's magic,' she said at last.

'I'm glad you feel it. Whoever built the Asklepion here on Temi, knew what they were doing. It's one of the great places of healing. You've not been to Epidaurus?'

'No.'

'Why are you smiling?'

'Was I? I suppose because that's just what Jacob Braun asked me. He thought it was . . .' She hesitated for a word. 'More peaceful than Kos.'

'And this is more so than either of them. When I realised that, and found what I found, I put it to the Greek Government that it should be spared the archaeologists' boots, and their trowels, and their arguments, and restored to what it had been, so far as was possible.' She smiled her strange archaic smile. 'I bribed them, really. Gold in such quantity is a powerful argument. But I am glad to say that in the end they really valued the place for what it has become. Become again. A place of healing; a home of reason. I just hope it lasts.' A cloud ruffled her calm face. 'It's so useful. Not just as a place of healing. When heads of state vanish from the papers and the public scene these days, they are often here, recharging their batteries, if you like. Breathing a little. Or, sometimes, talking to each other, away from the noise and the cameras.' She paused, as the musicians finished a movement. 'Haydn, I think. You'd be surprised how well you know the pianist. From the papers, I mean. He comes here every year, if he can.'

'Shall I meet him? Meet them . . .'

'The guests? It depends entirely on them. Solitude, if they wish; company if they prefer it. This is a big place, though it is so enclosed in its valley. I think that's one of the reasons the genius who designed it thought of the circular shape. To give the greatest possible feeling of space, in the close confines of the valley. My architect had a terrible time working out how he achieved his curve, when it came to the restoration. Genius was his word, not mine.'

'It's the right one. Was it all originally built at the same time?'

'We think so. Do you feel up to seeing some more of it? This is the first precinct. My quarters, and the admissions section. The valley widens out above us, so the next circle is larger. How do you feel?'

'Marvellous,' said Daphne. 'I'd love to see some more.'

'Good. But tell me the moment you begin to feel tired. I'm afraid I'm an unbridled enthusiast when it comes to this place.' She was leading the way as she talked round the curve of the cloister to where the stream came bubbling out of a Triton's mouth. 'The next circle is guests' quarters,' she spoke quietly. 'We'll go through the middle, not to disturb them.'

This circle, too, had twelve pillars, but they were very much more widely spaced. Here, vines replaced the bougainvillaea, climbing freely on to the cloister roof and along a double row of lower pillars on each side of the stream. Walking through the green shade, Sophia continued, quietly, her voice blending with the babble of the water, and the next movement of the Haydn, which came from the cloister on their right. 'The vines act as camouflage from above. The Greeks very kindly agreed that no planes would be routed over Temi, but in fact you'd be amazed how hard it is to spot the buildings from the air, what with the curve of the valley and the pains we took. One problem the original designer didn't have. I wish I knew what the approach was like then. It must have been difficult, because of the line in Homer, but I don't think it can have been as difficult as it is now. Just imagine the organisation required if you had to stay on Kos and arrange to be guided in. You'd have been dead, or cured, before you even got here.'

'Jacob Braun said he thought a lot of people probably were cured just by the journey.'

'I'm sure he's right. That's not the case these days. I never heard of anyone being cured by modern travel, though I did hope you would get a bit of rest on Kos. I didn't mean you to get hit on the head.' She laughed. 'A useful reminder to me that I'm not omnipotent. It's a dangerous tendency I have, lately, because of ruling so absolutely as I do here on Temi. It's not good for one, that.' They were passing through the top of the second circle and paused for a moment to look back across it. 'This is the treatment area,' she went on as they plunged into a labyrinth of dimly lit corridors. Low voltage bulbs lit the one they were in, but dark openings to right and left suggested some monstrous, subterranean spider web and Daphne caught her breath, fighting panic. 'We only light what's in use,' Sophia went on. 'One of these days I'll have to get a new generator, but until then, we economise. And, of course, the dark threshold to the sacred place was part of the old concept. It was amazing how little change we needed to make in the original design. The pool was always in the centre, full of light, with the treatment rooms radiating out from it as they do now.' She smiled at a woman in a sage-coloured tunic who had emerged from a lighted corridor to their right. 'How is your patient today, Hermione?'

'Much better, Kyria. He has had his massage and is resting a little before I take him to the pool. He says he will swim the circle twice today.'

'I hope he does, but don't let him tire himself. It's a boy from Kos,' she turned to Daphne. 'He broke his leg last winter and it got set rather badly. We've had some trouble with it, but I think he'll be as good as new soon. He means to be an Olympic swimmer, so it's important to him.'

'I should think so.' Daphne drew a great breath of relief as they emerged from the shadows to stand on the marble verge of the huge round pool that lay open and quiet under the sun. 'What a beautiful pool.'

'Isn't it? Fed by springs, so no problems of changing the water. You didn't much like it back there, did you?'

'No. It's stupid.'

'Claustrophobia's not stupidity, it's bad luck. Or, maybe, bad management. We'll have to see what we can do for you. In the meantime, perhaps we should call this enough for today. If you find this bit claustrophobic I'm not sure you're up to the Tholos area yet. Or would you like to go quickly through there and out to the view from the top? That would give you a real feeling of the place.'

'Oh, yes, please. I'd like that. But, what's a Tholos?'

'You'll see. But not today.' She led the way along another corridor, off which an open door showed a large, modern gymnasium, lit by a huge skylight. 'Nobody's at work today. There aren't many guests. Autumn's usually a slack time, with people picking up the threads of their lives for the winter. That's why I waited until now to invite you, so I could make the most of you.' She paused at a pair of huge, intricately-wrought bronze doors. 'These are original, of course. If you don't mind, we won't talk as we go through the Tholos area. I'll tell you about it afterwards. I'm afraid you won't like it. Hold my hand if you want to.'

'I'll be all right, thanks.' The heavy doors swung silently inwards on enormous hinges and she followed Sophia into a vaulted corridor lit by dim lights in wall niches. Here, the quietness was so complete as to be oppressive. They had lost the voice of the stream, and she missed it. The air was chill and, looking up, she saw that this corridor had not been built, but hollowed out of the living rock. No wonder it was so cold. She reached out and Sophia's hand found hers, warm and comforting.

They came to more bronze doors, set in a wall that curved away to right and left. 'The Tholos is in there.' Sophia's hand, gently guiding, steered Daphne to the left, following the circular wall around half its circumference until they reached the counterpart of the first corridor. This one sloped slightly upwards, and Daphne, breathing hard, was relieved to see more doors ahead. 'Well done,' said Sophia quietly as she swung the doors open into a glorious blaze of light. Marble steps, facing them, led up to an open portico. 'This is the sacred area,' Sophia went on as they climbed the steps. 'Or the recovery room, if you like. We all worship our gods in our own ways. We did as little as possible to the temples up here.' They passed through the portico and out on to a wide, paved terrace, drenched in sunshine. 'Asklepios on the right. We re-erected his statue and the pillars. You shall see him another day, when you are stronger. But today: the Lady.' She turned to lead the way up shelving steps to a smaller temple, whose pillars, Daphne now saw, were caryatids, huge, calm-faced women with archaic smiles very like her companion's.

Here, as in the guests' circle, a vine did duty for a roof, letting dappled sunshine through on to the paved floor, and as Daphne's eyes got used to the half-light after the strong sunshine outside, she saw the huge, throned figure facing her, friendly hands outstretched.

'Oh,' she sighed, and moved a step forward. The statue's extraordinary eyes held hers, pierced through her, probed her to her depths. She was crying, not hard or painfully, but easy, relieving tears, the kind she had never been able to shed on her mother's lap.

'Come.' Sophia put her arm round her. 'That's enough for today. But I am glad you felt it, Daphne. I thought you would. Now we are going to sit among the trees, and look at the sea, and be quiet for a while.' She guided Daphne, her eyes still blurred with tears, back down the temple steps and up the slightly sloping terrace, past an altar covered with a blue-flowered creeper and so to the edge of the pine grove that lay above the terrace at the very top of the valley. 'There.' She settled them on a marble bench, warmed by the sun, and commanding a view between the two temples, across grey-brown broken ridges to the deep hyacinth of the sea. 'Let them come,' she said. 'Let the tears come, Daphne. They're good tears, healing ones.'

'What a mess I am,' Daphne said at last.

'Just unhappy.' Sophia silently handed her a clean handkerchief. 'And unoccupied, which is worse.' She sounded pleased with herself. 'I'm glad I brought you up here,' she said, confirming this. 'We haven't time, alas, you and I, to do things the slow way. It's good you're strong, Daphne.'

68

'Me? Strong?'

'I've seen men who thought themselves strong have hysterics when they met the Lady's eyes. I ought to be ashamed of myself, really, for bringing you up so ruthlessly fast. What would I have done, I wonder, if you had failed me?' She reached out to give Daphne's hand a friendly pat. 'No need to wonder. You didn't.'

'She saw right through me,' said Daphne. 'But — it's only a statue?' Despite herself, she made it a question.

'Yes, if you can use the word "only". Another lost art, those eyes. When we found her we knew this must be a place of healing again. My dear friend David was already ill. We'd had aerial photographs taken; he spotted this place and the outer way to it up the valley. It merely meant digging through the spur at the bottom where the earthquake had blocked it. And here it all was. The Lady, sitting there . . . Those eyes . . . We were so happy, planning how to use it, at first I didn't realise that David was dying. If only we had found the inner way, and the Tholos, but that came later, after he was dead: too late. And now it is getting late for me, Daphne. Time is running out on me.'

'Time,' said Daphne thoughtfully. 'You said something earlier about time, about not hurrying, about having all one needed. And now, you say . . .'

'That we have not very much, you and I. I'm glad you noticed that. It runs counter to all my principles to say it to you; but then, so does what I have done to you today. I have never brought anyone so swiftly up to see the Lady. But you are my kin, and I feel already that I know you well. I hope you feel the same about me. Because time has caught up with me. There is not a great deal left. I am eighty,' she answered the unspoken question. 'But that is not all of it. There are other things . . . other threats to Temi. I should have seen them sooner. I have been alone too long. Solitude is a dangerous drug, Daphne, an addictive one. You and I are going to be very good for each other, I think.'

'I do hope so.' Daphne longed to ask about Sophia's friend David, but knew that the moment had not yet come.

6

'Tell me about the Tholos,' Daphne asked, reaching for distraction as the bronze doors closed behind them and she felt her chest tighten at sight of the shadowy passages ahead.

'I think it's where it all started: the heart of the matter. A most extraordinary place. I suspect it's the original of all the Greek tholoses – or tholoi, if you want to be pedantic about it. That's why the archaeologists have never been able to understand the workings of the others; because they were imitations, not functional like this one.'

'How do you mean, functional?' Now they were skirting round the curved wall of the secret place itself.

'It provides a very drastic form of treatment. Natural forces enhanced by man. Again, I've not wanted to let the experts in, but I read, just the other day, about some new discovery in the magnetic field, something called magnetic monopoles that nobody seems to understand. I've wondered, in my great ignorance, if something like that might not to be at work here. All I know is, that it works, amazingly. I may let you try it presently. I don't know. You may not need it. And you're most certainly not up to it yet. It's strong stuff. Take my hand, cousin. You're exhausted, aren't you?'

'And frightened.' Extraordinary to be able to admit it. 'I hate the dark.'

'Foolish.' Her tone took the sting out of the word. 'Dark is good, like sleep. You don't hate that.'

'No.' The second pair of doors swung open upon what now seemed the comparative brightness of the treatment area. 'Except that I have bad dreams.'

'We'll talk about those. But not now. Now I'm going to

take you to my rooms for a rest before lunch, while I come back and take a look at a patient.' She settled Daphne in a lounging chair in her courtyard which opened off the first circle, not far from Daphne's. 'Lie there; try to relax. Do you know how?'

'I've never been much good at it.'

'You'll find the sun helps; think about breath and life; think about the Lady; concentrate on her eyes . . .' Her voice died away as Daphne breathed her way gently into a great quietness.

'You look better.' Sophia's voice woke her. 'That was a tough morning I put you through. But we've so little time.' She reached out a cool hand to take Daphne's pulse, then bent to look at the wound on her head. 'Healing beautifully. I don't think you need use the salve again. It's a great thing to be young. Enjoy it, Daphne; use it.'

She pulled up a chair to settle by Daphne in the shady court.

'Use it? How do you mean?'

'You've not done a great deal with your life – with yourself so far, have you?' She smiled, softening the criticism. 'What do you plan for yourself?'

'Plan?' She thought about it. 'I don't really know.' But she felt betraying colour flood her face. She had meant to live her life as Mark's wife and friend, to help him with his work and bear and rear his children.

'May we talk about him? About your Mark?'

'Not my Mark.' She was no longer surprised at the way Sophia read her mind. And then, glad to be able to admit it, 'I wish he was.'

'You love him still?'

'Yes. I can't help it.' And then, 'I keep dreaming about him!'

'I see.'

Daphne was afraid she did, and wondered, and was ashamed of doing so, what her cousin's relationship had been with the friend who had died.

'David and I loved each other very much.' Once again, Sophia answered the unspoken question. 'But I was forty, when we met during the war. And David –' She paused. 'David had been a prisoner of the Nazis. We had no hope of children. Temi has been my child. Given me the pleasure of creation. Still does. I love it. Why did you part, you and Mark?'

'He fell in love with someone else.' It still hurt hideously to say it. 'A friend of mine.'

'He's still with her?'

'I don't know. I lost them both, you see. It was horrible ... It had been going on for ages, when I found out. I ... I couldn't believe it at first. It made our life together, mine and Mark's, that I had thought so happy, it made it disgusting. All those lies ...'

'How long had you been married?'

'Not long married. We'd been living together three years. I'm not sure Mark really wanted to get married.'

'But you did?'

'Oh yes! You see: my mother. I didn't want to behave like her. You know so much. Do you know about my mother?'

'Yes, I know.' The brown hand touched hers for a moment, warm with life. 'Why didn't Mark want to marry?'

'He said it would devalue me. That marriage was a primitive, patriarchal concept and we would have none of it. When we did get married I didn't take his name.'

'So what made him change his mind?'

'I don't know. I hope I hadn't put pressure on him. Sophia, I think it was at our wedding that his affair with Anne started. Isn't that horrible? She'd been abroad, you see, teaching. I was so *glad* she was back, and could come. My dearest friend. Mark helped her get a job in Oxford. I was so pleased. And all the time ... Horrible.'

'Horrible, yes, but not necessarily surprising. Not if he hadn't really wanted to get married.'

'But he did! He said he did. Said he'd found how badly he needed me. Because of his dyslexia, his reading problem. He wouldn't admit to it, poor Mark. Thought it was disgraceful, somehow. So he didn't get the help he might

72

have. He said he'd never have managed without me.'

'I've read his books. I found them very interesting.'

'I loved helping with them. He let me do a lot of the research, and of course I had to do all the typing. It was much easier after we managed to get a tape recorder. We were so poor! We got the tape recorder with the advance for the first book. After that I didn't have to be at home all the time in case he needed me to take something down. He could just record it.'

'Very handy. But, surely, the first book, *Women in History*: I had rather imagined you actually worked with him on that?'

'Oh yes, I did.' She hesitated for a moment. 'Actually, it began as an idea of mine, for my doctoral thesis. We talked about it a good deal, and then I went and mucked things up and only got a second, so no grant, no doctorate.'

'How exactly did you muck things up?'

'All the usual ways. Not working enough; not sleeping enough; maybe not thinking enough. There was so much going on. Of course, reading classics, Mark didn't have finals that year and he had started a paper. A weekly called *Inside Oxford*. It did terribly well.' She heard the defensive note in her own voice.

'Until it was banned. You did all the typing for that?'

'Oh, I hadn't even got a typewriter then. I did it in longhand. I write a very clear hand, luckily. Mother bought me a typewriter as a kind of consolation prize when I got my second. Well, I think she felt bad about not having paid her share of my college fees. She was supposed to, but she never could. Nor Mark's parents either. And of course she hoped typing would steer me into safe, secretarial channels. In a way it did. It made the whole difference to Mark's last year.'

'He got his first?'

'Oh, yes. He's brilliant, Mark. Only, it's so hard for him to decide how to use it.' And then. 'How odd, that's what you said to me, isn't it?'

'Yes. It's the basic problem, after all. Surprising how many women still don't face up to it. Take it for granted it will settle itself for them. I've done it myself, in my time. Still am, maybe?'

Daphne could not help laughing. 'You say that, Cousin Sophia? You who have brought Temi back to life?'

'Thank you, nice child. But don't you see, that was really something that happened to me. If my father hadn't decided to come back to Greece in 1912 ... If the man I loved when I was young hadn't been killed fighting the Turks in 1922, I imagine I'd be a formidable old Greek grandmother by now, not a doctor at all. Nor the boss of Temi. Sometimes I wish I was. A dear old grandma. Grandchildren are not the responsibility Temi is. What did you think of Andros?'

'Andros?'

'The man who brought you here yesterday.'

Daphne thought for a moment. 'Not very much. He was kind . . . He didn't make much impression on me.'

'That's the trouble. He's the nearest I've got to a second in command, here on Temi. My fault, in a way. At first, after David died, I couldn't bear the idea of a substitute. Some people, both men and women, who might have helped me, left the island because, I suppose, they felt there was no future for them here. I was stupid. And now, there's Andros; he's very able; but I can't feel my way through to him. As you say, he doesn't quite make an impression. I think maybe it's because he doesn't mean to. He's lunching with us; think about him a little, Daphne. Meanwhile, there's another problem which I shall indulge myself by sharing with you. A luxury I've not had since David died. It doesn't seem to work with Andros. We don't think the same way. There's a block somewhere in his mind; I can feel it. It's not that he can't think with me; it's that he won't. I wish I understood ... It seemed such a good idea to have a man as second in command. It's equality we want, not a new kind of dominance.'

'We?'

'Women. Men complicate: women simplify. We're the gentle ones, mostly, the conciliators, the healers, the pacifiers. Men compete. They've been running the world, and fighting over it, since recorded history began. Everything we found, here on Temi, suggested an older civilisation where the female element prevailed. Women functioning as women, not like imitation males. You know what I mean: the Amazons, or Joan of Arc, or Margaret Thatcher. All competitors for power, in a man's power-oriented world. David felt just as strongly about it as I did. He hated the male chauvinist element in Judaism almost as much as he hated Hitler's form of tyranny. When we found the Lady, understood what she meant, we thought we saw a chance to go back to the golden age, to Atlantis, call it what you like. Temi seemed to prove that it was not a dream, but a lost reality, trampled on by generations of fighting men. By St. George and St. Paul and all the other dominating, competitive males down to the politicians and trades unionists today who enlist women for their votes and then leave them to make the tea and mind the children. Or treat them as sex objects, which is worse. We thought, if we could only achieve it here, the gentle civilisation, use Temi as what it used to be, a place of peace and healing, we might start something, get something across.'

'But I thought you didn't want people to know about Temi?'

'There you are! You've put your finger on it, the basic weakness of my position.' She rose and moved restlessly across the little courtyard. 'We were such optimists, David and I. We thought people would have learned from the horrors of the war. Would at least be wanting to learn. That we could build up our peaceful enclave here; let it gradually become known. Be an example, if it doesn't sound too smug.' She came back to stand by Daphne's chair and look gravely down at her. 'Nothing to be smug about now. Things aren't going right. Nothing you can put your finger on, but I can feel it. That's why I decided I needed help.'

'Help?'

'I didn't send for you just for fun, Daphne. And I did some pretty hard thinking before I decided you were the one to send for. If I was wrong, you'll have to forgive me.'

She ran a hand through her hair. 'It's maddening. I'd meant to have the next few weeks clear for you and me and some guests I have asked to meet you. Some thinking time for us all. But Andros brought me a message, this morning. There are a couple of very important people indeed who want to use this island for a quiet talk. One of them has been before and knows this for the one place where he can meet a public enemy without the world getting to know of it. He's an old friend of David's. I owe it to him; I owe it to the world to give him the chance for this meeting, however inconvenient it is to me. But I wish so many people hadn't "coincidentally" turned up at the same time. This island is altogether too popular right now. Andros also brought me notes from both the men you met on Kos. Left at the Zephyros: Madame Costa thought she'd better send them on. I like the sound of Jacob Braun. He says some polite things about you and some interesting ones about Temi. I think we might let him come. I'm not quite so sure about the other one: Christopher Maitland. Writes a very civil letter indeed. Fine-flowing, old-fashioned courtesy.'

'He would. He's the kind of man who would keep dodging round you in the street to protect you from the traffic.'

Sophia laughed. 'You make me long to meet him! And he seems to know a surprising amount about Temi too.'

'I forgot to tell you. He'd heard about it on Rhodes, he said. He thinks it would make a marvellous scoop for his architectural paper.'

'Does he so? How come he told you this, Daphne? He didn't know you were coming here?'

'Oh, no. I was careful not to tell him. It just came up when he was talking about the paper he's writing.'

'So how did he know that a letter left at the Zephyros would reach me? It's just addressed to, "The Owner of Temi." But it does raise a question, doesn't it? I suppose it really was an accident, his hitting you?'

'What else could it have been?'

'Handled right, and if he knew who you were, a clever way of getting a toe in, here on Temi.'

'But, Sophia, how could he have known? Unless he'd met Jacob Braun, of course. He did know. But how in the world would it have come up?'

'It does seem unlikely. I wonder if there is some leakage on Kos. I'll get Andros to look into it. And I really think we'd better ask both men here, don't you, and look them over. I'd like to meet Jacob Braun anyway, and I expect it will turn out that Christopher Maitland really did hit you by accident and took a not unreasonable fancy to you.'

Daphne laughed. 'Better for my morale! He certainly put himself out to be agreeable, but I got the feeling that he did that with all the girls. He's dreadfully handsome. I rather think he expects us to fall for him in rows.'

'I take it you didn't.'

'Mark's pretty good looking, too.'

'You're immunised? Well, that's something. I think we'd better tell Andros about this. It has a good deal of bearing on the arrangements we make for the guests we are going to have next week. If there is a leak, we must find it quick. Ah, Andros. Let me introduce you to our guest, my cousin, Daphne Vernon. You can hardly be said to have met the night she arrived.'

'I am glad to see you looking in such good health,' said Andros rather formally. 'You gave us a fright the other night. You should have told me about your injury.' He was short, dark, thickset, a typical Greek with a closed, careful face.

'I'm sorry. It was all so strange. I do thank you for bringing me.'

'It was nothing. I am quite sure we were not followed,' he told Sophia.

'No,' she said. 'They are still trying.' Over lunch, she told him about the two notes and the possibility of a leak on Kos. 'I've decided to invite both men,' she concluded. 'Next week, when the other guests are coming.'

'So we can take a look at them? I agree with you. I'll put the arrangements in train at once. As to your idea of a leak, I find it hard to believe.' A quick glance at Daphne suggested that he thought her responsible. 'But of course I'll check.'

77

He finished his coffee and rose. 'If you will excuse me, ladies?'

'What good English he speaks – Well, you all do,' said Daphne when they were alone.

'Andros particularly, and with good reason. You must have noticed his American accent? He was one of the children the communist guerrillas kidnapped during the Greek civil war. He was just a little boy and his sister younger still. Their mother managed to get them out. She was killed doing it. It was one of the stories that catch the fancy of the world's press. So they got adopted, he and his sister, by rich Americans, grew up there into their teens. Then, I don't know, they got homesick perhaps; something went wrong between them and their adoptive parents. So . . . they came back to Greece and that wasn't easy either. I happened to hear about them. A lucky day for me. Like the one when I remembered about you. I'm sorry we're not going to have more time alone together, Daphne, before our other guests arrive. It's lucky you're one of the patients who cure themselves on the journey, even if it was only a four-hour flight from London and an accident on Kos.'

Daphne smiled. 'Before that,' she said. 'I think it was getting your letter. Being invited. Being wanted. I . . . Cousin Sophia, I'm so ashamed.'

'Oh?'

'The night before your letter came. I'd lost Mark, you see. He was – well, everything in my life. All the family I had. My reason. My life, I suppose.'

'Foolish,' said Sophia gently.

'I suppose so. But, you see, mother . . .'

'I know.'

'The teaching helped; the job; the people. Then I lost that. Couldn't get another. No money. No future. Nothing. I almost killed myself, Sophia. I really meant to; had it all ready.' She could taste the strong whisky; feel the bottle of hoarded pills in her hand; the sordid plastic bag.

'But you didn't,' said Sophia. 'That's when you started to cure yourself. Starting's the hardest. Like deciding to go to a psychiatrist. I'm glad you told me, Daphne. I could see there was more to your trouble than a blow on the head. And I'm glad, too, that my letter didn't arrive until after you had fought your battle, and won. Otherwise we'd never have been sure. I said you were strong. And now, we've talked quite enough. What do you say to a swim? It would do your head good. It's very special water, you'll find.'

'I'd love it.'

'Good. Put on your things and I'll meet you by the pool. Can you find your way? Will you mind?'

A test, perhaps? Daphne remembered those oppressive corridors. 'I'll see you there,' she said.

Back in her room, she found her bikini laid out on her bed, with a dark blue tunic of the finest possible towelling and a huge blue towel. There might be no telephone on Temi, and she seldom saw the saffron-tunicked staff, but the place seemed to run like magic. Changing quickly, she wondered about the other guests Sophia had spoken of. Was there, perhaps, some kind of committee concerned with the affairs of Temi, whom she was to meet? It seemed unlikely, granted Sophia's apparently unlimited authority, but who else could it be?

She had to make a conscious effort to leave the afternoon light of the guests' circle and plunge into the shadowy corridors of the treatment area, where, it seemed to her, there were fewer lights even than in the morning. Hating it, she nevertheless made herself walk slowly, timing her breath with her footsteps, holding irrational fear at bay. Or almost. When a white door opened on her right, she could not suppress a quick gasp of fear, then smiled an apology at the woman, Hermione, whom she and Sophia had met that morning. 'How's your patient?' she asked.

But Hermione only looked at her oddly, muttered something in Greek, and brushed past her. How strange. Perhaps the staff were not supposed to speak to guests. She must ask Sophia. And on the thought, emerged into the blessed sunlight of the open pool and saw her cousin's sleek head plunging in and out of the water in an elegant, controlled crawl. She pulled off her own tunic and dived neatly into the most amazing water she had ever felt. Champagne, she thought, feeling it sparkle and fizz around her as she struck out to join Sophia.

'How do you like it?' Sophia had turned over to float lightly beside her.

'Marvellous! What is it?' She trod water, feeling it buoy her up.

'A thermal spring. There's another one at Therme on Kos, where Andros picked you up. It's hotter, but this one is better for you. We must start you on your glass a day. You'll be amazed how well it makes you feel. But don't forget, it's strong stuff, a glass a day is enough, with what you swallow swimming. We don't have it in the pipes; they're from another spring; just water.'

'This is better than the sea,' said Daphne. 'I never really liked pools much, but this is different.'

'Yes. I'll race you to the edge.' She gave Daphne a head start and beat her easily.

'You can't call yourself old!' Daphne looked with admiration at the firm brown body in the black one-piece suit.

'As old as you feel, they say.' Sophia laughed it off. 'Today I feel young again: your age, Daphne, with it all before me.'

Did she say something else, before she plunged back into the sparkling water? Daphne thought so, but, plunging in after her, could not be sure.

'That's enough for today.' Sophia was waiting for her at the other side. 'It's strong medicine, this water. Go and change, child. I'll stay in a little longer, and expect you in my rooms for dinner at eight.'

'You rested?' Sophia greeted her with a smile and a cloudy glass of ouzo.

'Beautifully, thank you.' It was still warm enough to sit outside in the bougainvillaea-shaded courtyard. 'Only, I kept thinking about the guests you said were coming. Cousin Sophia, who?'

'I rather thought I'd let them be a surprise, if you don't mind. Aside from Mr. Braun and Mr. Maitland, of course.'

'Will they come the way I did?' She found herself wondering how Chris Maitland and Jacob Braun would get on.

'Very likely. I leave all that to Andros, and he waits until the last moment, taking advantage of any favourable circumstance like the power cut the night you came. It's tiresome having to take such precautions, but there it is. The quietness of this island is so much of its secret. Imagine what it would be like if we had tourists flooding in and out.' She smiled. 'I was actually approached by one of the cruise companies. They wouldn't tell me how they had heard of Temi, but they were prepared to pay handsomely for a weekly visit. I gave them a pretty short answer, I can tell you. If there's time, I'll take you down and show you our watergate tomorrow. You weren't noticing much when you arrived, were you? You've made a good recovery.'

'I feel a different person. Oh, listen!' The first quiet notes of the piano came down to them from the guests' circle. 'It's the Moonlight Sonata.'

'He said he'd play for us tonight, bless him. The other two are gone already, by way of Rhodes, so just piano. He came earlier for a farewell glass of ouzo. I'm sorry you're not going to meet him this time but he says he'll be back when next things get on top of him. I told him I'd introduce you to him then.'

A little chill ruffled through Daphne's mind. But why? She was already hoping Sophia would ask her to stay on. She picked up her glass for a warming draught. 'You let your patients drink?' It was the most trivial of the questions surging to be asked.

'In moderation. Wine's a good friend, if you let it be. It depends on the patient, of course. So many of them are more guest than patient.' She gave a little sigh. 'One of the diplomats who are coming to talk here doesn't drink at all, and that's a problem too. Funny it should go with disliking women.'

Back in her own room, much later, Daphne prowled about restlessly, looking at the books by the bed, trying to sort out the manifold impressions of the day. Sophia had talked as if she meant her to stay indefinitely, as if she really

81

wanted her, needed her . . . But what for? Marvellous to be needed, but suppose she was not up to it? 'You've not done much with your life,' Sophia had said, and it was true enough. Start again? Try again?

It took her a long time to get to sleep, and when she did, it was restlessly, dreaming and waking, fleeing endlessly down winding corridors . . . She was looking for Sophia, who could save her, but when she found her at last, she looked at her blankly and spoke to her in unintelligible Greek.

Despite the bad night, she woke early, and, remembering something, got out of bed to look in the bookshelf. Yes, there it was, a modern Greek grammar. It looked appallingly complicated, but she had always enjoyed languages. She got back into bed and began to read.

Half an hour later Zoe brought her breakfast and a message. 'The Kyria begs you to forgive her, but she will be busy with a patient this morning. He had a bad night. This afternoon, she will show you more of Temi, and, perhaps, if you were to be swimming before lunch she would be able to join you.'

'How is her patient?'

'Not well, I think. She says she is very sorry.'

'So am I. But tell her I am busy learning Greek.'

Zoe smiled. 'The Kyria will be pleased.'

It was restful to sit in the shady corner of her courtyard and apply her mind to the complexities of Greek grammar. When had she last really made herself study something? Ever since the bitter disappointment of her finals, she had been mentally coasting along, doing only the thinking Mark asked of her. It was good to do her own, for a change. And, thinking this, thought that in all the frightening complexity of the night's dreams, Mark had played no part. Someone had. Who?

If Sophia had not said she might meet her at the pool, Daphne would not have gone. With the night's shadows still upon her, she felt very reluctant indeed to plunge into the dim corridors of the treatment area. Presumably, Sophia was in there somewhere with her patient, but this was small comfort as she hesitated in the sunshine at the entrance, wishing herself safe at the pool. Ridiculous. She had been trying to learn Greek verbs and recited them to herself as she walked swiftly but steadily through the corridors and wished that Cousin Sophia had installed a stronger electric generator.

Today there was no sleek head in the pool and she felt oddly lonely as she plunged in. Three days ago – was it only that? – she had taken loneliness for granted. What had Sophia said? Loneliness is bad medicine. True, but not helpful. She made herself swim the whole sweep of the circle before she emerged to lie in the sun. She had brought her watch in a concealed pocket of the towelling tunic and waited for Sophia until it was well after one o'clock. Then, at last, reluctantly, she pulled on the tunic and started back to the first circle.

And, again, one of the flat, anonymous doors opened, revealing Hermione hand in hand with a smiling Greek boy. '*Herete*,' said Daphne, remembering the basic Greek greeting.

And, 'Good morning,' said Hermione. 'May I present my friend and patient Loukas?'

Stranger and stranger. 'Hullo, Loukas,' said Daphne. 'How are you today?' And got a puzzled look and another smile.

'He speaks no English,' said Hermione. 'But he is much better, thank you.'

'And the Kyria's other patient?'

'Not well. The Kyria has been with him all morning. It is not often that she misses her morning swim. You must see to it, kyria, that she swims tonight.'

'I will,' said Daphne with a warm feeling of responsibility that took her through the rest of the corridor and out into the sunshine of the guests' circle. Walking down the centre, under the trees, she was aware of activity over where the pianist had had his rooms and was tempted to pause in the hope of meeting him. Possible names flickered through her mind. But Sophia did not want her to see him. Not this time, she had said. She looked the other way and hurried past to the next cloister and her own room.

83

7

That day set the pattern for a peaceful week. Sophia was much preoccupied with her patient, and spent most mornings with him, meeting Daphne at the pool when she could. Sometimes she arrived looking so tired, so drained, that Daphne was anxious for her. 'I told you the Tholos was a drastic treatment,' Sophia explained. 'I don't often use it, or not to this extent. If it makes me tired, imagine what it does to him.'

'But it's working?'

'I'm not sure; not yet. I'm sorry, Daphne, I'm being a wretched hostess, after all.'

'Not a hostess; family.'

'I'm glad you feel it, too. And the rest is doing you good. You look a different creature, had you noticed?'

'Nothing like a suntan.'

'And health. Our guests arrive tomorrow evening. Will you forgive me if I leave you alone all day? There's a lot to do, and I think I'm going to double my patient's treatment.'

'You'll be worn out.'

'It doesn't matter. And — he does. I don't think I've ever wanted to heal someone so badly in my life.' She reached out to pat Daphne's hand. 'You're a dear good child not to ask me about him. I'll tell you it all when he's better.'

'I'm glad you don't say if.'

'I won't. So — have a quiet day tomorrow and join me for a drink at eight. Our guests are all arriving late; one lot from Kos, one from Rhodes. Andros has been busy getting it organised, but in fact it's easier with people from Rhodes; the island's so much bigger than Kos. More private places to leave from. A longer boat trip, of course. I hope they won't mind it.' She smiled lovingly. 'And you're a honey, not asking me who they are. Good night; sweet dreams.'

But Daphne dreamed of Mark and woke sweating, and wanting him. Zoe, bringing her breakfast, paused in the doorway. 'A bad night?'

'Yes. Does it show?'

'A little. Rest today, for the Kyria's sake. I wanted to say – we all want to say how happy we are you are here, Kyria Daphne. You probably don't know what a difference your coming has made to the Kyria. We were getting – a little anxious about her. Now, with you here, she has come through even this last terrible week.'

'Terrible?'

'The treatment of the Tholos is terrible, they say. She has never before spent so much time there. The patient is on the mend, but the Kyria is exhausted. And more guests today. I am glad you are here to help her entertain them. We are all glad. Remember that.'

'Thank you!' The heart-warming words had given her an appetite for her breakfast. Finishing the last crumb of croissant and drop of coffee, she made herself spend an extra hour on Greek grammar, before she braved the dark passages to the pool.

The sparkling water took away the last heaviness of her bad night and she emerged feeling herself again, spread out her towel on the sun-warmed verge and drifted into light sleep. Waking with a start, she sat up in one swift movement. What had she heard? What had waked her? Nothing had changed; the pool lay quiet in the sun; the only sound the soft, steady rush of water in at the top, out at the bottom. No, she was wrong, the noise had changed. Water was slapping against the sides of the pool and she could see an eddy towards the middle. On the thought, she was diving in, swimming strongly under water towards where the movement had been. Something there. Someone there? A threshing in the water. Reaching out, she felt a hand, lost it again. Her own breath was giving out. Searching blindly through the water, she felt hair, grasped at it. Her head was beginning to swim. She clasped the ears; felt the whole body go limp, surfaced, gasped, and struck out strongly towards the edge of the pool.

Why had she been so sure it was Sophia? Towing the light body towards the shallow end she wondered how in the world she was going to get her out of the water. 'Here, kyria, this way!' She dared not look round but followed the sound of the woman's voice, reached the edge, felt strong hands reach down to share her burden.

Hermione and the boy, Loukas. Between them, hardly speaking, they got Sophia out of the water and Hermione bent instantly to artificial respiration. 'I know how. We all do.'

It took only a moment. Sophia shuddered; sat up. 'I fainted! In the water. I remember plunging in ...' She looked up at their three anxious faces. 'Who saved me?'

'The kyria,' said Hermione.

'Thank you, cousin.' She ran her hand through wet hair. 'Stupid of me. I'd have told anyone else to take things easier long before this. And thank you too, Hermione. And, please, all of you, we will say nothing about this.'

'But, Kyria.' Hermione seemed to have grown more anxious as Sophia recovered.

'Nothing,' Sophia repeated. 'Give Loukas his swim, Hermione, and Daphne will see me to my rooms.'

And that was that. Reaching her own rooms in silence, Sophia touched Daphne's cheek lightly. 'I owe you my life,' she said. 'I like it. And I'm sorry I may not thank you publicly as I should. But I cannot, just now, afford the excitement this tiresome episode would cause. We have more important things to think about, you and I. Dear Daphne, I must rest, and so should you. I will see you at eight as we planned.'

That was a strange afternoon. Daphne could settle to nothing. What would have happened, here on Temi, if Sophia had died in the pool? Who would have taken over? Andros, that strange, silent man? It made her realise how little she had found out about the island in the week she had been there. Sophia had learned a great deal about her, and she almost nothing about Sophia, who was not, somehow, a woman you lightly questioned.

Perhaps this would change now. But when she joined Sophia in her courtyard it was as if nothing had happened. Sophia was working at a piece of embroidery. 'Dear child.' The words said a great deal, but they were all. She exhibited the half-finished tapestry of the virgin and the unicorn. 'Instead of a cigarette,' she explained. 'Have you ever thought how much easier men would find life if they had something harmless to do with their hands? The Greeks have worry beads, and a good thing, too. They need them. What do you do, I wonder?'

'I used to knit.' Pullovers for Mark. Losing him, she had lost the will to do it.

'You should start again. Speak to Zoe; she runs our occupational therapy department and will find you some wool. But, now, I think you deserve a drink.'

'I'm sure I do.'

'And so do I. One doesn't brush quite so close to death every day.' She smiled at Daphne. 'It makes two of us, doesn't it? I find – did you? – that it clarifies the mind wonderfully.' She reached for the ouzo bottle and poured two generous measures. 'Ice?'

'Yes, please.'

'I'm glad our guests are late tonight.' She watched the colourless liquid cloud round the ice. 'More and more, since you saved my life, my conscience has been pricking me about letting you meet them quite unprepared.'

'Oh?' At last.

But Sophia seemed to go off at a tangent. 'I wanted to get to know you as fast and as well as possible. And – I wanted you to get to know yourself a bit better. It didn't sound – forgive me – from what I learned about you, as if you knew yourself very well. So – I have invited a group of people who, I hope, will help you get things a bit clearer– and me, too, for the matter of that. You're going to find it a bit like appearing on one of those drastic television programmes, I'm afraid. They haven't all accepted, but –Yes, Zoe?' Her tone was as near to anger as Daphne had heard it.

'Forgive me, Kyria, but the first party have just arrived, and Andros wishes to speak to you.'

'Very well.' A smile for Daphne. 'Drink up, and meet us in the guests' dining-room in half an hour? And – forgive me for being an interfering old woman who had begun to love you even before today.'

Left alone, Daphne found herself fighting tears. Can one cry from pleasure? Apparently one could. To be loved by Sophia . . . Even before today, she had said. It made her, suddenly, value herself as she had not since parting from Mark. Mark! One of those drastic television programmes, Sophia had said. *This is Your Life?* So: Mark one of the guests? Fantastic thought; one that sent her blood racing. Would he have come if Sophia had asked him? Of course he would. Mark had never resisted a dare in his life. And, besides, he had always wanted to come back to Greece. She had been surprised that they had not done so when the money started pouring in for *Women in History*. Had he been tiring of her already, already involved with Anne? She had always suspected that that affair had been going on for a long while before she came home early that Monday afternoon and found them in bed. In her bed.

She sighed and finished her second drink. Time to be looking for the guests' dining-room. It was dark now, but a glow of light at the top of the guests' circle indicated the dining-room, its small courtyard screened by the enveloping vine. A woman was sitting there, half-turned away, drink in hand, her backless red dress a startling note in the muted light. She had not heard Daphne and now rose to move impatiently over to a table of drinks.

Breath caught in Daphne's throat. Sophia's warning should have prepared her for this. 'Mother?' she said.

'There you are at last! A fine welcome I get to the end of nowhere. Devil of a journey. Then shown to my room and dumped like a parcel. Wear this! Do that! Sit here! Go there! Boarding school!' Frances Vernon poured herself a generous slug of Greek brandy. 'No gin of course! No vodka! What kind of a hotel is this anyway, and where's this lady bountiful? Begs me to come here and then can't even be bothered to say hullo when I arrive! Well, what's up with you, Daph? Lost your voice?' She reached for a second glass. 'Have a drink!'

'Not yet, thanks.' The moment when she should have kissed her mother had passed somewhere in the course of her speech. 'I'm so sorry, mother, I didn't know you were coming.'

'Don't keep calling me mother, for God's sake. Making me sound out of the ark. Like this cousin of yours, I suppose. If I've asked you once to call me Fran I've done it a million times. You mean to say that woman invited me without even choosing to mention it to you? What's she like anyway? Fine sort of hostess doesn't bother to meet her guests.'

'She's got a very sick patient. And she's pretty tired herself. It's not a hotel, mother, it's a hospital, kind of.'

'Don't call me mother.' Frances Vernon spoke through clenched teeth. 'Not a hotel? She said — a holiday. Expenses paid, she said. Not much of a hotel on Rhodes, if you ask me, and as for the journey! They fetched me at no notice in the middle of the night. Hardly time to pack. And then miles and miles of those gruesome roads in the dark to a bloody pebble beach. I broke a heel on the stones. My best sandals. And the boat trip! I never could stand small boats!' She broke off. 'Well, don't look now, but it sounds like company at last.' They could hear voices from across the guests' circle. 'Now, mind, Daphne, the less of this mother business the better you and me are going to get on. I've got a life to lead, just like you, and between you and me, this invitation came in handy. I'm broke, stony. Someone I was fond of did me down . . . I hope this cousin of yours is going to turn up trumps. What's she like, anyway?'

'Hush,' said Daphne, full of an old, familiar despair.

'Mrs. Vernon!' Sophia came through the vine-hung entrance, hand outstretched. 'I do deeply apologise for not being there to greet you. We've had rather a crisis here today, I'm afraid, but it's no excuse. I hope your daughter has been making you welcome.'

'She didn't even know I was coming!' Frances grumbled.

'And me dropping everything to come and stand by her.'
Her bright eyes flickered past Sophia to the group of
blue-tunicked men behind her. 'Well,' with satisfaction, 'it
may not be a hotel, but it does seem to be a party. Old
home week, eh? How are you then, Mark?'

Daphne's heart jumped. But she had been sure, really,
when she saw Frances, that Mark must have been invited
too, had been waiting, full-stretched, for this moment.

'I'm fine, and so are you, I can see.' Mark bent gallantly,
as he always had, to kiss Frances on the cheek, and Daphne
had time to relearn him by heart: the tall, easy carriage,
the handsome head, the eyes that melted her. 'Daphne!' He
turned to her now, his deep voice a caress. 'It's been so
much too long.' Would he kiss her? What would she do if
he did? No, he held out a friendly hand.

'Mark!' What could she say while his touch worked the
old magic? 'It's nice to see you.' Banal. Ridiculous. She
looked beyond him, to greet the two men who stood
watching. 'Hullo, Chris. How are you, Mr. Braun?'

'Glad to be here. I wish you would call me Jacob.' His
voice was almost lost in the general babble of greeting,
from which Daphne gathered that her mother had come
from Rhodes, while the three men had made more or less
the same journey as she herself had, from Kos. She also
noticed that Mark and Chris were not liking each other
much, and was not surprised. Two beautiful men. Mark
was surely more handsome than ever. She relearned him
sensuously, the crisp dark hair, the imperial brow over
deepset eyes that went on holding hers.

'How is your new patient, Kyria?' Jacob had gravitated
to Sophia as they settled with their drinks. 'I'm afraid he
must have found the crossing pretty rough.'

'It took a while to get him settled. That's why I have
been such a deplorable hostess.' Sophia's friendly, apologetic smile swept the little group. 'And you must all be
starving, after your journey. Let's eat, shall we?'

'Another patient?' Daphne asked her, as they moved
towards the table.

'An emergency.' Preoccupied. 'I thought you should sit

between Mark and Mr. Braun, Daphne. If I may call you Mark?' She smiled at him.

'I wish you would.' He was at his charming best. 'I've not had a chance to thank you for your invitation. I can't begin to tell you how glad I am to be here. It's a privilege!'

'It most certainly is.' Unlike Mark and Chris, who wore theirs with elegance, Jacob Braun looked faintly ridiculous in his dark blue tunic, all elbows and knobbly knees, but it did not seem to bother him as he pulled out Sophia's chair for her. 'There's so much I want to ask you, Kyria, about Temi and its history. Past and future. I'm not sure that what you are doing here isn't even more interesting than the past. Do you find it's working?'

'You know about it?' He had her full attention.

'Daphne.' Mark's voice dragged her back from Sophia. He leaned closer. 'You look terrific. Tell me about this miracle-working island of your cousin's. You're certainly an advertisement for it.'

Why did she feel reluctant to do so? Was she afraid Mark might laugh if she told him about the Lady in the temple? You could never quite tell with Mark. So, with one ear cocked for Jacob Braun's increasingly lively conversation with Sophia, she confined herself to generalities about the buildings, the way of life, the remarkable pool. Across the table, Frances was holding forth about the discomforts of her journey from Rhodes to Christopher Maitland, who was proving a receptive listener, ready to charm and be charmed.

When coffee was brought in, Sophia rose. 'Will you forgive me? I must go and see to my patients. Daphne, will you pour the coffee for me?'

'Glad to.' It was her first chance for more than the merest of greetings to Chris, who came leisurely over to pass coffee cups for her.

'You look marvellously better.' His tone made it a compliment.

'Thank you. I feel it.' She wanted to ask him how he had found out where she was, but could not think how to do it.

'I hope you didn't mind my tracking you down like this.' He might have read her thoughts. 'I couldn't just let you vanish into thin air like the princess in the fairy tale.'

'How did you find me?'

'Oh, there aren't many secrets on Kos; not if you're more or less a resident like me.' It was hardly an answer. 'What baffles me is how the professor got on to Temi.'

'The professor? Oh, you mean Mr. Braun? He's some kind of an archaeologist, I think. He's got a theory about Temi.'

'Haven't we all? Will you show me round some time?'

'I'll have to ask my cousin. I hardly know my own way yet.'

'She's your cousin?'

'Kind of.'

'And the lady in red is really your mother? It's hard to believe.'

'I'll say!' Frances had been talking to Jacob Braun on the other side, but now leaned across Chris to join in. 'Practically in my cradle I was when I had her. Not my fault if she won't make the best of herself.' She put down her coffee cup with a sharp click. 'I can't stand this sweet Turkish muck; how's about we move back to where the drink is? I could use another brandy. Pour me a good one, Chris, would you? I need it.' She linked her arm through his and led him across the courtyard to where the drinks still stood on their marble table.

Daphne sighed. She had seen it so often before. The swift appraisal of a group of men; the instant decision, followed as instantly by action.

'Your mother's not changed.' Mark had always been able to read her thoughts. 'We have to talk, Daphne, you and I. Later? I'll come to your room.'

'No.' It surprised her, but she meant it. 'It's been a long day. Let's talk tomorrow.' And then, because she could not help it, 'How is Anne?'

'How should I know? We parted before Christmas . . . God, I've missed you, Daphne. What a hellish year. Why didn't you tell me Anne can't cook? And so damned busy with that social work of hers. Do you know, she seriously suggested we invite one of her unmarried mums for Christmas dinner? That's when I stuck; when we split. But what about you, Daphne? How have you been?' He turned the full force of his charm on her.

Tell him? No. 'I've managed.'

'Crazy couple of fools we were. I shouldn't have let you go, when you took that high line about Anne. I knew it soon enough.' Perceptive when he wanted to be, he recognised her withdrawal. 'I don't blame you if you're going to put me through it. I deserve it all for being such a clot. Nothing's gone right since you left me.'

'I'm sorry.'

'My new book's been turned down.'

'Oh, I *am* sorry.' She knew what it must have cost him to tell her. He had never found failure bearable. 'Not the one about women in ancient Greece?'

'Yes. They said it wasn't a patch on my earlier stuff. What was the matter, they asked. I could hardly tell them I had lost my inspiration. I didn't realise, Daphne, just how much you meant to my work. But we'll talk about that tomorrow.' He refilled his glass. 'You can see what a miracle it seemed when I had your cousin's letter inviting me here. Everything I need: You — and a chance to take a look at some Greek women.'

'They're not exactly typical ones here.'

'No, of course not; the phoney chitons and all that. What I want to see is the village. That's where I'm counting on you to help me. I rather get the impression the old dragon tends to keep visitors away from there.'

'Old dragon?'

'I beg your pardon. Your fierce cousin, then. Has she got a surname? I don't know that I'd dare call her Sophia.'

'People mainly just call her Kyria.'

'"Call me madam"?' And then, aware as always of her reaction, 'Sorry, I'm sure. She puts the fear of God into me, but if you like her, love, I'll not say another word. Only, you will get her to let you show me the village, won't you?'

'I don't know, Mark. Sophia doesn't talk about the village much. I'm surprised you know about it.'

'Well, there has to be one, doesn't there? The staff here: Andros, the boatman and all those pretty young things in ballet costume. They have to live somewhere. The tale is there's a village tucked away on this island, with no way in or out except through here, and customs going back to God knows when. I've just got to see that.'

'You know a lot about this place.'

'Well, naturally. Anything that concerns you, concerns me, Daphne love. And I'm in the business, after all. That first book you helped me with, *Women in History*, got me quite a bit of connection. So – I asked around. I suppose in more or less the same places Braun did. He seems to have come up with some of the same answers. Not many hard facts, but some interesting rumours. Mind you, he has a powerful advantage with the old witch.'

'Don't call her that!'

'Sorry! You've really taken to her, haven't you? And she to you, God bless you. So it's not going to matter that Braun has such an edge with her.'

'What do you mean?' But Mark had always thought of life in terms of competition.

'The old lady must have told you about her great and good friend David? The brains behind this place, I suspect. I did some research on him too. He was Professor of Archaeology in Vienna before the Anschluss; didn't have the wits to get out; had a pretty rough time before he did manage to escape. He was on one of those boats the British wouldn't let land in Israel. Ended up in Cyprus; got from there to Greece and ended as a key man in the resistance to the Germans. That's when he met our hostess, of course. They sound to have had quite a thing going. I wish I knew what they did that got them a whole island for themselves. Has the old thing told you yet?'

'No! And I'd hardly call her an old thing.' She turned away from him almost with relief as Sophia appeared in the courtyard entrance.

'I do apologise for having abandoned you for so long.'

Sophia made the apology general. 'And now I have a request to make. Some unexpected guests are arriving tonight, or rather, guests I had not expected so soon. I have promised them the most absolute privacy, and must ask your help in securing it. I have arranged that they shall sleep in the conference suite, which is off the treatment area, so that you can get to the pool without disturbing them, but for tonight I must ask if you will all very kindly go to your rooms, so that the place is quiet for their arrival. I expect you will be glad of an early night after your journey.' She directed this appeal to Frances, who was sitting very close to Christopher. 'The outside lights will be turned off in half an hour,' she went on. 'So, I hope you will all be safe in your own rooms by then. I do apologise to you all,' her smile of apology merely served to accentuate fatigue lines in the brown face. 'Daphne, would you come to my room for a moment?'

'Of course.' She turned to her mother. 'Good night, m—'

'Don't call me that,' said Frances viciously. 'You'll see me safe home, Chris, won't you? I'm scared of the dark.'

The men were all on their feet now, and good nights were quickly said, Daphne breathing a sigh of relief for the command from Sophia that had made it impossible for Mark to come to her room. But this time he bent to brush a whisper of a kiss across her cheek. 'Tomorrow then?'

'What about breakfast?' Frances paused in the cloister, still leaning on Christopher's arm.

'It will be served in your rooms,' said Sophia. 'After-wards, I hope Daphne will be able to show you a little of my island.' She smiled at Daphne and linked an arm through hers. 'Come along, it's time we were all in bed.'

It was cooler now, and black dark beyond the lights, but as they all moved out together into the cloister, Daphne was aware of movement below somewhere, towards the water-gate, and Sophia excused herself for a moment to go down there. The others paused at the entrance to the guests' circle.

'"You that way and we this,"' said Jacob Braun to Frances.

'I beg your pardon? Oh,' her laugh was forced. 'That nonsense about one side for the men and the other for the women. Out of the ark! You'll come back for a drink in my room, Chris, won't you? I'm sure you can persuade one of those ballet girls to find us one.'

'The Kyria asked us to go to our own rooms,' said Jacob Braun.

'Yes, please.' Sophia rejoined them. 'As a favour to me.' But it was a command. 'Come along, Daphne, I won't keep you more than a minute or two.'

Reaching her own courtyard, she moved wearily across it into the room beyond and sat down almost heavily in a high backed chair.

'You expect your guests soon?' Daphne asked.

'One of them is here already.' She closed her eyes for a moment. 'He's the "patient" your nice Jacob Braun spoke of. When he arrived on Kos so unexpectedly early, Andros sensibly wrapped him in bandages and brought him along. But it worries me, Daphne. Something's going wrong with my arrangements; someone is interfering. I don't like the feel of it. I'll be glad when the other one is safely here. He's the one most at risk, David's friend. If anything were to happen to him . . .'

'Happen?'

'There have been too many accidents. Too many oddities. At first I just thought it was someone trying to discredit what I am doing here on Temi; now I wonder if it's not more serious still. I'm glad you're here, Daphne.' She was silent for a moment, her eyes closed. 'Be a lamb and fetch me the bottle from my bathroom shelf. And a glass. It's a poor doctor who doesn't do her best for herself. And it's been quite a day. What with passing out in the pool . . . I haven't thanked you properly. Hermione says it was touch and go.'

'Do you often faint?' Daphne had wanted the chance to ask it.

'Never in my life. Hermione was surprised, too. But the treatments I've been giving have been tough. I've promised Hermione I won't swim again alone. Lucky you're here, cousin.' She reached out to press Daphne's hand. 'Very lucky.'

'It smells delicious.' Returning from the green marble bathroom, Daphne poured and passed golden liquid.

'Herbal.' Sophia sipped. 'And honey-based.' She sat, silent and totally relaxed for a few moments, then sighed and straightened, her dark eyes studying Daphne. 'Have you forgiven me for springing our ill-assorted guests on you, Daphne, and will you be able to manage them for me tomorrow, do you think?'

'I'll do my best. As to forgiving ... It's going to be quite interesting, don't you think? I'm –' she felt herself colouring, and was enraged – 'I think I'm glad to see Mark again.'

'Unfinished business,' said Sophia. 'I like your Jacob Braun.'

'Hardly mine. It's you he came to see. Sophia, Mark wants to see the village, and I imagine Jacob would like to, too. Would it be a good idea if I took them there tomorrow? Got them out of the way?'

'I don't usually allow it. The villagers don't like it much. It wasn't in our agreement.' Colour was ebbing back under the brown skin. 'But I think for tomorrow it's a good idea. If you can get your mother along the path. It's rough going. But if the men go, as they will, I expect she'll manage.'

'I'm sure she will.' Sophia had clearly summed up Frances. 'Where does the path start from?'

'I'll get Zoe to show you. And have her send a message up to the village first thing, warning them. You can lunch at the taverna; that should be an experience for all of you. They're kind people; it's the old hospitable Greece. And they'll do it for me, if I ask them. Only – warn our guests, Daphne, that they must behave themselves. If you can persuade your mother into a chiton, so much the better, if not, at least no trousers. And covered shoulders. Particularly if she wants to go into the church. They will welcome you there, too, my friends in the village, but they will also watch how you behave.'

'It's Sunday tomorrow. I'd quite forgotten.'

'Yes, that was the excuse given for advancing the date of the diplomatic meeting here. Both my guests are theoretically having quiet weekends at home with their families.'

'You don't want to tell me who they are?'

'I think not, if you don't mind.'

'I'm not sure I want to know. It's enough that you feel it's so important.'

'Important? You could say it was a kind of global life or death.' She looked at her watch. 'The lights will go out in five minutes. Good night, dear child, sleep well, and wish me luck.' She was on her feet now, slim and strong-looking as ever. 'I must go down to the watergate to welcome my honoured guest.'

'You don't much like the other one?'

Sophia laughed. 'Don't start reading my mind, that's a dangerous game.' She brushed a butterfly kiss against Daphne's cheek. 'But I think I like it.'

8

Daphne bolted her door that night, surprised at herself for doing so. But she knew Mark well enough to be sure that if he wanted to come to her Sophia's request would mean nothing to him. She thought he would come. But did she want him? Of course she did. That quick, light kiss had stirred up depths she had been trying to forget. But – quick, light, and confident. He thought he could take her for granted. After all the misery, he thought he could smile, and beckon, and she would come running. Even if he was right, she was not going to let him see it; not yet. And was she sure he was right?

Something roused her from her first, exhausted sleep. A hand, trying her door? Mark's hand? Or just her imagination. She slept again at last, restlessly, then plunged at first light into a deep sleep from which Zoe woke her, knocking on her door, obviously surprised to find it bolted. 'Your breakfast is waiting for you in your courtyard.' Her tone suggested affront, and Daphne hastened to apologise.

'I had the horrors a bit, last night,' she said. 'Something about those secret guests got at me, I think.'

'The Kyria did not sleep well either.' Zoe accepted the implied apology. 'She is breakfasting with one of her new guests. I have sent a message to the village; the Kyria says I am to take you there. Will you tell the other guests, or shall I?'

'Have they had their breakfasts yet?' Extraordinary to find herself in charge of this odd group of people.

'No. The Kyria said I should come to you first.'

'Then would you kindly ask them to meet me in the guests' courtyard –' She looked at her watch. 'Perhaps at eleven? Could you maybe arrange some coffee then? Nescafé, please, for my mother.' This, too, was an apology.

99

'She really is your mother?'

'Yes.' She would not apologise for Frances.

'But no kin of the Kyria?'

'No. The connection is through my father. Thank you, Zoe.' Left alone, she drank freshly squeezed orange juice and thought about her father. If Sophia had invited her mother, surely she would have asked him too, since it was he who was her kinsman? Would he turn up as unexpectedly as the rest of the guests? And what would she feel if he did? Would she even recognise him? It was over ten years since their last, sad meeting. He had gone back to America straight after it. There had been occasional letters for a while; Christmas presents that she remembered as always subtly wrong; chosen for too old a child, or too young a one. Her mother had made half-hearted efforts to make her write and thank him, but had been too absorbed in her own affairs to trouble herself about it much. She hardly blamed him for giving up.

Half an hour later, she found the three men awaiting her in the guests' courtyard, and from their sudden silence suspected that they had been discussing her, or Sophia, or both. Which was natural enough. Now they spoke all at once, in greeting and amazed comment on the place as seen by daylight. 'The mosaic by the stream is out of this world,' said Chris.

'I wonder what genius planted the vine and the bougainvillaea.' Jacob braun hitched up his tunic. 'It must make the place practically invisible from the air.'

'That's what my cousin said.' Daphne smiled at him. 'Keeping it Temi of the secrets.'

'Are we really getting to see the village?' Mark interrupted her. He was in one of his dark romantic glooms this morning. It must have been his hand at her bedroom door last night.

'Just as soon as my mother arrives and we've had some coffee.' She turned. 'Ah, here it is, thank you, Zoe.'

'Why don't you call your mother Frances like the rest of us?' suggested Jacob Braun diffidently. 'You'll find it gets easier as you go on.'

'Thanks! You're absolutely right, and I'll try. Habit's a terrible thing.'

'A bad master,' he agreed. 'But a useful servant.' He turned with a smile to say something in quick Greek to Zoe, who was busy with the coffee cups.

She smiled and answered in Greek, then turned with natural good manners to Daphne. 'The kyrie is surprised that we make real coffee the French way here on Temi.'

'Yes, my – Frances will be pleased,' said Daphne, and got an approving smile from Jacob. 'Would you very kindly tell her the coffee is served?' she asked Zoe, knowing her mother's unpunctual habits of old.

'And that we all await her eagerly,' added Jacob Braun.

They started at last some time later, after Daphne had managed to persuade her mother to change scarlet shorts and high heeled sandals for a chiton and espadrilles. She was helped in this by all three men who were eager to be off and blandished Frances shamelessly into agreeing. Watching them persuade her that they longed to see her wearing the chiton Daphne felt curiously revolted, both with them for manipulating Frances and with her for laying herself open to it.

'Bear with us.' Jacob Braun fell in beside her as they followed Zoe up by the stream across the guests' circle. 'It's the only way, you know.'

'That doesn't make me like it any better.' How odd to be discussing her mother with this stranger.

'Of course not.' But he was interrupted by Mark, who moved in between them and took her arm, his gloom apparently gone as suddenly as it had come. 'Did you remember your sunburn cream, love? I've not forgotten how you burned on Rhodes.'

'I've got some on, thanks.' She coloured, remembering where she had burned, and sure that he did, too.

'That's all right then. What a place this is!' He paused in the pillared entrance to the treatment area and looked back across the vine-hung second circle. 'Do you think your cousin would mind if I took some pictures?'

'I'm not sure. I'd rather you didn't until we've asked her.'

'O.K. Which way now, Zoe?' He had wasted no time in getting to Christian names.

'Through here, and to the left.' Zoe swung open the door of the treatment area. 'The pool's along there, any time you want to swim.' She pointed down the corridor Daphne knew so well. 'If there's time, we'll take a look at it on the way back, but right now they'll be expecting us in the village.' She turned on the lights of a corridor that slanted off to the left. The usual anonymous doors on its right and a blank wall on the left suggested that they were skirting the very edge of the hollowed-out treatment area.

'Extraordinary! The whole place has been cut out of the rock?' The three men were clustered round Zoe now, eager with questions. This was Jacob Braun. 'Do you know when?'

'Not precisely.' She laughed. 'A long time ago! They built well, our ancestors. The Kyria says she only had to have it made good here and there. This wall is still just the rock, whitewashed, as you can see.'

'She put in the modern doors and wired it for light, I take it,' said Jacob. 'It must have been pretty formidable by torchlight.'

'Are you all right, love?' Mark fell back to take Daphne's arm. 'This isn't exactly your scene, is it?'

'No! Thanks.' Grateful for the tingling reassurance of his touch, she was nevertheless listening eagerly as Zoe told Jacob how Sophia had built her modern clinic on the lines of the old buildings.

'I hope she kept records,' said Jacob, and, 'Monstrous not to have the experts in,' said Chris.

'You'd better talk to her about that. There are most certainly records.' Zoe paused at a dead end where a larger door faced them and reached into the pocket of her chiton for a key. It turned smoothly in the lock and the door swung outwards on to a welcome blaze of sunlight.

'Wow!' Mark pulled Daphne forward to stand beside him on the little plateau that must be the mouth of an old quarry, with the door on its back wall. Ahead of them, a mountain path climbed diagonally across the bare, brown hill. 'Are we going over there?' he asked Zoe.

'I'm not,' said Frances.

'It's easier than it looks.' Zoe locked the heavy door behind Jacob. 'The Kyria said you were all young and strong. It is no distance to the village once one is over the brow of the hill, and the path gets better all the way. They are expecting us in the village; there will be roast lamb at the taverna.'

'Come along, Fran,' said Chris. 'I'll help you over the rough bits. There'll be brandy at the taverna too, won't there, Zoe?'

'We make our own,' said Zoe.

'You wouldn't be able to see a thing from the air.' Chris had turned to look back at tangled thorn and cistus on the lip of the quarry. 'Natural camouflage, like the vine and the bougainvillaea. What an extraordinary place. I do thank you for my invitation, Daphne.'

'And so do I!' Jacob was walking ahead with Zoe, but turned to smile at Daphne. 'I wouldn't have missed this for all the coffee in Ceylon. I suppose the quarry is where they carved the stone for the temples, all those years ago?'

'That's what the Kyria says,' Zoe smiled at him. 'She thinks it was all open here before the great earthquake.'

'That figures. They'd never have got the rock through that tangle of passages.'

'I'm beginning to wonder if you're going to get me over this damned hill.' Frances was tired of being ignored. 'And I've got a stone in my shoe.'

'Here! Let me give you a hand.' Chris was all attention at once, and Daphne breathed a grateful sigh. 'And then how about that taverna, and the roast lamb.' The stone safely extracted, he applied himself to keeping Frances cheerful, and Daphne blessed him again as she and Mark started up the hill behind Zoe and Jacob. Luckily, though it was steep, the path was wide enough for two to walk abreast. 'It's no worse than what passes for the high street on Symi,' said Jacob Braun. 'A perfectly good mule track. I suppose all the village supplies come this way, Zoe?'

'What we can't make ourselves,' she told him. 'The Kyria is a great believer in self sufficiency.'

'Kyria this and Kyria that,' Frances broke in impatiently. 'Anyone would think she was Hitler or someone.'

'Or someone,' said Jacob quietly, and a little uncomfortable hush fell on the party. It lasted until they reached the brow of the hill and saw the fertile valley below, with its whitewashed typical Greek village, its church and pattern of brown plough and golden harvest, of silver olive and dark green orange groves.

'Good God!' Jacob stopped in his tracks. 'The Promised Land.'

'That's what my mother said.' Zoe turned to him with sudden warmth. 'She's told me many times. After the sea voyage, and the dangerous channel, and an uncomfortable night camping above the watergate, they climbed up to here, and looked at each other, and cried a little, and shook hands.'

'Who do you mean, "they?"' Frances bent to take another stone out of her espadrille, leaning heavily on Chris.

'The First Comers. The founders of the village. Has the Kyria not told you about them?'

'There's been so little time,' Daphne said. 'Do tell us. I don't know about anyone else, but I could do with a rest.'

The men agreed tactfully as Frances slumped down with a sigh of relief on a convenient stone.

'The First Comers built the village.' Zoe was looking at it with pride. 'When the Kyria found what she found on Temi, she needed workers, she and the Kyrie David. They let it be known that there would be a good life here for people uprooted by the war. This was almost forty years ago, remember; there were many, many Greeks who had suffered under the Germans, or the Italians, or the Turks.' She turned aside and spat, suddenly and shockingly, into dry grass. 'My mother was one of them. She had lost everything, everyone, on Crete. German reprisals. Her whole village. Wiped out. She had been away, guiding an American airman to safety. When she got back, carefully, as they always came back, she found nothing but smouldering embers. After the war, she heard of the Kyria's offer, and came. She met my father here, on this path. It was really rough then, and she was tired. He carried her bundle for her. He was from northern Greece, what is Albania now.' Once again she spat. 'We owe everything to the Kyria,' she summed it up. 'Time to go on! Downhill now.'

'Downhill's much worse than up.' But Frances got grumbling to her feet.

'So the whole village is new,' said Jacob, looking down at it.

'Was new forty years ago,' Zoe told him. 'The Kyrie David was sure it was on the site of the classical village, but no one has ever found a trace of that. He said the earthquake that preserved the temples must have destroyed everything on this side. It closed the gap to the sea, too.' She pointed to a fold in the mountains. 'That's where it must have been; a narrow way down to the harbour. Now there is no possible way through. Generations of small boys have looked for one and not found it.'

'And not even room for a helicopter to land,' said Mark.

'No.' She turned to give him a sharp look. 'The boys keep asking for a football pitch, and the Kyria has always said no. And the village elders,' she hastened to add.

The whole village seemed to have turned out to greet them. 'It is not often we entertain the Kyria's guests,' explained Zoe, introducing the head man, a handsome old bandit with black moustaches and the classic Greek kilted breeches.

'That's funny,' Jacob fell in beside Daphne as they walked down the narrow, paved alley that angled in to the village centre. 'The first thing she said to him, very quick, was, "One of them speaks Greek. " What do you make of that, Daphne?'

'I don't think I like it very much.'

'It could just be good manners; not wanting him to say something careless, thinking we couldn't understand.' Was he trying to convince himself or her?'

'I suppose so.'

'Talk about model villages!' Mark had not heard Jacob's low-voiced remark to Daphne. 'Almost too good to be true.'

'Their flowers are lovely.' Frances bent to pick a sprig of scarlet geraniums that erupted from an old petrol tin. 'But where's this taverna? I'm dying of thirst.'

'It is one o'clock.' Mark knew Frances' habits of old. 'Tell you what. Why don't you ladies go and put your feet up at the taverna while we three have another quick look round? O.K. with you, Zoe?'

'Well.' The girl looked doubtful. 'The Kyria didn't say . . .'

'We'll be as good as gold.' Mark was at his charming best. 'And Braun here can talk to the natives if need be. Come on, Jake, let's go! Who knows? Maybe you'll find evidence of that lost classical village old Sophia's boy friend missed.'

'I very much doubt that,' said Jacob dryly. 'But it's true, I would like more of a look around.'

'So would I,' chimed in Chris. 'It's an absolutely fascinating bit of town planning; all the character of an old village, but a hell of a lot more convenience. That David must have been quite a guy if he designed all this. Did he, Zoe?'

'He and the Kyria between them.' Zoe obviously did not much like the division of the party, but there was nothing she could do about it short of actual rudeness, so she yielded gracefully. 'Very well, we'll expect you at the taverna in – half an hour perhaps? It's up at the top of the village, beyond the church.'

'Another hill,' grumbled Frances. 'Then let's get going, for God's sake. I'm dry as the Sahara and I need to powder my nose. I'm sure I look like hell.'

'You couldn't if you tried.' Mark had always been able to manage Frances. 'See you soon, ladies.' His smile was for Daphne.

'This way then,' Zoe started up the whitewashed steps that were the village street. 'Would you like just to stop and look at the church as we go by? The service is over, and I know the Papa would be proud to show it to you. There is an icon . . .'

'Christ, no.' Frances interrupted rudely, her manners gone with the men. 'I'm for the taverna, the ladies' room, if any, and a drink, in that order, but quick.'

Daphne, aware of the black-clad figure of the village priest hovering outside the church, hoped passionately but without conviction that he did not understand English, and they climbed the last steps to the top of the village in constrained silence.

Something else beside her mother's rudeness had been worrying her. 'Is it right, our coming to the taverna?' she asked Zoe, remembering small villages on Rhodes where it had been obvious that she was entertained very much on sufferance, as an appendage of Mark.

'Three women, you mean?' Zoe took her point at once. 'Oh, yes. This village is different. You'd have seen, if it hadn't been Sunday. It's a pity about the church, though.' She shrugged expressively. 'Maybe for the best at that.' Daphne was afraid she thought Frances might have said something disastrous, and equally afraid she was right. 'Here we are, and here is the proprietor, waiting for us.'

'Good gracious,' said Daphne. The proprietor of the Temi taverna was a tall dark-haired woman with the build of one of the female statues on Kos.

'Welcome, the Kyria's guests!' She moved impressively forward to greet them in fluent English, a handsome figure in black blouse and permanently pleated black skirt. 'But where are the others, Zoe?'

'They wanted to look around a bit more, Anastasia. They will join us soon.'

'Where's the Ladies?' Frances interrupted her. 'I'm a mess whatever young Mark says.'

'This way, madame.' Anastasia turned to Zoe. 'Take the kyria out on the terrace, Zoe, and give her a drink.'

'What a heavenly place!' Daphne stood at the front of the vine-hung terrace looking down on the gold and green patchwork of the valley. 'But is there no one else here?'

'Sunday's a quiet day. If you'd like to sit here, Kyria Daphne? And shall I get you an ouzo?'

'Yes, please. I'm afraid I need it.' Tone as well as look were an implied apology for her mother. 'Surely it's very unusual to have a woman running a taverna?' she asked.

'Temi is a very unusual village.' Zoe paused, her hand on the back of a chair. 'Men and women are equals here, in everything. It's true at the Sanctuary, too, only there are so many more women than men there that you wouldn't have noticed. It was part of the understanding on which people were accepted for Temi in the first place. My mother says she couldn't believe it at first. That it would really happen.'

'And has it?'

'Well, not entirely,' Zoe admitted. 'There have been problems; with the women as much as the men. And then there is the Papa — the priest. He is getting old: perhaps it is understandable that he is sliding back to the ways of his youth. But he did promise the Kyria and Kyrie David. They all did, the First Comers.'

'You have a head man, though?'

'Only this year.' Zoe smiled. 'We hold it year about, men and women. Last year it was Anastasia, and I tell you she made the village jump. Not everyone liked it,' she added. 'Specially not the Papa. He does rather think women are for cooking and scrubbing floors. Anastasia made him whitewash the steps of his church,' she smiled with remembered pleasure. 'He did *not* like that. I think it must have been he who started the trouble with the new government.'

'Trouble?'

'Oh.' Zoe's face changed. 'Has the Kyria not told you yet? I am sure she will. But perhaps, if you will forgive me, she had better.'

'Yes, of course.' Daphne found herself liking Zoe very much indeed. 'Are you going to have an ouzo too?' It was the best way she could register how she felt the relation between them had changed. How could she have imagined Zoe a servant?

'I don't think so.' Zoe took the suggestion in the spirit in which it was meant. 'We tend not to drink when we are working.' She smiled, and Daphne saw that she was beautiful. 'Anastasia keeps white grape juice for people who want to look as if they are drinking. I shall have some of that and no one will know except you. What will your mother want? Ah, here she comes.'

Frances demanded brandy. 'That place is out of the ark,' she told Daphne, 'but I will say it's water, and it works. You going before the boys turn up?'

The men were late, of course, and Anastasia, bringing Frances her third brandy, brought an even more lavish supply of mezes than before. 'It will be hot, I'm afraid, walking back after lunch.' A note of warning in her voice.

'Don't talk about it.' Frances reached out to the plate of small hors d'oeuvres. 'Smashing little sausages, these. Have one, Daph?'

'Thanks.' Daphne had always hated the shortening of the name her father had given her. 'Do you make these on the island?' she asked Anastasia. 'They're delicious.'

'Yes, we have pigs out on the hillside as well as goats and sheep. One of the many advantages of life on Temi is that the only predators are animals; we can let the livestock roam at will with no problems of thieving. Ah, here comes one of your wanderers.'

'Terribly sorry to be late.' Jacob had been hurrying; there were sweat patches on his tunic and his breath came fast. 'Oh, the others not back yet either?'

'You split up?' Daphne's anger was as much for herself as for him. Sophia had put her in charge of this party and what a mess she had made of it.

'Why, yes. I wanted to get down to the gap where the path to the sea must have gone through. I hoped to find traces of it, but I'm afraid I didn't do any better than the generations of small boys Zoe spoke of. Oh, thank you, Zoe.' She had silently handed him an ouzo. 'A lot of water, if I may. It's delicious, your island water, kyria.' To Anastasia.

'You've not drunk from the stream, I hope? The animals rather have their own way here on Temi.'

'Oh, no. I've more sense than that. I begged a drink from a lady at the bottom of the village. I was hard put to it to persuade her I only wanted water. They're a hospitable lot, your — do you call them Temians or Temans?'

'Temiotes.' Her smile deprived the correction of its sting. 'I would have thought you'd have known that, speaking Greek so well as you do.'

'Dear me! Your intelligence system is good.'

'We like to know what is going on.'

'Are we your only guests today?' Jacob was glancing about the empty tables on the terrace.

'For now, yes. We make rather an institution of the Sunday meal, here on Temi. It was the Kyria's idea, back at the beginning, that families should get together, at least once a week, to talk things over. It's our political system, you could say. If you could stay until this evening, which I am afraid is not possible, since the path back is not safe in the dark, you would find all the heads of households gathered here, for a friendly drink, and to compare notes. To report for their families, if you like.'

'Your form of local government?' And then, colouring in the rather endearing way he had, 'Forgive me, do you understand that?' He broke into resonant Greek.

She smiled at him, reminding Daphne more than ever of the statues on Kos. 'Thank you. In fact, I understand your English, and was interested, as you must have been, to notice how differently the same thought comes out in the two languages.'

'You saw that too! Kyria, may I come and talk to you again?' But he was interrupted by the appearance of Mark and Chris, quarrelling. 'I said by the church.' Mark looked about the terrace, focusing at once on Anastasia. 'I do ask your forgiveness for being so late, kyria. I have been waiting for my friend here outside your church, and he tells me he was waiting for me down by the school, of all stupidities.'

'It's what I said, just the same.' Chris spoke to Daphne. 'Mark here suggested the church and I said no, I wanted to do some drawings of the ingenious way the modern school has been blended into the traditional village. And here they are! You said no photographs, Daphne, but I'm sure Sophia wouldn't object to honest drawing.'

'They're good!'

'No need to sound so surprised. It's my job. But I am

sorry we've kept you so long; you must be starving. Total idiocy. First we waited all that time, and then Mark came down by the main steps and I went up the lane by the stream. So of course we missed each other and had to start all over again. How about some lunch? What have you got for us?' Turning to Anastasia, he asked it abruptly, as to a menial.

'Lamb,' she told him succinctly. 'But you will wish to tidy yourselves before you sit down with the ladies. This way, gentlemen.'

'That's quite a gal.' Frances put down her empty glass and looked at it regretfully. 'Has she a husband at all?'

'No, she never married,' Zoe told her. 'From choice, I hardly need tell you. Her father built the taverna; she inherited it. And she's been very active in the village.'

'How did it go when she was boss last year?' asked Daphne.

'It wasn't her first time by any means,' said Zoe. 'But her first time under the new government. It was odd; you'd have thought that with our new socialist regime there would be more equality for women. I voted for them,' she said it almost defiantly, 'because I thought that. But it doesn't seem to be working that way. Anastasia has had all kinds of problems we've never had before. Some silly little ones, like having official letters addressed to Kyrie instead of Kyria, and more serious ones like not getting listened to when she was trying to tell them something important. Even here in the village, things have changed a bit.' She did not enjoy admitting it. 'This year's head man is a nonentity. It's the Papa, the priest makes the trouble; he never did think much of women. If he met the Virgin Mary, pregnant, he'd run a mile. He has a wonderful boys' choir,' she summed it up. 'Girls not wanted. I must go and help Anastasia with the food.' She left them precipitately.

'That was a mouthful,' said Frances. 'Doesn't like men much, would you say, our Zoe? Pity. She could be attractive, if she only tried.' She gave her daughter a thoughtful look. 'Well, so could you, come to that. I never did go for your natural look, but I must admit it seems O.K. here.

Are you going to have Mark back then? He seems to think so.'

'Has he said anything?' Furiously, she felt herself blushing deeply.

'Doesn't need to; stands out a mile. I'd have him, I think. He's a bright boy, that Mark. He'll go far.'

'Yes, but where to? Here they come,' she added, noticing that all three men seemed to be arguing now.

'I want to ask that splendid landlady to join us for lunch,' said Mark.

'And I say if we do we must invite Zoe too.' Jacob had obviously said it before.

'Bossy young –' Mark was stopped by a quelling glance from Daphne who could see Zoe approaching with a tray.

Chris took the law into his own hands. 'Won't you and the kyria join us for lunch, Zoe?'

'I was intending to,' she gave him a look of sparkling amusement. 'As to Anastasia, I'll ask her. Sunday is a quiet day, as you can see; she might be able to.' She handed the tray to a sullen-looking boy who had been laying a checked cloth on a table at the front of the terrace, spoke to him in swift Greek, and vanished through the kitchen doorway.

'Wrong-footed again,' Chris shrugged. 'I don't altogether get the set-up on this island, do you, Daphne?'

'Zoe was telling us about it. Sophia – my cousin – and her friend seem to have established a kind of equality of the sexes here. It was part of the agreement with the First Comers.'

'Good God,' said Mark. 'Believe that, you'll believe anything.'

'Haven't you changed your views a bit since we wrote *Women in History*?' Daphne challenged Mark as he sat down beside her.

'We?' His hand, finding hers under the table, took the sting out of it. 'Wow!' The exclamation was for Anastasia, who had covered her black shirt with a heavily embroidered tunic that made her look more like some archaic priestess than ever. He rose to greet her, probably surprising himself as much as he did Daphne, and seated her at the head of the table.

'Do please, tell us,' Jacob had taken the place on Anastasia's other side, 'how it comes about that your English is so good, kyria. And Zoe's too.' He turned with a friendly apologetic look at Zoe, who had slipped in between Anastasia and Mark. 'I know most Greeks speak it well,' he went on, 'but you speak it almost like natives. Don't tell me you all come to England for a year, or something of the kind.'

'Oh, no.' Anastasia looked at him gravely. 'The Kyria has always been against that. She says, forgive me, that for people like us who must live at subsistence level, the life of great cities like yours can only be corrupting. She is always a little anxious when our young people go to mainland Greece to finish their education. And, of course, she is right. Many of them do not come back. Or come back with different ideas.'

'They might be better ones,' said Mark.

'They might.' She left it at that. 'But as to our English; that is simple enough. It was one of the stipulations in the original agreement, signed with the First Comers. The Kyria and her Kyrie David thought that modern Greek was an inflammatory language, politically, that is. And this was to be an island devoted to peace and healing. They made the First Comers promise that they would learn enough English so they could conduct their village affairs in it.' She smiled at Mark. 'If you were to come here this evening, you would hear us all planning next week's activities in fluent English. It's a great inducement to learning the language, you can see.'

'You mean,' Chris leaned forward from beside Frances, 'everyone in the village understands English?'

'Just about.'

'Ouch.' He and Mark exchanged glances.

9

The lamb was delicious, the lunch took a long time, and Daphne, monopolised again by Mark, found herself trying to catch bits of the animated talk between Jacob, Anastasia and Zoe who were laughing a great deal, and switching from Greek to English and back again. 'We're talking about language,' Jacob caught her eye at the coffee stage, and explained with a note of apology, 'and how often it conceals as much as it reveals. American and English, for instance, just think of the possibilities for misunderstanding.'

'All I understand,' Frances had finished her wine, 'is that I could do with a brandy.'

'I'm sorry.' Zoe got up. 'But we really ought to be going. The path is not at all easy once the light begins to go.'

'Oh hell!' But the sense of this was obvious. 'No more sightseeing then?' Frances sounded as if that suited her well enough.

'Not today. The mill and the bakery will have to wait; and the wine press. Another day would be better anyway; nothing much happens on Sundays.'

'You take your religion seriously?' Mark suddenly sounded as if he was at work.

'It depends what you mean by religion.' Zoe turned to Jacob, who had reached into his pocket for a wallet. 'Good gracious, no. You are the Kyria's guests.'

'And mine,' said Anastasia unanswerably. 'It has been a pleasure to entertain you.' She too had risen, effectively breaking up the party, and spoke directly to Daphne. 'If you should ever need me, send Zoe and I will come at once.'

'Why, thank you,' said Daphne puzzled.

The food and wine had been good, the day was still hot,

they walked back mostly in silence, punctuated by an occasional grumble from Frances, who had annexed Chris again and leaned heavily on his arm whenever the path made this possible. Since Mark had equally taken over Daphne, Jacob was once more left to walk ahead with Zoe, and Daphne could hear a steady stream of question and answer, sometimes English, sometimes incomprehensible Greek, and grew almost jealously curious about what they were saying. Why had she talked about herself so much to Sophia in the last week, and asked so few questions? Or had Sophia perhaps wanted it that way? Answering Mark in monosyllables, she hoped she would find a message from Sophia awaiting her when she got back, a chance to talk to her alone.

But someone was waiting for them just inside the door in the hill. Someone who whispered swiftly to Zoe in Greek. 'There's been an accident.' Zoe turned back in the doorway to speak to them. 'A serious one. Would you mind waiting here for a few minutes? I'll come for you as soon as I can.'

'What's happened?' asked Jacob.

'We don't know yet. It's Hermione. She was on her way home to the village; she must have fallen in the passage, just the other side of the door. They're fetching a stretcher for her now. If you wouldn't mind waiting . . .'

'Of course not,' said Daphne. 'But isn't there something we could do to help?'

'Not right now. I'll let you know if there is. And just as soon as you can come through.' Zoe closed the big door gently in their faces.

'Well I'm damned,' said Chris. 'Never a dull moment on Temi.'

'Island of secrets,' said Jacob thoughtfully. 'I thought Zoe sounded really bothered.'

'Yes. I am sorry.' Daphne suddenly felt the burden of her responsibility for the party.

'Not your fault.' Mark pressed her arm reassuringly. 'And no use standing here like a bunch of refugees waiting for the soup kitchen to open. One good thing, we're not the only people who've waited here. I take it this is the staff entrance, and it looks as if they have to wait about until they're let in, too. Interesting, wouldn't you say?' He led the way across the quarry floor to where a shelter of bamboo canes had been built to throw shade over a group of benches and tables. 'I didn't notice this before, did you?'

'No.' She sat down beside him because he obviously expected her to do so and then regretted the chance to ask Jacob what else he had learned from Zoe. But he was busy finding a comfortable place, half sun half shade, for Frances, and she felt a wave of gratitude to him.

'What a bore.' Frances settled herself with her back against the warm rock. 'I was just about ready to put my feet up with a drink and here we are stuck at the back end of nowhere.' She leaned back and closed her eyes.

'I expect it's a bore for Hermione, too.' Chris got out his sketching block and settled at the edge of the quarry. 'What a place! Even the door is camouflaged. If you didn't know, you'd have no idea that either the village or the cave existed.'

'Come on, relax, be comfortable.' Mark's arm came round Daphne's waist to pull her down until her head rested on his shoulder. 'You must be tired. Rest, love. There'll be time for talking.'

The old magic worked again, the warm, exciting feel of him, the thrill as his encircling hand brushed her breast, momentarily, as if by accident, through the light chiton. She felt her whole body respond, and willed him not to feel it too. 'Lots of time.' His voice was low. 'I've missed you so much, Daphne. Every way.'

'I must say, I am quite tired.' While part of her thrilled to his touch, something else resented the public appropriation. She closed her eyes, pretending instant, wine-brought sleep, and was shocked awake by a sudden stir around her.

'Door's open,' said Mark. 'Come on, love, time to go. How's the patient, Zoe?'

'Patient?' Zoe looked older, drawn, anxious. 'Hermione? I'm afraid it was a very serious accident indeed. She's dead.'

'Dead?' Jacob crossed the plateau in three strides. 'What on earth happened to her?'

'We don't know. She must have fainted, fallen and hit her head. The Kyria is examining her now. In her room. She asks that you go back to your own rooms and wait there for further news.'

They were all silent and subdued when they emerged into evening light at the top of the guests' circle. 'We can find our own way now,' Jacob told Zoe. 'You want us to stay in our rooms, right?'

'If you would. It is the time of the Sunday meeting. We have one here too, of course, and the Kyria will want to talk about the accident. Dinner will be late, I am afraid. In the guests' dining-room, at nine. You will find drinks in your rooms.' She anticipated a protest from Frances.

'Very well.' Jacob answered for all of them. 'Thank you for our day, Zoe. Tell the Kyria how sorry we are. I don't know about the rest of you, but I'll be glad enough to settle with a book for a bit.' He turned away.

'I'll see you to your room.' Daphne took her mother's arm, anticipating a move by Mark. 'And go straight on to my own,' she told Zoe. 'Where does your meeting happen?'

'In the lecture room. It's in the treatment area. No swimming tonight, I'm afraid.' She looked quickly at her watch. 'I must go. Forgive me.'

'Stay and talk a while.' Frances poured straight brandy and drank it off. 'I don't fancy being alone, and we've a lot to talk about, you and I.'

'I'm sorry. There might be a message from Cousin Sophia.' Their time for talking had passed years before.

'Quite her fair-haired little pet, aren't you? You and all the other girls! Charming set-up, if you ask me. Zoe and Anastasia and Hermione and God knows how many others . . . Had you stopped to wonder why she invited you, not your father? She doesn't reckon much to men, does she? That David she keeps talking about must have been queer as they come.'

'Goodbye, mother.' Daphne had had enough. Pausing at the entrance to her own courtyard, she thought how quiet it all was. Usually, though one seldom saw anyone, there were small sounds of life going on, of unseen hands at work. Now, with the human silence absolute, natural noises took over, the stream talked quietly to itself, evening crickets chattered . . . There was a note on her table, held down by a bottle of ouzo against any evening stirring of wind. 'Dear child: I am so sad this disaster has happened to your visit. Wait in your room; I will come to you on the way to dinner.' And a bold 'S'.

Two glasses by the ouzo bottle on the tray. The staff work of Temi was impeccable as ever, despite the disaster. Disaster? A strong word surely for however unhappy an accident. 'Send for me if you need help,' Anastasia had said, and meant it. What was happening, on this island of secrets?

She moved about mechanically, showering, putting on the heavy silk chiton that lay ready on her bed, her mind swinging all the time like a metronome between the problems of Mark and of Sophia. Strange things had been happening ever since she reached Kos, but strangest of all, it seemed to her, was that Mark wanted her back. I dance to his tune, she thought, pouring ouzo on to a ready lump of ice. Should I?

Half an hour later, Sophia found her still sitting there in the half-dark, gazing down at melting ice. 'A bad day.' She bent down to switch on a table lamp. 'My poor Hermione. It was no accident, Daphne. She was killed. Someone struck her from behind; once; hard. I am so very glad that you and your party were safe in the village at the time.'

'Safe?' asked Daphne. And then, 'Oh, poor Hermione. But, Sophia, I'm not even surprised. I think I knew it was no accident. Odd things have been happening; ever since I got to Kos.'

'Odd things?'

'Little things. Just as you said. Too many accidents; too many coincidences. Sophia, what is going on?'

'I wish I knew. I think, perhaps, various things, all happening at once. Zoe says she told you something about the new government.'

'That they are making things difficult for you? Yes, she did. Why?'

'They want the island. They want an incident that will justify them in taking it away from me. My title is as good as our lawyers and the government of the time could make it, but it's only a piece of paper after all, and you know how much that is worth in the world today. All they need is a good public excuse.'

'But why? What would they do with the island?'

'That's the question, isn't it? Not what I do, that's certain. Use it for defence, perhaps. Temi is frighteningly near Turkey. Or tourism. Do you realise what a fortune someone could make here?'

'Yes. And all their other sites being so crowded now . . . But surely, they must recognise the value of this place? The healing pool . . . That extraordinary figure up at the temple . . . The Tholos you spoke of . . .'

'You'd think so. But modern governments seem more interested in killing than curing. They talk peace and make war. I've been wondering if this attack on Temi may not be directed at it as a centre for peace, not just as a place of healing, or a possible tourist site. Imagine if I were to send for the police, just while my two guests are in the thick of their talks?'

'You aren't going to?'

'No. We have agreed, at our meeting, that this was an accidental death, and will be treated as such. In that case, my only duty is to notify the authorities on Kos in the usual way.'

'You'll lie to them?'

'I see no other course. And yet I'm afraid that then something else will happen, some new "accident". But at least I should have got my distinguished guests safely off the island first. They have talked all day. They are very close to agreement. That is more important than anything. They must be left in peace.'

'You mean there is a murderer loose on Temi and you are going to do nothing about it?'

'Oh, no, we mean to find the murderer ourselves,' said Sophia quietly. 'And turn him over to justice. Zoe says you separated in the village?'

'Yes, I'm very sorry. There seemed no way to prevent it.'

'Short of actual rudeness? I know. But at least you and your mother and Zoe were together all the time, I understand, though the three men split up?'

'Yes.'

'How long for? Could one of them have got back to the door in the hill?'

'If he had hurried? Yes, perhaps. But he couldn't have opened it.'

'It was open when Hermione was found,' said Sophia bleakly. 'As senior staff, she had her own key. It was in its place, on her body, but you see there is no way we can tell whether the door was opened before or after her death.'

'So it could have been someone from the village?'

'Or one of your three men, if you think they had long enough.'

'To meet Hermione? And kill her? But Sophia, why?'

'Ah, if we knew that! We know so little about them. I am afraid, Daphne, that we have to recognise, you and I, that one of those three men may be a murderer. I do beg you to be careful.' She sighed. 'Nothing has gone as I meant it to. I wanted you to have time. Time to remember your life. Sort it out, with the evidence in front of you. Find yourself. But there is no time. It has caught up with me. Daphne, there is something I have to ask you to do for me. Far too soon . . .'

'I've been wishing I could help.'

'You are, immensely, just by being here. Not to mention saving my life! But this is more: the patient I've been taking for daily treatments. I'm going to have to ask you to take him over while I am occupied with this dreadful business.'

'What treatment?' But she knew, and was afraid.

'Yes, it's the Tholos. But there is nothing there for you to fear, Daphne. It is a most extraordinary place, but I promise you there is nothing supernatural about it. Nor any danger. As a doctor, I can see its results, but I'm not scientist enough to understand their cause. One of these days, I shall have to get the experts in to study it, but I am so afraid that to do so would put an end to its usefulness. If only we had found it before David died, he might have understood . . . It might even have saved him. No use thinking about that. What happens, happens. But there is no question: for certain mental and nervous conditions, it works. It seems to have the same effect as electric shock treatment, but without the horrors: a kind of shaking back to sanity.'

'Sanity? You mean this patient is mad?'

'No, no! Now I really have frightened you. I'm sorry, Daphne, I'm . . . I'm feeling my age tonight. He's not mad at all, but mentally shaken. And physically! He's had a bad time. A very bad time. He will probably tell you about it. I think I would rather leave it to him. That will be good for him, too. To talk it out . . . and to you.'

'So what do I do?' She made her voice matter of fact.

'He has his treatment every morning, the earlier the better. Tomorrow, I am summoning a meeting of everyone who could possibly have been involved in Hermione's killing, which means practically everyone except you and your mother and Zoe.'

'And Anastasia.' Daphne remembered her strange last words.

'And Anastasia, of course. So, as soon as you have had your breakfast, you go to the treatment area, room seventeen. There is a plan on the left as you go in, I don't know if you have noticed?'

'No.' Daphne did not like to confess how fast she tended to scurry through the treatment area.

'Follow it; switch on all the lights you want; there is no one there just now to be disturbed. My other guests are in the conference suite, on the other side. You will find your patient waiting for you. Take your time, but take him to the door of the Tholos. Here's the key, let him in and wait for him outside. He knows what to do. Then go on to the open area. He's not up to swimming, but the Lady and the fresh air do him good. There is absolutely nothing to be afraid of, Daphne.'

'Except fear. You've not told me his name.'

'He'll tell you, if he wants to. And now, we must go to dinner, our guests will be waiting.'

Daphne bolted her door again that night, and again woke, this time, to the clear sound of knocking. 'Daphne.' Mark's voice. 'Let me in. I've got to talk to you.'

Pretend to be asleep? But he knew how easily she could be waked. If she let him in, he might tell her something that would be useful to Sophia. Which half of her was arguing that?

'Daphne.' His voice came again. 'I know you're awake. Come on; let me in. There's something your cousin needs to know before tomorrow's meeting.'

She was out of bed, marble cold under bare feet, a shaft of moonlight guiding her to the door. 'What is it?'

'Open up, Daphne. I can't stand here whispering at you for everyone in the circle to hear. You won't like it if I have to come out with it at the meeting tomorrow. Much better discuss it now. I warn you; I'm going to stay here, knocking, until you let me in.'

Her hand, shooting the bolt, seemed to do it without her volition.

'That's better.' Mark was into the room in a flash, bolting the door behind him. 'You're shivering.' A warm arm round her. 'Back to bed with you, love. No need for you to freeze to death while we talk. There.' He tucked the light duvet round her and sat down beside her, his arm still supporting her, his hand casually, intimately busy at her breast.

'No!' She tried to pull away. 'No, Mark. You said: "talk". What is it Sophia needs to know?'

'Don't panic, love.' His hand remembered too well what pleased her. 'We're going to talk. I'm going to tell you just what Sophia needs to know about Jacob Braun and Chris Maitland. But first there's something you and I need to clear up between us. Why did you fail me so? Why didn't you fight me for Anne?'

'Fight you? Fail you? What do you mean?'

'You know what I mean. That time when you found us in bed. That scene you made. Anyone would have thought it was the end of the world.'

'It was the end of my world.'

'Nonsense. It was just a passing thing, a happiness, me

and Anne. If you'd laughed, and said she couldn't cook, and left us to it, I'd have been over her in a few weeks. But you had to make a full five act melodrama of it, and just look where it got us. Both wretched. No, don't contradict, love, I know you well enough to know you haven't been happy. Things have been wrong with you, badly wrong. I can see it. My fault, of course, but yours, too. Let's give it another go, shall we? I can't manage without you; I began to see that when the new book went so wrong. We're a team, you and I. Besides, my darling puritan, we need each other. You feel it just as much as I do, don't try to pretend anything else.' He moved suddenly, hard against her, and all the old, passionate mix of love and wanting surged up to yield her to him.

It was madness; it was ecstasy; it was better than it had ever been between them. Much, much later, waking in his arms to a gleam of morning light, she felt him rouse beside her and put out an indolent, loving hand to restrain him. 'But what was it you had to tell me about Chris and Jacob?'

He laughed and bit her ear. 'A ruse, love. A ruse to get to you. And see how happily it worked.'

10

'What time is your meeting?' A quick, anxious glance as Zoe appeared with her breakfast had reassured Daphne that Mark's visit had left no trace. Except on me, she thought.

'Nine o'clock. We'll all be settled in the lecture hall by the time you get to the treatment area. The Kyria sends her love and says, don't worry about anything.'

'I do hope the meeting goes well.'

'So do I! If only it turns out to have been an accident after all. Poor Hermione . . . We never exactly made friends, she and I. Well, she was older, and an outlander, not born here, and not one of the original settlers either. It does make a difference, though we try not to let it. They kept themselves to themselves somehow . . . I mustn't stay here talking; I've your mother's tray to take.'

'Give her my love. Tell her I'll come and see her as soon as I am free.'

'The Kyria told me to suggest a restful morning in bed.'

Out of harm's way. They exchanged a smile of friendly understanding.

Emerging into the colonnade of the first circle half an hour later, Daphne found the quiet absolute. Strange to think that now the meeting had started she and her mother would be the only people in the two circles, though presumably someone must be on duty down at the watergate, and others in attendance on the important guests in the conference suite. She shivered. If Hermione had been attacked, could it have been by a stranger, someone who had contrived to get on to the island unobserved? And might be lurking anywhere among the shadowed porticoes or the dark corridors of the treatment area. But that was impossible or Sophia would never have sent her on this errand. Just the same, crossing the guests' circle she was actually tempted to pause for a moment's talk with her mother, simply as reassurance. Absurd. What reassurance had Frances ever had to offer?

The plan of the treatment area was lit by a little strip light and showed room seventeen on a corridor off the one leading to the swimming pool. Daphne turned on all the lights as Sophia had suggested, but lights in the main corridor only emphasised shadow and silence in the network of passages opening off it. And all horribly quiet. If she waited a moment longer, she would turn and run for the sunshine. And fail Sophia. She took a deep breath and started down the silent corridor. Reaching the turn-off for room seventeen, she paused, surprised. Surely this was where she had met Hermione the time she had behaved so strangely? Or was she imagining things again? One of these white, impersonal corridors looked very much like another. She was probably mistaken.

Room seventeen. She thought of Bluebeard's wife as she raised a hand to knock at the door. Wife. She had been refusing to think about Mark. Was she afraid to? Afraid to face the fact that she had slept with him without protection of any kind. Ecstasy. Madness. Her hand finished its movement and knocked firmly on the white door.

'It's on the latch; come in. I'm a bit slow on my feet.' The muffled voice sounded more clearly as she pushed open the door and went in. Clearer and familiar?

Her first feeling was one of overwhelming relief. The room was not subterranean as she had expected, but lit by a huge skylight, and it opened on to its own enclosed courtyard. More light came from there, and the small sound of water. The nightmare of the dark corridors safe behind her, she looked at the man who had risen with difficulty to greet her. A skeleton of a man. Shocking white hair above the gaunt, tanned face. Why shocking? Because it was in such contrast with the painfully alive blue eyes that were studying her.

'Well?' He hitched the crutch more securely under his

left arm. 'You've grown into quite a girl, Daphne. How's your mother?'

'Father?' It was half a question still. And yet, in a way, in her heart, had she been expecting this?

'Right.' Pleased. 'And with an apology for you, long overdue. It was bad, that last time, wasn't it? That walk we took. That wretched goodbye. Not all your mother's fault, either, and don't ever think so.'

'No?' She thought about it. 'It wasn't just bad, it was unbearable.' And, admitting it, felt a weight slip quietly from her shoulders. 'It was the not understanding that was worst. If you'd only told me, explained . . . The way you used to come and go. And, that time, you didn't even come in. Like a stranger, a casual guest; not my father at all.'

'That's the way she said it had to be. Your mother. I'd tried so hard to persuade her to come back to the States with me. That was the last time. I knew already it was no good. That I was losing you. What could I have said to you that wouldn't have made things worse between you and your mother? I don't know.' The blue eyes stared, unseeing, into the past. 'Maybe I'd have handled it better if I hadn't been so wretched myself. I adored you, Daphne. Never forget that.' He smiled the remembered smile. 'Still do. Always will. But your mother held all the cards. Technically, I had abandoned the two of you. I had to, Daphne. Please believe that. What I was doing was so important.'

'What were you doing?' She could not quite keep the note of reproach out of her voice.

'You don't know much about me, do you?'

'No. Mother said –' What had Frances said? 'He's nuts; probably mixed up with one of those crazy sects.'

'Said I was crazy, I expect. I suppose I was, in a way. Anyone who lets an idea ride him looks mad from outside. But how are we to get anywhere if we don't throw our heart over the moon sometimes? I'm just sorry it came so hard on you. But you're all right now?' This was a question.

'I'm not sure.' Last night, and Mark, screamed in her mind.

'Too soon to talk about it? O.K.' From time to time his accent modulated into American. 'We've got plenty of ground to cover, you and I. Where shall we start?'

'Ought we to start with your treatment?'

The blue eyes clouded. 'Yes. Get it over with. It's . . . drastic, Daphne. You mustn't be frightened if I come out talking a bit strangely. It passes, I promise you, and it is,' he paused, bright eyes looking inwards, 'it may not be curing me, but it's doing me a hell of a lot of good. Sophia didn't tell you? About me?'

'Nothing.'

'I was kidnapped. By a super power. I still don't know which. They wanted something I had; an invention of mine. They wanted it badly; asked for it hard.' His eyes flickered down to the crutch. 'It was all in my mind, you see. I'd kept it there, because it seemed the safest place. Only . . . it wasn't as safe as all that.'

'You told them?'

'I don't know. I can remember neither all I knew, nor whether I told them. The fact that I got away seems to suggest that I told them, and yet I'm not so sure . . .'

'How did you get away?'

'Sophia. That's a powerful lady, that cousin of ours. She wrote me, when she started looking for her family. Same way she wrote you, I suppose. My gaolers were interested in everything about me; the letter got through to them and they showed it to me. They wanted to know all about Sophia. Well, I knew almost nothing. I don't know if they believed me. All I know is, they dumped me on her. Lucky for me; not so good for her. They're bound to have had me followed. The question is whether her people managed to shake them off. It begins to look as if they didn't. Poor Hermione. I feel a murderer.' He spoke in odd, short sentences, as if he had trouble controlling his thoughts. 'I was off my head at the time I got here,' he said as if in excuse. 'I don't remember a thing, which doesn't exactly help. So, let's go and get this treatment over with.' He slipped his right arm through her left one. 'I can walk quite well, now, like this. Not bad, when you think I came

127

here on a stretcher, babbling of green fields. This place is something; they mustn't be let destroy it.'

'They?'

'Whoever they are. In my gloomier moments, Daphne, I find myself believing in forces of evil.' They were out in the corridor now, his crutch thudding dully on marble paving. 'Well, Sophia's a force for good, if ever I met one, and I suppose there's a con to every pro.' They had passed the pool and reached the huge, bronze doors of the Tholos area. 'You've the key? Good.'

Daphne's hand shook as she inserted it in the immense lock. As the door swung open she felt the cold breath of the solid rock inside and shivered.

'Steady.' His hand comforted her as Sophia's had before. 'The same key opens both locks.' The distance to the second pair of doors was shorter than she had remembered. 'Open it for me, Daphne, let me in, and wait outside.'

'Can you manage?' Like the first one, this door opened silently on well-oiled hinges, revealing blackness absolute.

'Yes.' He slid his arm from hers. 'The passage is so narrow, it holds me up. I just have to keep going forward.' She felt him take a firmer grip on the crutch. 'I won't be long. There is nothing whatever to be afraid of, either for you or for me.'

How could he be so sure? The soft thud of the crutch dwindled slowly and died. A narrow passage to what unimaginable goal? Suppose he never came back? Suppose it was too strong for him, whatever it was that lurked there in the darkness? Was she more afraid for herself or for him? For herself. Shameful. Don't panic. Think about something else. About Mark? A glow of happiness, last night's ecstasy still a liquefaction of her bones. Mark loved her, needed her. It had just been a passing madness, the affair with Anne. He was right. She should have been more patient, not forced it to an issue. Perhaps she should even have agreed to his suggestion that the three of them live together. Given it time to sort itself out. She should have known that Anne, whose new career mattered so much to her, would never be able to give Mark the help he needed.

She would make up for it all now. They would write a great book together, she and Mark. And if, by any wild chance, she found she was carrying his child, that would be happiness, too. Their child. A team, he had said. But he had been talking about his work. What kind of father would Mark be?

The warm glow faded. Cold began to gnaw at her bones. How long had she been standing here, looking at blackness? But now, at last, she heard the distant thud of her father's crutch.

'Told you I wouldn't be long.' His voice shook, and his hand, as he slid it under her bare arm, was cold with sweat. 'Now for the sunshine, and the Lady.' At least he was making sense. And it was he guiding her now as she locked the great door and they started clockwise round the curve of the Tholos wall. When they left it and began to climb the slope, she felt him lean more heavily on her arm, and was aware of the effort each step cost him. He was almost at the end of his strength.

'Not far now.' She turned the key in the last door and took a breath of relief as it swung open into sunshine. Now she could see how drawn he was, how drained of strength, and forgot her own terror in anxiety for him. 'This way.' She guided him across the terrace and with difficulty up the steps to the little temple with its caryatid pillars and the great statue brooding over all. 'Here.' A broken pillar, warmed by the sun, made a seat. 'Sit and recover.'

'You, too.' They let the silence fall companionably between them, sharing the sunshine and the quietness of the place. At last he raised his head to meet the statue's amazing eyes. 'I've remembered,' he said. 'Let's go up to the top, Daphne, and I'll tell you.'

'Yes.' She was glad to go. Last time, those strong eyes had made her cry, good, healing tears. Why could she not meet them today? She reached down to pick up her father's crutch, which had slipped from his hand to fall just out of reach, in a patch of sweet marjoram. 'Let's go.'

Settled at last on the marble bench at the top, his back to a pine tree, he turned to her eagerly. 'I remembered it all,' he said. 'I must tell you quickly, in case the darkness falls again. You will remember, if I do not. Won't you?'

'Of course!' She made herself concentrate on him, forcing her own problem down to a lower level of consciousness, where it waited, grumbling.

'I'd found a way to heal people's minds,' he told her. 'Your mother thought I was crazy, but I had. I know I had. It worked. Quite simply. A kind of retraining . . . reprogramming. Erasing the tape, if you like, and starting again. But of course it needed development, backing, money . . . Everything I hadn't got. That's why we went to the States. I thought the chances would be better there. Well, they were and they weren't. Everyone wanted my idea; but they all wanted to use it for their own ends. I got very good at spotting them; the ways they set about getting it out of me. It's so simple, Daphne, so important, and, in the wrong hands, so dangerous. A way to cure people of all the negative, dangerous reactions that have been built into them since birth. Since before, come to that. I don't like to think of the things that happened to you in your mother's womb.'

'You can sort me out?'

'I'd like to try. It was so simple . . . so easy. A repatterning. Something one could teach to any intelligent person once they had been straightened out themselves. In a way, everything that was hoped for from psychoanalysis, only so much simpler. Not hypnosis either, though there are similarities. Only . . .' He shook his head, as if to clear it. 'No, there's still something missing. But so much has come back to me, so fast, since I came here . . . Surely the rest will come if I keep up the treatment?'

'I'm sure it will.' Reassuring him, she wished she could do as much for herself. Had her father's captors decided that if they could not have his secret, no one should? Or had they sent him here to be cured, and followed him? Might that explain Hermione's death? 'How much does Sophia know?' She turned to ask him and was glad to see him looking remarkably better, relaxed in the hot sun.

'Everything I have remembered so far. It's been coming back gradually. At first I only knew I had a secret my captors wanted; had no idea what it was. Or who they were. Well, I still don't know that. Anonymous cells. Anonymous food. They talked to me in a different language every time. Different people, different races; always fluent, like natives. So far as I could tell. Sometimes they needed interpreters. I speak a bit of Russian, but no Chinese ... No African languages. Those were the worst times of all; the long wait for translation; for the questions; for the torture to start. They wanted it badly, my gift. Now I remember what it was, I understand. Just imagine such a technique in the wrong hands. They could programme an army of serfs, or – just an army. No need for nerve gas, any of the modern horrors. Oh, God, Daphne, I hope I didn't tell them.' She felt him rigid beside her now, remembering horror. 'I think we had better stop talking about it. For a while. Can we talk about you a little? But one thing, first of all, your mother is here, Sophia tells me. I do beg you not to tell her about me. Not yet. I don't think I can face her yet. Poor Frances. I did her a great disservice by marrying her, but I can't absolutely regret it; not with you sitting here beside me. We were so young, you see. She was so lovely. More beautiful than you, Daphne, which is saying a lot. And – empty. I learned that when she started you. An accident, of course. She didn't want children. I didn't know that either, when I married her. One should talk about these things ... Before ... When she found she was pregnant, she was furious. Did everything she could to get rid of you. I had to watch her like a hawk. And then, maybe because she was so angry, it was a terrible, long birth. She fought you every inch of the way, poor Frances.'

'Poor me!' But she said it lightly. 'No wonder she hustled me off to boarding school the minute she decently could. How I loathed it!'

'But you've survived. It's made you strong. I can feel it in you.'

'More than I can sometimes. I'm a bit of a mess, father.'

'Sophia says you married and it didn't work out, which doesn't altogether surprise me. Not with your unlucky background.'

131

She was not ready to talk about Mark. A quick look at her watch. 'How long do you usually stay up here? I do think we should tell Sophia what you have remembered just as soon as her meeting is over.'

No answer. Turning quickly, she saw that he had fallen lightly asleep. Part of the cure? Almost certainly. She was sure she should not disturb him, and sat there, feeling his light weight sag against her, trying to keep anxiety at bay, lest it infect him. It seemed a long time before he stirred, looked at her, smiled. 'Daphne? That's wonderful. Sophia said you'd come; it seemed too good to be true.' And then, gradually taking in where they were. 'I've had my treatment? Don't look so frightened. I'm not mad; it's just, my memory slips to and fro a bit. You took me to the Tholos? Tell me, did I remember anything?'

'You don't know?'

'Sometimes I don't. Sophia says not to worry; it will come gradually. But did I?'

'Oh yes,' she said, 'but should I tell you? Does Sophia?'

Somewhere behind them, a bird screeched suddenly, startled from noonday hush. A fox? Or – a listener? She looked round quickly; nothing but dark trees in the strong sun, closer than she had realised. Perfect cover. Hermione's attacker? How much could they have overheard?

Her father had noticed nothing, thinking about her question. 'Not always,' he said now. 'She says it's best to let things come back naturally. I don't think Hermione said anything either. I wish I could remember.'

'Hermione?'

'She brought me once. I do remember that. I think. Or, maybe I remember Sophia asking me about it after she was killed, poor thing.'

'I think we should go back.' She tried to keep her voice steady. Hermione had listened to his rememberings. Hermione was dead.

'What's the matter?' He had sensed her fear, and she felt him begin very quietly, very basically to shake. 'What's the matter, Daphne?'

'Nothing, I hope.' Even with his memory betraying him,

he was not someone to whom one lied. 'But I do think that we should tell Sophia what you have remembered as soon as possible. Are you strong enough to go down?'

'Of course.' But she felt the effort it cost him to get to his feet, and felt, too, a wave of cold hatred for the people who had done this to him. 'It was important, then, what I remembered?' he asked, as they started slowly back down the slope.

'Not really.' She pitched her voice as loud as she naturally could. 'Interesting, but not enough of it. We'll just have to keep up the treatment, I suppose.' At least, if there really was someone listening that might be some protection for him. They would know that they needed him alive, to go on remembering. Because if there was someone there, listening, it surely meant that his captors had not broken him and secured his secret; they still wanted it, and would kill for it. They? Who?

'He doesn't even know who they are.' After the grim, dark passages, it had been unbelievable relief to find Sophia waiting for them in room seventeen.

'No. I had gathered that much.' Sophia had given the two of them one comprehensive look, reached into the small bag she always carried and produced a hypodermic syringe: 'Sleep for you, my friend, and good dreams.' Now Paul Vernon was fast asleep in his bedroom while they talked quietly in the enclosed courtyard.

'He told me they talked to him in different languages every day.' Remembering it made Daphne angry all over again.

'A refinement of cruelty. Totally disorienting.'

'Horrible. But I don't think he told them what they wanted to know.'

'Nor do I. That's what this is all about, I'm afraid. What did he remember, Daphne? I can see it was important. Did he remember what it was they wanted from him?'

'Almost.' She repeated what her father had said, as close as she could get to it.

'To heal people's minds,' said Sophia thoughtfully when

she had finished. 'No wonder they wanted him, whoever they are. To mend them or to bend them would be very much the same process. And it could be easily taught?'

'It was simple, he said. At first I thought he'd remembered how. He thought so himself. Will it always be like that, his memory?'

'I hope not. It's strong medicine, that Tholos.' She anticipated Daphne's question. 'No time for that. You can see it works; that's enough for now.' She ran a distracted hand through crisp hair. 'You've given me a lot to think about, Daphne. But I can set your mind at rest on one point; there is absolutely no way anyone could get up to the temple valley without my knowledge. There is only one key to the locks, and I keep it. I've never given it to anyone I don't trust absolutely. You must have been imagining things. Not surprising, in the circumstances.'

'No. Poor father. Do you really think the people who kidnapped him may have followed him here? Have something to do with Hermione's death?'

'It seems wildly unlikely. Why let him go in the first place? Besides, Andros and Niko are certain no one has come through the channel.'

'And you trust them?'

'Oh, absolutely. And that reminds me of one really good bit of news. My secret conference is over: well over. My friend and his enemy have finished their talks, and Andros got them safely off the island while we were holding our meeting this morning. That's one problem the less. And I hope one world danger less as well. They really seem to have come up with something positive at last. It's marvellous what the chance to talk in peace and quiet will do. Makes me feel Temi is worth all the trouble. Did you know Jacob Braun got up at the meeting about Hermione and urged me to send for the police? Crazy. If I let them in, it would be the end . . .'

'What happened at the meeting?'

'Nothing very positive, I'm afraid. Not that I had wanted to find evidence that it was one of us who had killed Hermione, but the fact remains, it has to have been. We managed to narrow down the time of her death quite a bit. She was expected for Sunday lunch in the village, around one o'clock. She was last seen in the Sanctuary at about twelve, and must have gone through the Village Door after you did, which was about twelve thirty. Right?'

'Yes.'

'And all the evidence, and the state of her body, tells us she was killed very soon after that.'

'So – when the three men were wandering about by themselves on the other side of the door?'

'I'm afraid so. But there's no possible motive for any of them. They hadn't been here long enough to get involved with Hermione. Only, being the lunch hour, everyone else seems to be accounted for. Except me.'

'You?'

'I was lunching alone with my guest friend. They had reached a hitch in their discussions; he was afraid it might prove an insuperable bar to agreement. He asked me to talk it over with him; we had a cold lunch in his room. He said it helped them to reach their agreement, which makes me very happy. But of course I could not possibly ask him to testify. Luckily my friends at the meeting took my word for it. And agreed that we must not let news of the murder get off the island. This is something we have to settle ourselves.'

'What about the other man? Where was he when you were lunching with your friend?'

'Quick of you. He was lunching alone in his room, but he's a man who likes to be waited on.' She smiled wryly. 'Lord, I'm glad he's gone. Compared with him, the government representatives I have coped with have been angels of light. For him, a woman should be veiled, totally submissive. I was a barefaced affront to his religion. It made conversation quite difficult. But there is no way it makes him a murderer. Besides, he had never been out of the conference suite except when he arrived. How could he have found his way to the Village Door?'

'It does seem unlikely. Unless Hermione guided him? Tell me about her, Sophia. Zoe says she was an outlander?'

Sophia smiled. 'You are learning about Temi. Yes, Hermione was one of my problem children. It's curious. Andros settled so well, but I've never been quite sure about Hermione. She was his younger sister, didn't I tell you? You can imagine how he feels about her death; he's not been himself since. They had been through so much together: the kidnapping by the guerrillas; the escape; their mother's death. And then the whole strange American experience . . . I'm not sure Hermione would have stayed here if it had not been for Andros. They were inseparable, those two. Well, he felt responsible for her. She was man mad, poor Hermione, totally promiscuous. Andros hated it, but always felt it his duty to tell me.'

'Brother and sister!' Daphne had been adding up this new sum. 'She must have been much older than she looked, surely?'

'Yes. You'd never have thought she was in her forties. I think something had stopped in her. I don't know when. She wouldn't ever talk about the past, so I don't know whether it was what happened to her during the time they were kidnapped. She was only tiny, poor little thing, but those were terrible, violent days. Her mother was certainly raped. Many times. I don't know about Hermione, but Andros said he thought his mother was glad to die.'

'Andros talks about that time?'

'Oh, yes. It was different for him. He was able to fight back, not just to suffer. He remembers it with pride, as something he managed to come through. The same with the American trouble, though it's true he never has told me just what that was. That's loyalty to their adoptive parents, and I respect it. But you can see why Hermione's death has hit him so hard. They were absolutely all in all to each other, except for Hermione's fits of sex madness. I'm sure that's why Andros never married, and of course it did complicate my problem over the succession here on Temi.'

'The succession?'

'I never finished telling you. Things are going too fast for me, Daphne; I'm letting them get out of hand. Which just proves how right I was to start facing it. I realised when the pressure from the new government began that there would soon be a need for strong young thinking here on Temi. I should have thought of it sooner. We've lost some of the best of our young people in the last few years, specially among the men. My fault: I must have let the pendulum swing too far; the men began to feel threatened. It's amazing how quick they are to take fright, poor things. And fright makes them violent. That's a lot of what's the matter with the world, I think. I really believed we were adjusting the balance here at last. Fair shares and equal responsibilities. It was a slow business, mind you, and David's death didn't help. To put it mildly. Partly because I missed him so. Maybe let things go a bit? And there seemed no way to replace him. Not then. Lately I've thought a lot about Andros. But there was the problem of Hermione. Aside from everything else, she wasn't much liked, poor woman. She kept herself too much to herself.'

'And Andros?'

'Oh, everyone respects him. There's something very powerful about him, in his quiet way. Well, the American experience was very developing. That's why I put him in charge of communications.' She sighed and ran a hand through her hair. 'Maybe he will marry now poor Hermione's dead. The right wife might solve it all . . . Zoe perhaps?'

'Does it have to be marriage?'

'No, of course not. I'm getting old and conservative; but marriage is one good old-fashioned approach to the partnership of a man and a woman. And that's what's needed here; I'm absolutely sure of that. A marriage of two minds.'

'Andros and Anastasia?'

'They don't get on. Her fault, I think. She never could like either him or poor Hermione.'

'Hermione.' Something had been nagging at the back of Daphne's mind. 'Sophia. I never told you; it didn't seem important. But the first time I came to the pool by myself I ran into Hermione on the way. There was something odd about her; she didn't a bit like my seeing her; I could tell

137

that. And it was only today I realised that she hadn't come from Loukas' room but from this corridor.'

'Hermione? But that's extraordinary. You think she had been visiting your father?'

'Is there anyone else in this corridor?'

'No. How very strange. I do remember, she was very upset after she took him for his treatment that time. As if something about his state had really got through to her. She said he was totally confused; made no sense. Can she have been keeping something back? But why? Unless she had taken one of her fancies to him. I do hope not.' She bent to take Paul's pulse. 'He's fine. I think we'd better leave him to have his sleep out and get back to my rooms. Andros should be back from Kos by now, and Zoe might have a report for me. I have named her and Andros as my assistants in the matter of Hermione's murder. Jacob Braun just does not understand what I would be laying myself — and Temi — open to if I sent for the police from Kos. Anastasia is investigating in the village. It's my good luck that there's no way those three can be involved.' She looked at her watch. 'It's late. You'd better run, Daphne, or you'll be late for lunch. Will you give my apologies to our guests? I'm afraid Hermione's death puts paid to my plans for entertaining them. At least for the time being. I had meant to spend this afternoon with your mother while you took the three men up the valley path to the temples. It's too rough going for your mother, I think, but you'd be able to manage it.'

'The valley path? There's another way? Not through the Tholos?'

'Surely I told you? There's a path that starts close to the Village Door. The two valleys almost converge there. Must have done so before the great earthquake. As soon as we found the ruins of the first circle we knew there had to be something up at the top. An Acropolis, a Parthenon . . . David had a wartime friend, a pilot. He did an aerial survey for us and we saw how the valleys lay. It was just a question of breaking through from the top of the guests' circle.'

'Yes, I do remember your saying something. But there

was so much to take in . . . You don't use the valley path now?'

'Not since we opened up the way through the Tholos. You'll see why if you go up it this afternoon.' She looked down at Paul Vernon. 'He'll sleep for a while. Come along and I'll show you where the path starts. Maybe you could persuade one of the men to take your mother swimming while you and the other two go up to the top. I know Jacob Braun is longing to see the temples, and I don't terribly want a lot of people going through the Tholos area right now.'

11

The treatment area was quiet as the grave, the pool's shining surface undisturbed, its edges dry. Whatever the three men had done since the meeting ended, they had not come here. Following Sophia, as she trod the corridors with quiet, espadrilled feet, Daphne felt reluctant to speak, the silence somehow oppressive.

Reaching the entrance to the guests' circle, Sophia turned to the right, towards the Village Door, then stopped, surprised, as Christopher Maitland came in sight at the far end of the corridor.

'Caught in the act!' His voice echoed strangely in the enclosed space. 'I hope you don't mind, Kyria, I was taking a look at the scene of the crime. If crime it was. I still think it's more likely that Hermione fell awkwardly and hit her own head, poor thing.'

'I wish she had,' said Sophia. 'Though it's heartless to say so. But the alternative's unpleasant.'

'I'll say.' He turned to Daphne. 'Have you heard that suspicion seems to lie between us three errant males and the Kyria? And believe that, you'll believe anything.'

'Thanks for the vote of confidence,' said Sophia drily. 'And now I think I'd better get back to my patient.'

'You won't be joining us for lunch?' he asked.

'I think not. I'd like to be beside our patient when he wakes. Oh, Daphne, the door you want is just this side of the Village Door.' She reached into her pocket. 'Here's the key. And, please, this time you will all keep together? Mind you take a look at the theatre. It's right up at the top, beyond the trees. I'm only sad I can't come with you.'

'Mysterious lady, isn't she?' Chris fell into step beside Daphne as they emerged into the guests' circle. 'Wants us out of the way, I suppose. Who's the patient, and what's all this about a theatre?'

Maddening not to have had a chance to finish her conversation with Sophia. But that slight stress on the word 'patient' had been a reminder that she must not reveal her father's identity. 'The patient's the one I took for treatment this morning,' she said. 'His mind's quite disturbed. As to the theatre, I didn't know there was one.'

'There usually is,' said Chris. 'But where?'

'Up at the top. Sophia suggests we go up there this afternoon. It turns out there's an outside path.'

'You'll like that better, won't you? Than those damned dark corridors.'

'You noticed, yesterday?' Surprised.

'I'm noticing you all the time, Daphne, don't ever think I'm not. But just now you've problems of your own to sort out. Right? Give me credit for doing my best to help.'

'Why, thank you!' Had he really been making his play for her mother for her sake? To give her time for what?

'Will your mother be able to cope with the path?' He must have been thinking along similar lines. 'She didn't much like the one yesterday.'

'No. Sophia says it would be too rough for her. She suggests one of you take her swimming while the rest of us go up.'

If she had hoped he would volunteer, she was to be disappointed. 'Tough,' he said. And then, 'Tell you what. I had a huge breakfast, no need for lunch. Give me the key, I'll go up and take a quick look round while you eat. I'll be back before your ma is ready to go swimming, the rest of you can be off with a clear conscience.'

'Nice of you. But Sophia specially asked us to keep together.'

'Oh, hell.' He stood back to let her go first into the guests' dining-room where they found the other three sitting over drinks.

'There you are at last!' Frances' petulant tone was explained by the fact that Mark and Jacob had only just joined her, having been down to explore the first circle and the watergate. When the afternoon's plans were mooted, she made her own position clear from the start. She neither wanted to swim nor to be left alone. Still less did she relish the idea of the rough path up the valley. 'I'll tell you what this place needs,' she said. 'A television room!'

'Greek television?' Chris smiled his charmer's smile. 'Have you ever tried it?'

'Of course not. But, video, for God's sake! Don't you even have that, Zoe?'

'I'm afraid not.' Zoe was helping her to stuffed vine leaves. 'The Kyria does not approve. She thinks it impoverishes the mind. There's a library on the other side of this circle.'

'I know! I've been there. George Eliot, and Proust, and a lot of dreary green paperbacks.'

'Virago?' asked Jacob Braun. 'I must take a look. As for this afternoon, I wouldn't mind a restful one. Why don't you and I start off with the others, Frances, and turn back when the going gets too rough.'

'After I've sprained my ankle? No, thanks! I've a bit of a head, actually. You run along and I'll take it easy in my courtyard and maybe get myself a bit of a tan.'

'Are you sure?' Daphne was amazed and pleased.

'Sure I'm sure. You may want to be mad British out in the heat of the sun. I've got more sense.'

'She's got something there.' Mark turned to Daphne. 'Ought you to go, love? Remember that time you nearly passed out on Rhodes? By the look of you, you've had quite a morning with that mystery patient. Why don't you and I take it easy too and let the he-men sweat their guts out up the valley?' His hand, butterfly-touching her thigh, suggested just what he meant by taking it easy.

'Goodness, no.' Her instant reaction surprised her almost as much as it did him. 'I'm longing to get up to the theatre. And I want to see what you three make of the Lady.'

But it was hotter today and they lingered a while over coffee, idly talking about moving, doing nothing. In the end, it was Frances who stood up. 'My head's killing me,

I'm for my bed. Don't wear yourselves out, and don't blame me if you get sunstroke, Daphne.'

'Crazy for you to go out in this hot sun.' Mark was walking Daphne down to her room. 'You look washed out already.'

'Thanks!'

'Oh, come on, Daphne. I'm still your husband, remember. I care enough about you to tell you the truth. I don't like to see that old witch Sophia using you for her own ends, wearing you out like this.' He put a hot hand on her shoulder, turned her into her courtyard and steered her gently, firmly across it to her bedroom. 'We've some unfinished business, you and I.' He turned her to face him, held her close. 'Don't fret about the others. They won't wait for us. I told Chris I'd persuade you to take a quiet afternoon. I will say for him, he knew just what I meant.' He was pushing her towards the bed.

'No!' She pushed him away with both hands, angry, and glad to be. 'No, Mark. Not like this. It's no answer. I let you in last night. I was crazy. I'm not now. We have to think, to talk, you and I, before we decide anything. Bed settles nothing. Besides,' she was actually laughing as she reached into her pocket and produced the key Sophia had given her. 'The other two won't get far without this.'

'Hell and damnation.' But she had won, and he knew it.

They found Jacob waiting for them at the top of the guests' circle, but there was no sign of Chris, who appeared, hurrying, five minutes later, from the direction of the watergate. 'Sorry to keep you. There was something I had to ask –' He broke off. 'Do you think you'll be all right in espadrilles, Daphne?'

'Oh, yes.' She looked rather doubtfully at his heavy shoes. 'I'm fine in these.' She led the way to the two doors.

This one was a path for goats, following the dry bed of what must be a torrent in winter. 'A summer-only path.' Jacob reached a hand to pull Daphne up what would be a waterfall when it rained.

'Thanks!' Letting go of his hand, she paused beside him at a turn of the path to look ahead up the dry, brown valley. 'Isn't this *good*?' She felt suddenly, glowingly alive.

'Glad to be out of the shadows?' Jacob smiled at her. 'That sanctuary of your cousin's is amazing, but it would take some getting used to. Myself, I'd like to see it thrown open, at whatever risk. I have the most enormous respect for the Kyria, but I do wonder if she has not made a mistake with all this secrecy. The cloak-and-dagger business can so easily work both ways.'

'What do you mean?'

But they were interrupted by Mark, who had gone ahead with Chris, now returned, all solicitude, to ask if Daphne had not had enough. 'I'll be glad to take you back, darling.'

'No, thanks.' The word of endearment seemed to stake a claim, irritating her. 'I'm enjoying myself. Go ahead, Jacob, I'll follow you.' Was it the first time she had used his Christian name? 'We don't want to lose sight of Chris.' Keep together, Sophia had said. Dear Sophia . . . But could Jacob be right about the secrecy?

'Hey, Chris,' he called from ahead of her. 'Hold on. We're supposed to keep together, remember.'

'Well, hurry up then.' Christopher's voice sounded unnaturally loud, doubtless magnified by the narrow valley. 'We haven't got all day, and we want time to explore.' He turned to look ahead. 'We're almost there, I think. It really has to be the top this time.' As the other three caught up with him, he pulled himself up by a dry root and vanished round the corner of a huge boulder. 'Golly, what a place.' His shout echoed back to them. 'Come on, you lot, we're there.'

Once they were over the top, the entire landscape changed. They were standing somewhere above the Lady's temple, Daphne thought, and the path, wider here, bore to the left through scrub and small firs towards what must be the top of the Asklepion. The men who had built the temples had not reckoned with the view from up here, and they formed a tantalising jumble of sun-warmed golden stone, strange angles, shadows and perspectives.

'Amazing!' Jacob had paused to let Daphne catch up. 'Can you tell which temple is which from here?'

'I think so.' She pointed. 'That has to be the temple of Asklepios, and the Lady must be below us somewhere.'

'Come on then,' said Chris impatiently. 'Let's get down and look.' Still gazing ahead, he started forward along the narrow path, tripped on a root and fell headlong, swearing once, vividly, then: 'God what a bore! I am so sorry. I've twisted my ankle. I hope to God it's not broken.' He was sitting in the path, tenderly feeling his right ankle.

'Bad luck.' Jacob reached him a hand. 'Try your weight on it. It may not be as bad as you think.'

'Want to bet?' Chris took the hand, pulled himself upright, let out another oath. 'Sorry!' He sat down again, heavily. 'You'll just have to leave me here. By the time you've had a look round I expect I'll be able to hobble back. If you could find me a stick, maybe, here in the woods somewhere?'

'No.' Daphne took command. 'I'm sorry. Sophia said we were to stay together. We'll all rest here until you feel up to it and then start back. If you two don't mind?' She turned to Mark and Jacob.

'It's a hell of a bore.' Mark was looking down towards the sun-drenched ruins. 'No law that says we can't split into pairs, surely? Why don't we draw lots, one to stay with the cripple, the other two to explore?'

'That makes sense.' Jacob, too, was looking longingly down at the valley. 'I'll even volunteer to stay with Chris, while you two have a look round.'

'Good of you.' Daphne smiled at him. 'But suppose we do that and then it turns out Chris can't manage the path back? Then one of us would have to stay up here with him while the other two went back for help. It would be dark before it got here, even up through the sanctuary. No fun at all, and Sophia would be angry.'

'Which heaven forfend,' said Mark. 'You're right, love, as usual. We'll all just have to sit here, like birds in the wilderness, until Chris gives the word.' He slumped down on a stone.

'I am *sorry*,' said Chris again. 'If you don't mind waiting a bit? Trouble is, I can't afford to crock myself up. I make a living on my feet.'

'I'm sure Sophia will be able to fix it for you.' Daphne, too, had sat down on the hard, dusty ground.

'Lean against my knees,' said Mark. 'You're getting the rest I prescribed after all.'

'Tremendous view.' Jacob stood leaning against a stubby fir tree. 'I wonder if we can see the theatre.'

'I don't know where it is.' As Daphne rose to join him, Chris got shakily to his feet.

'Give me a hand, Braun, would you?' This time, he seemed to be able to take some of his weight on his right foot. 'Just a sprain, thank God. I think, if you don't mind, I'd like to start back now before it stiffens up. The downhill slope's going to be a help; I can do most of it pretty well on my rear end.'

'Hang on a mo',' said Mark. 'I'll see if I can find you a stick.'

'Don't bother.' He lurched and got hold of Mark's shoulder. 'It would be more trouble than help downhill.'

The backward journey was a slow, trying business, and tempers began to fray. Jacob soon took over from an increasingly and obviously impatient Mark to help Chris as much as he could, but Christopher's tight lips and an occasional suppressed oath showed what the climb was costing him. By tacit consent, Daphne and Mark stayed a little behind the other two, so as not to seem to hurry them. When they finally reached the door in the hillside, Chris sat down, sudden and heavily on a ledge of rock beside it. 'I've had it,' he announced, as Daphne and Mark caught up. 'I bet that capable Kyria has a wheel-chair and she's certainly got enough willing hands. No –' he anticipated Jacob's offer – 'I'm not letting you two carry me; I'm a hell of a load; muscle weighs heavy. Stay with me, Daphne, keep me cheerful while they get me some help?'

Oddly, she found herself exchanging a quick considering glance with Jacob. 'Right.' They had agreed, tacitly, that this made sense. 'We'll be here,' she told Jacob. 'No need to lock the door. Tell my cousin how sorry I am . . .'

146

'Not your fault,' said Chris, as the door closed behind the two men. 'Mine for being an impatient idiot. But at least it's got me a chance to talk to you, Daphne. I've wanted to, badly; couldn't make up my mind whether I should or not. It's a damned difficult thing to do. None of my business, you might say, and I don't think I'd have the nerve to say any of it if I didn't think you'd pretty well made up your own mind already. He acts as if he owned you!' He burst out with it. 'Told Braun and me, confident as you please, not to expect you two this afternoon. Other plans for you, he implied. And I with no right to shut his mouth. It was touch and go, I can tell you. My temper never was my strongest point. And then there you were, cool as a cucumber, bless you, with Mark fuming behind you. I could have kissed you. Maybe it was because I was so pleased, so hopeful, all of a sudden, that I went and stumbled like that. You've distracted me, Daphne, ever since we met. Tell you the truth, I've never been much of a one for girls. They're so easy, most of them. You're different. I knew it when you wouldn't come back with me, that night at the Coral. I didn't even dare kiss you. Me! And then, next day, when I rang up, you'd gone. That was a knockout, I can tell you. It wasn't easy to find out where you were. They close ranks pretty tight on Kos when it comes to the Kyria and Temi. But I was one determined man. I think old Madame Costa at the hotel was sorry for me, in the end. Gave me the clue I needed. And then, by God, I come out on the boat with a man who claims to be your husband and talks as if he owned you, bag and baggage. Come to collect his property!'

'That doesn't sound like Mark.' Was she quite sure of this?

'You haven't heard him when he's among men. Well, obviously! And I feel a cad telling on him, but this is too important. You are too important. Daphne, don't say anything now, except, if you will, that you forgive me for speaking out of turn. But remember, I'm here, at your service, to use an old-fashioned phrase. Not much use at the moment, I'm afraid.' With a rueful look at his ankle, which he had contrived to prop awkwardly enough on an outcrop of rock.

'It doesn't look too bad actually.' She absolutely did not know how to respond to his remarkable outburst. 'It's hardly swollen at all.' She leaned forward from her own perch on the other side of the door in the rock to look at the muscular ankle in its dusty shoe.

'I'm a quick mender. Like you, Daphne. I'll never forget how gallant you were, that day at Tingaki. Nearly killed, and came up smiling. Doc Manson ribbed me about it afterwards. Said he'd never thought to see me knocked for six like that. And I don't believe you even noticed. Not the kind of girl who goes round taking it for granted men will fall for her in rows.'

'Well, they don't.'

'This one has. That's why I'm going to trust you, Daphne; ask you to trust me.' He stood up, took a step towards her. 'There's something I've got to tell you. Confess to you. I'm on a job here.'

'A job?'

'Yes. I thought it was just big business at work — and what a chance! But if that poor woman was really murdered . . . And, besides, there's something about this place, isn't there? It gets to you, the quiet. I'd hate to see it spoiled. I thought I'd be bored rigid, here, but I'm nearer to happy than I've ever been. Mind you, I've been pretty busy with my drawings.'

'You've done more?'

'That's what I'm here for.'

'I don't understand.'

'That's what I'm trying to tell you, explain to you. You'll make my peace with the old lady, won't you? Oh, damnation!'

'Well, you must be recovering.' Jacob Braun surveyed the little scene with a hint of amusement. 'Did we waste our time bringing this luxurious vehicle?' He stepped aside to let a man Daphne had not seen before manoeuvre a wheel-chair through the narrow doorway. 'Thanks, Petros. How does it feel, now you're on it?' he asked Chris.

'Not so bad as I feared, but I'm more than grateful for this.' He let himself carefully down into the chair. 'Tell you the truth, I was talking to Daphne and forgot all about it for a moment.'

'A good sign, I'm sure.' Now his smile for Daphne was one of pure amusement, and she felt her colour rise.

'Well, let's get going then.' Mark had followed the chair through the door and moved solicitously across to Daphne. 'Time you got in out of the sun, love. I should never have let you stay.'

'You didn't let me, I made up my own mind,' she told him levelly. 'I can do it, you know.' And got such an appreciative look from Chris that she rather wished she had not said it.

'Well, what next!' The business of getting the wheel-chair down the steps into the guests' circle must have waked Frances, who appeared, flushed and sleepy-looking, at the entrance to her courtyard. 'I didn't expect you back for hours. What happened then?' She surveyed the little procession.

'I ricked my ankle, like an idiot. Nothing to make a song and dance about.'

And indeed when Sophia had strapped it for him and supplied him with a crutch like the one Paul used, Chris seemed able to get about the corridors of the sanctuary.

'How exactly did it happen?' Sophia had summoned Daphne for a drink in her rooms before dinner.

'He tripped on a root up at the top, just where you get to see down into the valley of the temples. He was looking at the view, rather than watching his feet. He fell heavily.'

'You saw it?'

'Oh, yes, I was right behind. We all were.'

'So – a genuine accident?'

'Well –' Had the shadow of doubt been in her mind too? 'He fell hard enough. He scraped his hands quite badly . . . You must have seen . . . Only, Sophia, it's hardly swollen at all.'

'I noticed that,' said Sophia drily. 'I couldn't feel anything. But then, one might well not. It's certainly a most convincing act, if it is one. The question is, what would he have gained by it, if it is an act, besides inconveniencing himself? You never got to see the valley of the temples at all?'

'No. Mark wanted one of us to stay with Chris and the other two explore, and Jacob even volunteered to stay, but I thought we should make sure Chris could get back all right. Besides, you did say we should stay together. But, Sophia, something else.' She felt herself colouring. 'When we did get down, Chris managed it so the other two went on to get the wheel-chair. And then he –' She thought about it. 'It was the queerest thing; he didn't actually propose to me, but he kind of made himself available.'

'Did he so? Quick work, wouldn't you say? And granted you're actually still a married lady!'

'Yes. It none of it seemed quite real to me. Oh – he talked a lot about Mark, about how he took me for granted. Made out he was jealous, I suppose: implied it had been love at first sight.' The more she talked about it, the less she believed it.

'Flattering!'

'If true. He said he wasn't much of a one for girls, usually. I believe that.'

'Ah,' said Sophia. 'So, what did you say?'

'Nothing, really. I didn't seem to need to. But, Sophia, there was more to it. What he really wanted to do was get me on his side. He was going to tell me, only the others turned up. From what he said, I think he's here to spy out the place for a tourist company; something like that. Only Hermione's death had shaken him badly; "I thought it was just big business," he said. I'm just his pretext.'

'I did wonder,' said Sophia. 'Do you mind?'

'A bit. Being used's not very nice.'

'No. And it does open up a vista or two, doesn't it? I must have a few words with Christopher Maitland just as soon as I can. I suppose he didn't happen to tell you what he was really doing up by the Valley Door when we met him there?'

'You didn't believe him?'

'No more than you did his declaration of undying passion.'

Daphne laughed. 'Not quite that! Funny, though, Sophia, it was good for morale in a way.' She thought she wanted to tell Sophia about Mark, to get her help in clearing her mind about him.

But Sophia was on her feet. 'High time we joined the others.'

They found the rest of the group already assembled, and Jacob raised the inevitable subject. 'May I ask if you have sent for the police yet, Kyria?'

'No.' She gave him a thoughtful look. 'I'm giving it another day. Andros, Zoe and I are still working through everyone's statements. There has to be a discrepancy somewhere. And that reminds me. Will you take our patient for his treatment again tomorrow, Daphne? I'm sorry.' She had seen Daphne's instinctive recoil. 'But I have to ask it. And my apologies to all of you, too, but I do hope to have this wretched business cleared up tomorrow, and then I can show you Temi as I planned to. In the meantime, may I suggest an early night? We have to face it that there is a murderer loose. I am putting guards on duty in both circles, and it will make things easier for them, and safer for you, if you go to your own rooms, and stay there.'

'Of course,' Jacob said. 'I just wish there was more we could do.'

'I promise to ask the minute I need anything. And now, come along to my rooms, Mr. Maitland, and let me have another look at that ankle of yours.'

'Oh, but it's nothing. I hate to take up your time.'

'Then let's not waste it arguing.' As she turned to say good night to Frances, Chris muttered something that sounded very much like 'obstinate old cuss'. But he went with her meekly enough.

'Old's not the first word I'd pick for the Kyria,' said Jacob thoughtfully when Chris had left them. 'What would you say, Daphne?'

'I quite agree.' She turned to him, pleased. 'You should see her do her daily ten lengths of the pool. I just hope I'm half the person she is when I'm her age.'

'You're not totally unlike her now, come to that.' For a curious moment it seemed as if they were alone in their corner of the dimly lit courtyard. 'If you went back to the Kos museum tomorrow and looked at those powerful ladies there, I think you'd see a family likeness.'

'Goodness, I wish I could!'

'Go back? No you don't.' He spoke with complete confidence. 'You're not the type who goes back.'

What could he possibly mean? While she thought about it, Mark left Frances abruptly and joined them. 'Time for bed. Boss's orders. Come on, Daph.' He took her arm and guided her the long way round the colonnade. Pausing at last in the shadows, he held her shoulders in a grip that hurt and looked down at her, louring. 'God, what a clot that Braun is! You get like the old woman! Not a chance in hell, praise be. Or like some dreary statue in a museum, come to that. Not just my idea of a compliment. Which reminds me, what were you and Chris Maitland being so confidential about, up at the Valley Door? Don't tell me I've got a rival!' He did not for a moment believe it. 'So what was he being so serious about?'

'I hope he's telling Sophia right now.'

'About those cute little architectural drawings of his? Get him to show them to you some time. They'll tell you a lot. Oh, and another thing, my gullible pet, don't let that creep Braun fool you with his faithful hound act. Something very fishy about him. Where the hell did he get to when we separated before lunch the other day? Looking for the way to the shore, he says. Well, believe that, you'll believe anything. I was up at the top of the village. I'd have seen him. So what was he doing? I don't exactly see him as one for the girls, but he could have gone back to the Village Door, made a pass at Hermione for some devious reason of his own. And then, maybe, gone too far, lost his nerve? He's doing his very best to soft-soap the old lady. He wouldn't want anything to get in the way of that. There's something he wants on this island, that's for sure, and don't go kidding yourself it's you, Daphne, love.'

'I wasn't,' she said drily.

'That's the girl.' A light, approving kiss. 'We've a lot of talking to do, you and I. But not tonight, Josephine. Mustn't annoy the old tartar. Just don't forget you're my wife. I'm sorry if I rushed things a bit last night, but you know you wanted it just as much as I did.' He was holding her closer now and something in her could not help responding to him. 'There'll be other nights, love. A lifetime of them.' He was entirely sure of this. 'For now, we'll play it slow and keep the old lady happy. But there is one thing: I'm going to chaperone you and that very important patient of yours in the morning. I like the old broomstick's nerve telling you to do it again when anyone could see how it had thrown you today. As your husband, it's my right and duty to go along and watch out for you.'

'What right? What duty?' She broke away from him, furious. 'You've changed your line about marriage a bit, haven't you? Anyway, if you ever did have any rights, as you so charmingly put it, you lost them when you walked out.'

'I didn't.' Now he was angry, too. 'You know I didn't. I wanted you to stay.'

'And cook-housekeep for you and Anne! Quite so. And here come the guards!' She was glad to see them.

'Forgive me!' He caught her hand, held her back for a moment. 'I don't know what I'm saying. I'm so anxious for you.'

She pulled away. 'Good night, Mark.'

On Sophia's instructions, Daphne was to get her father's treatment over with first thing next morning, and everything was quiet when she left her courtyard. Morning sun made leaf patterns on the mosaic floor; the stream talked to itself; for a moment she recaptured the magic of the place as she had felt it that first morning when Sophia took her up to the temple. Could she really have been two weeks on Temi? Did it seem more, or less?

Entering the guests' circle, she was surprised to see Niko, the boatman, approaching from the women's side, then realised that he must have been one of the night guards, now dismissed in the reassuring daylight. Doubtless tired, he returned her greeting with a gruff good morning.

Absurdly dashed by this break in the uniform island friendliness, she paused in the entrance to the treatment area, reluctant to face its shadows alone. Could Jacob be right in thinking Sophia's emphasis on secrecy a mistake?

As she thought about him, Jacob emerged from his courtyard on the men's side of the circle. 'Good morning.' He greeted her quietly, aware as she was of other people still asleep. 'I thought I'd come and wish you luck with the treatment.'

'Thanks. I rather feel I need it.' Remarkable how the confession and the short, friendly exchange seemed to fortify her for the plunge into the treatment area.

Her father was awaiting her eagerly, his door ajar. 'Good to see you! What's going on, Daphne? There's something in the air; I can feel it. Nobody's told me anything! What's happened about poor Hermione? The more I think about her death the more afraid I am that it has something to do with my coming here. You thought someone was listening yesterday, up at the top, didn't you? I didn't somehow take that in until after you'd left me.'

'I'm not sure. I . . . I wasn't comfortable.'

'A fine understatement.' He was actually laughing at her, and she liked it very much. 'Sophia is convinced that no one can get up to the temple valley. Says she has the only key. But she could be wrong. And there's a murderer loose. I think we'll play safe and come straight back here today. And – something else – are you feeling brave, Daphne?'

'Not very. Why?'

'Because I don't think we should separate today. Which means you will have to come through the Tholos with me, the way Sophia does. Can you face it?'

'Do you think I can?'

'Yes. You're in a bit of a muddle, aren't you, but strong enough underneath.'

She laughed. 'Thanks. But oughtn't we to ask Sophia?'

'No time. Besides, asking Sophia might involve telling someone who'd better not know.'

'What do you mean? You can't think Sophia . . .?'

'Of course not. But maybe someone close to her? Anyway, you're really only making excuses, aren't you? If you can't face it, say so; but I'd much rather not have you waiting outside by yourself. I'd be worrying about you, for one thing. Distracting. One needs to concentrate, there, or let oneself be concentrated. It will be drastic, coming with me, but safe. I'll get the full charge, you'll only get the aftershock. Won't do you any harm; might do you a lot of good. Sophia said she rather enjoyed it.'

But Daphne knew how exhausted Sophia had looked afterwards. 'Suppose I go off my head?'

'You won't. No one ever has. Sophia told me that before I went in the first time. Interesting the things I remember, isn't it, and the ones I don't. But one wouldn't lightly forget about Sophia's Tholos. It's a very powerful place, Daphne. I wish I knew more about it; understood more. But you can understand why Sophia felt she couldn't have it investigated. She'll have to in the end, I think. My bet is, it will turn out this is the original Tholos, the others, Delphi, Samothrace and so on, just copies. It's hard to imagine just this combination of power and light coming together more than once. It's what Temi was all about; no question of that.' He reached out and touched her hand lightly. 'I'm sorry; it's not fair to keep you here talking. Let's get it over with, shall we? Please, Daphne.' He sensed her recoil. 'Do this for me? Or – you don't owe me much – for Sophia?'

She took a strong breath. 'Yes.'

'Good. Maybe let's play safe and not talk much in the corridors. Or on an indifferent subject. Can you think of one?'

'I'll try.' She thought about it. 'We went up the outside path to the valley of the temples yesterday afternoon,' she began as they emerged from his room. 'The three men and I. But Chris sprained his ankle, and we had to turn back.'

How very strange. She had forgotten, yesterday, climbing that hot valley, about the morning's imagined listener. She must remember to tell Sophia.

'What's the matter?' Paul's hand tightened on her arm.

'Just something I remembered. Here we are.' The huge key turned in the lock of the first door, and they fell silent as they moved at his slow pace up the curving slope. As they approached the second huge pair of doors, dim light from above picked out a detail here and there of their carving. A nymph. A face like that of the Lady up at the temple? Like Sophia?

Her father's hand pressed her arm in welcome reassurance. 'Lock the doors behind us, Daphne. There. Now we are really alone. I am so very glad to be here with you. It seems something I owe you – we owe each other – after all the years of neglect. Put your hand on my shoulder, and remember, you are younger and stronger than I am. Anything I can bear, you can most certainly bear better.'

'Stronger?' There was no light ahead of them. As she shut the heavy door behind them the darkness became absolute. There was a smell of cold and damp and ancientness. Her breath came faster. She reached out, desperately, in the darkness and found his shoulder. Gripping it, she felt the bones painfully prominent, forgot her own fear in a surge of anger at what had been done to him.

He was moving slowly forward, and to the left. His crutch thudded softly. His other hand must be steadying him against the rock wall of the narrow passage. Her right hand still gripping his shoulder as if for dear life, she reached out with her left and touched cold rock. They were climbing slightly. She could feel his breath come quicker. With effort? With terror, like her own? They were inside the solid rock now; she could feel it looming above them, so close, she thought, that a tall man would have to stoop. Horrible. I have never been so afraid in my life . . . Presently, I will stop breathing. I have never . . . In a moment she would be saying the words aloud. And what would that do to Paul? She swallowed them with an effort. What had Sophia said? Dark is just dark. Something like that?

Jacob had said something too, about the journey, the search for healing.

Was that a gleam ahead? Her father was walking faster now; he turned sharply, and, following him, she stopped, astonished, dazzled, bathed in a great flood of light from above. Sunlight, it must be, but focused, channelled, intensified as it shone down its narrow opening through all that depth of rock. The chamber was tiny. As her father stepped forward into its centre she could still keep her hand on his shoulder and so when the electric charge surged up through him it echoed into her. He was vibrating like some piece of fine-tuned machinery and she felt the waves of it pass down her arm and shake her to her centre. She was whirling out of control; a mad set of atoms let loose. And then, as suddenly, it was over. The kaleidoscope she had been was shaking and reassembling. Order out of chaos. Pattern out of nonsense. Reason . . . Her father stepped forward into darkness, and, following him, she just missed the bright centre and was not even sure whether she was relieved or sorry as they plunged back into a darkness more absolute still but now unimportant, immaterial. The walls were close and cold as ever, the ceiling loomed low above her; it mattered not at all.

12

The dark corridors held no terror now. Extraordinary. Daphne started to say so, but her father pressed her arm. 'These passages must be practically an echo chamber.' He made the warning casual. 'I imagine in the old days there was a priestess somewhere, listening and taking notes for use by the oracle.'

'Was there an oracle here?' She picked up his safe subject as she unlocked the outer doors.

'Must have been. Divine answers were always part of the treatment. Still are. You wouldn't want your health problems handled entirely by computer, would you?'

'And the doctor's the divine answerer?'

'You could say so. A responsible job.'

'Yes.' The subject took them down the now harmless corridors to his courtyard. Reaching his room, she turned to him, smiling. 'I'm cured.'

'What of?' He was smiling too.

'All kinds of things. Claustrophobia . . . fear . . . Mark.'

'Mark?'

'My husband. That was. Oh hell! I do hope I'm not pregnant.'

'By him? Is it likely?'

'It would be damned bad luck . . . I wonder if he wants me pregnant!' It had not struck her before. 'Tied to him. He's been trying hard enough. But why?'

'Well,' said Paul mildly, 'it might be because he loved you; found he'd made a mistake.'

'Thanks!' She smiled at him, enjoying this new relationship. 'But it's not, you know. I'm sure of that now. So — why?'

'I've never met the young man.' Paul sat rather heavily

on an upright chair. 'But Sophia thinks him something of an opportunist. If he thought there was a chance she'd name you her successor here on Temi? It's quite a place. He'd be sure to find it tempting. Had it struck you she might be looking around for an heir?'

'She did say something. About Andros and the succession.'

'Andros? Which is he?'

'He and Niko are the two people who know the channel. One of them must have brought you here. I suppose you don't remember?'

'Not that. No. But I think I've remembered everything that matters. Would you fetch Sophia for me, Daphne? I'd better tell you both, right away. Just in case I forget again.'

'I'm sure you won't.' Her own new confidence made her sure for him. 'But I'll get her.'

Reaching the guests' circle, she paused, amazed. From below, from Sophia's circle, came a clamour of strident voices, a most extraordinary sound, here on quiet Temi.

'What's going on? Sounds like a riot!' Frances emerged from her courtyard.

'I don't know.' Entering Sophia's court together, they found it full of people, all talking at once.

'Quiet, please.' For once Sophia's voice did not win instant attention.

Andros pushed forward to stand beside her, clapping his hands. 'Silence. The Kyria will speak.'

'Thank you, Andros.' She looked small, suddenly, almost frail. 'When was Niko last seen?' She addressed the crowd, and then, to Andros: 'You say he wasn't at breakfast?'

'No. We always agree the day's arrangements then. When he didn't appear, I went to his room; the bed hadn't been slept in. Then I began to ask ... I've found no one who has seen him since supper last night. He said then that he was going down to the watergate to check the boats. It seems impossible that he should have had an accident; always such a careful man. There's no sign of him there; everything is in order. I checked at once.'

'Niko? But I saw him this morning.' Daphne had been

159

waiting for her chance to speak, felt her mother suddenly tense beside her. 'In the guests' circle, the women's side. I thought he must have been one of the guards. Wasn't he?' And realised, as she spoke, what this must mean.

'No, he wasn't on guard,' Sophia said. 'You've thought of something, Daphne?'

'Well, I think I know where he spent the night, but that's not the point, is it, since I saw him this morning.'

'What time?'

'Early, when I was on my way to the Tholos. Just after seven.'

'Did you see anyone else?' asked Andros.

'Why, yes, Jacob Braun.' A quick glance had shown that neither he nor the other two men were present.

'Braun?' said Andros thoughtfully. 'That's very interesting. Very interesting indeed.' He turned to Sophia. 'Where are our three guests this morning, Kyria?'

'I don't know. When you didn't turn up, Zoe and I started comparing yesterday's statements. But they must be in the sanctuary area since they haven't keys to any of the doors. Zoe, would you see if you can find them?'

'And in the meantime,' said Andros, 'perhaps the Kyria Daphne would tell us where she thinks Niko spent the night, since it may well have bearing on what has happened to him. He was missing most of yesterday afternoon, too. While the party of guests were up the valley path.' He managed to make the combination of events sound faintly sinister.

'I don't like to . . .' Daphne looked first at her mother, then at Sophia.

'Oh, hell,' said Frances. 'Why make a song and dance about it? Niko was with me, yesterday afternoon and last night. But that doesn't mean I know anything about why he didn't turn up for breakfast. I expect he has fish of his own to fry. He's the still waters type, if you ask me. Deep. And handsome,' she finished reflectively. 'I hope nothing's happened to him, but I'd have thought he was one could look after himself.'

'Could he have gone to the village?' suggested Daphne.

'Not before breakfast,' Andros told her. 'The door is never opened until after. Ah, here come our guests.'

Zoe had found Jacob Braun in the library, and Mark and Chris in Mark's courtyard, arguing. 'We were trying to decide what to do with ourselves,' explained Mark. 'While we waited for my wife to get back from the treatment area.'

They had none of them been down to the watergate or seen Niko that morning. 'I suppose I just missed him first thing,' said Jacob. 'I went back to my room after I saw you, Daphne, and waited for my breakfast. I've been in the library ever since. That's a very interesting archaeological collection you have, Kyria.' He turned with his usual courtesy to Sophia, contriving somehow to re-establish her as the centre of the enquiry, a position that had been disconcertingly slipping towards Andros.

'Thank you,' she said mechanically. And then, with decision: 'No use standing here talking. Andros, you will organise a search party. Zoe, will you go over to the village, just in case anyone there can throw any light on this? And, in the meantime, may I ask our guests to stay together, in order to make things easier for the searchers?'

'Yes, of course,' said Jacob Braun. 'Why don't we all go in swimming? Unless we can help with the search, Kyria?'

'Better not, I think.'

'As if she'd let him, when he may so easily be involved!' Mark was walking Daphne to her room. 'I told you there was something fishy about that Braun.'

'I'm the one who saw Niko.'

'Emerging from dear Frances' bed. What are we going to do about your mother, love?'

'We aren't going to do anything.' She turned to confront him in the entrance to her courtyard. 'It's over between us, Mark. Please, face it with me.'

'I won't. Daphne, I can't. I need you, don't you see? Can't manage without you. And you need me right back. Don't pretend you didn't enjoy it the other night. Starved, you were. Mad for it.'

'I know. But that's not enough. If I truly loved you, I

might be ready to give up my life to yours, to let you swallow me whole. But I don't. I know that now. Oh, you can make me shiver with a touch, but what does that prove? That I'm female, I suppose. There has to be more to it than that. Anyway, you'd only get bored with me again, and turn to someone else, and that's not the way I want to live. I want my own life, Mark. If I can share it with someone, so much the better, but you're not a sharer. You don't know how.' She stood firm in the entrance to her courtyard, barring the way.

'What's got into you, Daph? You sound different, somehow. Tougher. If I swallowed you, back in Oxford, as you say, it's because you were a pushover. Lying down to be trampled on. Nurse-tending me. A man doesn't want a nurse, he wants a wife. Maybe we've both learned something, here on Temi. Maybe we could start all over again, from the beginning, better. A real team. The best book of all together. This place is crying out to be written up. It would make me a fortune.' He touched her lips lightly with a finger. 'Don't say anything now. Think about it, love, and remember I love you.'

'I'll think, but I won't change. The guards are coming, Mark.' She had been watching them pace slowly round the cloister. 'I'll see you at the pool.'

They were a subdued party. 'It seems wrong to be enjoying ourselves while the Kyria has all this on her hands.' Jacob pulled himself strongly up out of the water to sit on the edge beside Daphne. 'She's suddenly beginning to look almost her age, have you noticed? I wish she would send for the police and hand the whole mess over to them.'

'I think she's afraid the Greek Government might use it as an excuse to take over Temi. She's been having a bit of trouble with them, she says.'

'That figures. But at least she's a Greek citizen. The trouble surely would begin if she wanted to hand Temi on to someone who wasn't. I wonder what their nationality law is like.' He was talking to himself as much as to her. 'But, of course the answer is international status of some kind. This place has such extraordinary potential. You're very quiet today, Daphne.' He turned to fix her with friendly blue eyes. 'Something's happened to you. Something good, I think. What?'

'I took Sophie's patient through the Tholos. I only got what he called the aftershock, but it was extraordinary. I can't describe it. As if I was shaken to pieces and put together again. The way I ought to be.'

'I wouldn't have said there was all that much wrong with you before.'

'Thanks, but there was. I was a terrible mess . . .'

'Oh, I know you've had a bad time, but you were coping; you'd have come out of it soon enough. Just as well you have, though. I think your cousin's going to need your help.'

'Mine?'

'Did you see how Andros was taking over back there? If he does it again, help me get the ball back into the Kyria's hands? I don't entirely trust that Andros.'

'But Hermione was his sister. Niko's his friend.'

'Sure, but he could be using what's happened to them to further his own ends. To work towards a take-over of Temi. Show the Kyria up as unable to cope. There's more to that man than he lets show, Daphne. I've seen him looking at you, once or twice, as if he didn't love you much. Which is understandable enough, in the circumstances. If I were you, I don't think I'd join him in any dark corridors.'

'You're not serious?'

'Never more so. There's violence loose on this island, and I think the Kyria is making a great mistake in taking it so coolly. She's been on her own too long. Power hasn't corrupted her. She's incorruptible. But I think it's made her just a little blind. She's not facing facts. And we're all in danger until this murderer is found. But I'm specially afraid for you, Daphne. I do beg you to be careful. I couldn't bear it if . . .' He paused. 'Daphne, there's something I must tell you . . .'

'No need.' He was going to remind her that he had only picked her up in the first place because of her connection with Temi. Why did she mind this so much?

'But there is,' he began, then broke off with an angry exclamation.

'You're very serious, you two.' Christopher Maitland had slid silently to the edge beside them, now pulled himself up to sit on the other side of Daphne. 'You've not even been in.' He looked with mock disapproval at her dry bikini. 'Come on, I'll race you round the circle.'

'You have to be joking!' But the moment of close communion with Jacob was over. She slid into the water and struck out beside Chris, who had slowed to her pace with an elegant, relaxed breast stroke. When they were at the far side of the pool, he put out a hand to slow her down. 'I need to talk to you, Daphne. Come out for a moment?'

She was glad to. The drastic experience of the Tholos had left her as tired as if she had walked ten miles or climbed a mountain. Hot sun beat down; there was no need of a towel. She settled on the edge beside him, running her fingers through short hair to settle her curls more or less into place. And found the gesture made her think of Sophia.

'It's about the Kyria,' Chris said. 'Your cousin. Daphne, I'm afraid for her. Hermione was bad enough, but now Niko . . . I wish now that I hadn't clammed up on her last night, but I was scared she'd turf me out. And I wouldn't blame her either. I feel a complete worm. I've got to tell you. That day I ran you down, Daphne, at Tingaki. It wasn't an accident. I was paid to do it.'

'Paid?'

'Handsomely. By a woman who wanted to find the way to Temi. She knew you were coming. All I had to do was pick you up, chat you up, get an invitation if I could, at least get an address of sorts. Naturally, I failed all along the line. I'm not much cop, Daphne. Not when the chips are down. And they are now. I can feel it. I'm . . . sensitive. I meant what I said yesterday. With you behind me, I could amount to something, get somewhere. Specially here on Temi. With something to do beyond teaching Dutch girls to windsurf.'

'But your architecture?'

'That's what it's all about!' He turned to her eagerly.
'That's what she said! They were going to make something
of Temi. High grade tourism. Wanted an architect to do
some drawings for them. A chance in a million! You can't
blame me, Daphne. I didn't know then what it was like
here. And all that money, just for helping her find the way.
God, she was angry when you vanished that night. I thought
I'd had it. But I managed to persuade old Madame Whatsit
I was a lovelorn suitor. She took my letter to you. That
was all I had to do.'

Despite the seriousness of what he was telling her,
Daphne could not help a wry smile. 'Not so lovelorn as all
that.'

'Not then. No. That came later. That's what I'm trying
to tell you. Daphne, you and I would be tremendous here,
running Temi . . . The old thing can't last for ever.'

'You were telling me about some threat to my cousin.'
His flippant tone had both alienated her and brought her
back to the matter in hand.

'Yes. That's it. You'll make it all right for me, Daphne,
if I tell you? I only did it for a laugh, and the money. And
the pleasure of your company, of course. And they're
really good, my drawings. How was I to know she was
dangerous? A made-up piece like that? A nothing . . . But
now: Hermione's dead; Niko's gone missing. He was the
one . . .' He stopped. 'If I could only have talked to her;
made her see . . . your cousin's security's too good, Daphne,
or not good enough.' He paused, looked across the pool.
'What's going on?'

Zoe was there, talking eagerly to Mark and Jacob. She
raised her voice. 'Could you two come, please? Quickly.
Niko's body's been found.'

The search party had found it, lodged in the rocks below
the watergate. 'It's a miracle it was found,' Zoe told them.
'If we hadn't searched at once it would have been gone.
The wind scours that channel.'

'Wind?' said Jacob. 'How did he die, Zoe?'

'We don't know yet. The Kyria is examining the body
now.'

'She's sent for the police, I hope,' said Jacob.

'Andros says it's impossible. The wind's getting up, the meltemi. Listen!'

Daphne had been vaguely aware that the quiet of the pool was not so absolute as usual. Now she realised that even here, in this sheltered spot, she could hear the far-off voice of the wind. Looking at the pool, she saw that though the ripples from her and Christopher's swift crossing had died away, vague tremors still troubled the usually quiet surface as if it shivered in sympathy with the rising gale outside.

'The channel's impassable when the wind gets up,' Zoe said.

'How long does it usually blow?' Jacob exchanged an anxious glance with Daphne.

'Three days at least. And another one, sometimes two, for the channel to calm down. Andros says it would be suicide to try to take a boat through now.'

'So we're marooned here with a murderer!' Frances' voice rose as she grabbed Daphne's hand. 'I wish to God I'd never come!'

'The Kyria is sure we will find the murderer now,' Zoe told her. 'She has called a meeting of the elders for this afternoon. They speak for the whole island. She asks you all to stay in your own rooms until then. Except for lunch, of course, in the guests' dining-room as usual.'

'Usual!' Frances' voice was somewhere between a scream and a hiccough. 'Niko's dead! What's usual about anything!' She reached out her other hand to Mark. 'Take me to my room, please, Mark, Daphne. I'm scared!'

Once there, she gave full rein to her hysteria, clutching first Daphne, then Mark, urging them not to leave her alone, convinced that whoever had killed Niko would attack her too. 'He was so pleased with himself,' she told them, between sobs. 'He said there were going to be great changes on this island soon. Give me some brandy, Mark. They're bound to think I know more than I do. Don't leave me, Daphne!' She reached out to the table beside her bed, grabbed a bottle and swallowed a handful of pills, washing

166

them down with brandy. 'Promise you'll stay with me! I might even sleep now.'

'I should rather think so!' Mark picked up the pill bottle as Frances buried her face in her pillow, still unevenly sobbing. 'These and brandy!'

'What are they?'

'Valium of course. The housewife's dangerous friend.' He bent down to pat Frances' shoulder. 'Don't fret. We'll stay with you. Both of us. That's a promise.' He smiled at Daphne. 'She knows I'm family, whatever you pretend.'

'I'm not pretending, Mark.'

Frances' sobs were gradually dying away. He took his hand off her shoulder and she turned into a more comfortable position, relaxing into sleep. 'That didn't take long,' he said. 'I hope she knows her dose.'

Here was a new anxiety. 'Should we get Sophia?'

'She's busy with another body, remember. No, they're the mildest possible. No need to worry. Come out into the yard and tell me what's going on.'

'How should I know?'

'Well, you've been having tête-à-têtes with a couple of the prime suspects. What had they to say for themselves?'

'Jacob and Chris? Do you seriously think they are suspects?'

'Face facts, love. Of course they are. So am I. So are you.'

'Not if Niko and Hermione were killed by the same person.' She was relieved at the turn he had given the conversation.

'Right. Count you out then. Count me out because I know I didn't do it. All the islanders seem to have alibis for Hermione's death, except Sophia, and I suppose we count her out, too.'

'Of course we do.'

'Which leaves us with Jacob and Chris. Do you wonder I ask what they had to say to you? Seriously, Daphne, this is no time to hold anything back. Nor to be bashful, come to that. Anyone can see you're the Kyria's pet. No wonder Andros looks at you so sourly. One can't even blame him, so sure as he must have been of the succession. So, let's take it as read that Jacob and Chris both propositioned you. What I want to know is what else they said. Hang on' – he stood up, poured them both ouzos, handed her hers – 'don't say it's none of my business. I'm your husband, remember. You could say, responsible for you. Or, if you don't want to say that, being in the feminist line right now, heaven help us all, then say I care about you, I'm someone you can trust.' He met her eyes and laughed ruefully. 'Well, in a context of murder, surely, if not in one of sex.'

'O.K.' She had never liked him so much. 'You're quite right. I don't for a minute believe you murdered either Hermione or Niko. If I was asked if you'd made a pass at my mother, I wouldn't be so sure.'

'Of course I did.' Impatiently. 'She expected it, didn't she? But I won't say it wasn't a relief when Niko took over. How many times do I have to tell you that I want you back, Daphne!'

'With your eye on the succession too?'

'Why not?' The old frankness. 'It's a doddle, Daphne. You and I and Temi. We'd be terrific. And the way to earn it is to sort out what's happening. So, what did those two say to you?'

She sipped ouzo, thinking about it. Outside, the wind was rising still, worrying at the vine, whipping loose branches this way and that, sending leaves scudding round the cloister. 'Jacob told me to watch out for Andros,' she said at last. 'He didn't "proposition me" as you charmingly call it. On the contrary.'

'How do you mean?'

'He reminded me, well, he started to . . .' Why was she telling Mark this? But his eager eye held her. 'He picked me up on Kos, you know,' she told him. 'He recognised my luggage labels, knew they meant I was coming here. Told me he had written to Sophia, asking to visit the island, hoped I would speak up for him.'

'And had he?'

'Written? Oh, yes. What I can't remember is whether I

ever told Sophia how he picked me out. By the labels. Could it be important?'

'I don't know. Better tell her, when she stops being the Grand Old Dame and you get a chance. In the meanwhile, that does seem to mean that Braun's not in the succession stakes – at least not through you. Maybe he means to make a direct play for the old lady. I wouldn't put it past him for a moment.'

'I wish you wouldn't.' The old argument.

'Where we came in, eh?' He was enjoying this. 'So – what about Chris Maitland, that dark horse?'

'Funny about him.' She found she wanted to talk about this. 'He told me he was hired to pick me up. Run me down with his windsurfer. He was supposed to keep in touch, find the way to Temi, through me. He said "she" was furious when I disappeared overnight.'

'You're sure he said she?'

'Quite sure. Then he persuaded Madame Costa, who ran the hotel, to forward a letter to me, and apparently that got him off the hook.'

'And an invitation for good measure. So, what was she after, this mystery woman?'

'Planning mass tourism, here on Temi. Well, no, not mass, very high class, Chris said. He hoped to be hired as architect for it. But something had frightened him. Hermione's death; Niko's disappearance. He talked about a threat to Sophia. He wouldn't tell her last night, but he was going to tell me, just now, only Zoe appeared with the news of Niko's death. Oh, my goodness!' She had remembered her father, presumably still waiting for her and Sophia.

'What is it?'

'A message I was supposed to give Sophia. About our patient.'

'It will have to wait, won't it? But that's another mystery. What part does he play in all this? And who is he anyway? I take it it's a man? So not Maitland's mysterious female employer.'

'Oh, no. He was here before I came, for one thing. But

Sophia thinks there is a chance he might have been followed here.' Surely it made sense to tell him this?

'Why?'

'He'd been kidnapped. By a super power. Interrogated . . . Tortured . . . When Sophia's invitation came, they let him go. Sophia thought they might have been using him as a lead to her, but Andros was sure they hadn't been followed.'

'It does keep coming back to Andros, doesn't it?' he said.

'Jacob thinks he's using what's happened to discredit Sophia. It can't be more than that. Hermione was his sister, remember. They were devoted, Sophia says.'

'So maybe Niko killed Hermione and Andros killed him in revenge.'

Suddenly this made sense. 'Sophia told me Hermione developed passions for men, was almost pathologically promiscuous. Andros hated it, she said. That would explain it, Mark!' She thought for a moment. 'But where would Christopher's mysterious female employer fit in?'

'Coincidence?'

'Not very likely, do you think?' She jumped up. 'Silly to be sitting here discussing it without the other two. Keep an eye on my mother, would you, while I fetch them?'

'I'll go.'

'No.' She was suddenly desperate to be off. 'She'd rather have you.' They both knew this to be true. 'Besides, I need to send a message to Sophia about the patient.' She was glad that she had contrived not to tell Mark who he was.

Emerging from the shelter of her mother's courtyard, she found that the murmur of the wind had risen to a roar. A branch from the vine scudded past her. The guards on duty in the courtyard were standing against a pillar, sheltering as best they might from the force of it. She crossed to them, fighting the blast. 'Would one of you take a message to the Kyria for me?' She explained what it was. 'I'm just going to ask the other two guests to join us,' she told them, and wondered for a strange moment whether they had thought of preventing her, might actually not have let Mark past.

The wind blew her down the other side of the cloister and

she fetched up, laughing and exhilarated, in the entrance to Christopher's courtyard. 'Chris? Are you there? May I come in?'

No answer. She raised her voice against the howl of the gale. Still no answer. Perhaps he was with Jacob, but better make sure. She stepped round the screening vine and stopped, horror-struck. Chris was collapsed against the table, his chair pushed back as if he had tried to rise, and failed. An ouzo bottle, water, two glasses on the table, one of them overturned. Two glasses. Did something stir in the comparative darkness of the bedroom? She crossed the courtyard swiftly, and as she passed him Christopher fell from chair to floor and lay still.

A body. Poor, golden Chris. But Jacob, lying just inside the bedroom, had a thread of life in him. He had been very sick, she saw without disgust, as she knelt beside him. A hint of a pulse. Eyes flickered open in the grey face. 'Daphne!' he whispered. 'Thank God. But, take care . . .'

She was back at the entrance to the courtyard, shouting to the guard on duty. 'Quick! Fetch the Kyria! Tell her it's life and death.'

The other man had not returned from his errand. She saw this one debate with himself whether to obey her and leave his post. 'Quick!' she said again, imperatively. And was obeyed.

Back to Jacob. His breathing so difficult . . . Get his head up, on her knees, surely this must be right? 'Jacob?' Leaning over him, beseeching him. 'Can you hear me?'

'Poison,' he just managed to form the words. 'Poor Chris . . .' The blue eyes opened again for an instant, cloudy, remote, then closed, but she felt his head settle, as if at home, on her knee.

How long? Five minutes? An eternity. Sophia in the courtyard: 'What happened?' She bent to touch Christopher's body, came over to Daphne and put a hand on Jacob's forehead.

'Poison, he says.'

'He spoke? Good. And he's been sick; it may have saved him, but we'll make sure.' She gave swift instructions to the guard who stood appalled in the entrance to the courtyard. 'Help me to get him on to the bed, Daphne. Nothing we can do for poor Maitland. He can wait. I'm a murderess, Daphne.'

'No!' A quick, relieved glance showed her the courtyard empty. 'You mustn't say such things, Sophia. They might be misunderstood.'

'Yes.' Dully. 'But would it matter? I've killed all three of them, Daphne, as surely as if I'd pointed the gun.'

'But there was no gun!' Jacob was heavier than she expected, and it was a relief to lower him carefully on to Christopher's tidy bed. 'No time for that now.' Was she actually afraid Sophia was going to break down? 'We have to save Jacob. Come in!' The guard was back, with Sophia's assistant, and the stomach pump.

A desperate half-hour later, Jacob opened his eyes at last. 'What a fool,' and then, to Daphne, with an attempt at a smile. 'I thought it was you. Thanks!'

'Do you remember?' Sophia was taking his pulse.

'What happened? Yes and no.' Speech came with difficulty still. 'We came back from the pool together, Chris and I. Poor Chris?' It was a question.

'I'm afraid so.' Daphne answered it.

'My fault. So stupid . . . Should have spotted it sooner. He was drinking faster than me. Well, he did. Talking nineteen to the dozen. A very frightened man. And right to be! He was hired to run you down, Daphne. Find the way here.'

'I know. He told me. Some woman representing a tourist business. Look!' A folder on the table by the bed was full of neat architect's drawings. A cruise ship moored at a modified watergate. A band playing in the centre of the guests' circle. The village street with tourist shops. 'Disgusting!' She turned to Sophia. 'But he did say he saw it was a horrible idea when he got here, poor Chris.'

'There has to be more to it than that.' Jacob sounded exhausted, drained. 'Chris was terrified. By Hermione's death. And Niko's. Of the woman. Had got deeper in than he bargained for. He was just beginning to tell me when he passed out. Between one word and the next. I'm not entirely a fool. I put my fingers down my throat; quick. Terrible mess. Sorry . . .' He was falling asleep.

'The best thing for him,' said Sophia. 'He's tough. Bit of luck he'll be all right when he wakes. Did Chris tell you any more, Daphne?'

'No. We were interrupted. But Jacob's right; Chris was terribly frightened, Sophia.'

'Right to be. The poison must have been meant for him. It was in his bottle of ouzo.' The yard had been tidied while they were working desperately on Jacob inside. 'We've got to clear this up, Daphne, before anything else happens. Let's go back to the beginning. Tell me everything you remember about your first encounter with Chris Maitland.' She pulled two chairs into the most sheltered corner of the courtyard. 'No one can possibly hear us against this wind.'

'We're really cut off?'

'Yes, and I'm glad of it. We must solve this ourselves. Niko didn't drown. He was killed by a blow on the back of the head; dead when he went into the water. It was the most amazing chance that his body was caught on those rocks. Whoever killed him must have been sure it would be dismissed as an accident.' She ran a hand through her hair. 'I've got guards – pairs of them – all through the sanctuary. Mark's with your mother?'

'Yes. What about my father, Sophia. Did you get my message?'

'Zoe's with him. And a tape recorder. It's wonderful if he has really remembered, but the murders come first. So, tell me about meeting Chris Maitland. It does seem that everything starts there.'

Telling the story of her rash plunge into the sea and its consequences, Daphne remembered one thing that had not struck her before. 'I saw a girl on the beach there at Tingaki who had sat next to me on the plane. Pam Slaughter, her name was. She'd tried quite hard to make friends, wanted to hitch a ride in my taxi.'

'The mystery woman? What was she like?'

'I wouldn't think so. Ordinary. Well,' she actually found

herself smiling, 'purple hair and talked about boy friends.'

'Easy to put on an act like that.'

'Yes. She knew where I was staying. Something she said at the airport. I thought she must have read my labels.' And this reminded her of something else. Something she had been purposely forgetting? 'Sophia! Did I tell you that Jacob Braun said he spotted me by my red luggage labels?'

'No. Did he? And if he did, you mean, someone else could have?'

'Yes. And there's more. I thought I recognised a man on the plane, that I'd seen him before somewhere. My memory's been so awful!'

'But you're better,' Sophia smiled at her. 'I'd noticed that.'

'Father took me through the Tholos; not right through; just holding on to him. Round the edge.'

'Drastic,' said Sophia. 'I wouldn't have chanced it, but here you are! So now you understand why we must save Temi at all costs. This man you saw on the plane. Have you seen him again anywhere?'

'No. Did my father have red labels when he came?'

'All my guests do. It speeds them through the formalities. So anyone could have been followed. Your father by his torturers; you, because of the connection with me. Time I retired, Daphne, that's one thing certain. How glad I am you are here. You'll do it for me, won't you?'

'I? Sophia, you can't mean —'

'I most certainly can. And I'm not the only one either. Zoe and Anastasia spoke to me after the meeting yesterday. They didn't say much, but it was enough.' Her smile was wry, self-mocking. 'I think they had seen my reason for inviting you almost before I did myself. One doesn't feel oneself growing old, Daphne. Only sees it in the faces of other people; in the way they treat one. I was slow . . . Andros had to help me quiet the crowd this afternoon. You make me realise what a fool I have been about those labels. I've laid Temi open to this trouble. I shall clear it up and then, at leisure, slowly and carefully, I will hand over to you. You'll cherish my island for me, won't you?'

'If you'll help me. I shall need so much ... I'm not a doctor, Sophia, I've got no training of any kind ...'

'I'll be your doctor, while I can. That would make me very happy. We'll look about for a replacement I can train. And I'm rather hoping your father will decide to stay with us.'

'But what about Andros? And, Sophia, can you just hand over to me? It's kind of Anastasia and Zoe, but what about the others?'

'You're quite right. I'm jumping ahead of myself again. The island is mine; I can leave it as I will, but by the terms of the contract with the First Comers, the elders have the right to vote for my successor. Naturally my recommendation will carry a good deal of weight. Do you think you could imagine working with Andros, Daphne? That would be an ideal arrangement.'

Every instinct cried no. 'Sophia, I don't know. Anyway, there'll be time to think about that. You're going to be mistress of Temi for a long while yet. If I can just help you a little, I'll be wonderfully happy. Working with you. Sophia, I can't tell you what this means to me. That you should want me; trust me. And Zoe and Anastasia, too. I'll try and live up to it.'

'I know you will. But first we must clear up these murders. Think hard, Daphne. Is there anything else, anything at all about your time on Kos that might have bearing on what's going on?'

She thought about it for a moment. 'Chris wanted to take me back to his room after he dined me at the Coral. But that would be just part of the plot to find out about Temi.'

'I'm glad you didn't go.'

'So'm I. But, Sophia, I've been a fool just the same. I let Mark come to my room. I could be pregnant.'

'Dear me.' Mildly. 'I must confess I rather hope you're not. I note you put it in the past tense. We don't have to think of Mark as a possible partner on Temi?'

'No, but, Sophia, I'm sure that's what he's thinking of.'

To her delighted surprise, Sophia threw back her head

and roared with laughter. 'Everyone thinking about the succession except me! I take it that's what poor Chris had in mind, with that odd proposal of his.'

'I'm afraid so.' She looked down at Jacob. 'At least he never pretended. It was always just the island with him. Sophia, do you think Mark could have found out about you, about Temi? Way back? That that was why he suddenly wanted to marry me?'

Sophia reached out a loving hand to touch her. 'I'm afraid it is a possibility. I think all our troubles probably stem from a rumour that got out about Temi two years or so ago. My fault. I let an archaeologist come, with promises of deepest secrecy. He went back promising eternal silence and was invited to a very good dinner at All Souls. Never forget, when you're running Temi, that when it comes to gossip men are quite as bad as women.'

'And Mark heard? Of course he would have. That's one in the eye for me. It makes his affair with Anne seem quite insignificant somehow. Oh dear, I do hope I'm not pregnant.'

'We'll cross that bridge if we come to it. Mind you, we could have a good time, you and I, bringing up a baby. A civilised male? But right now we're wasting time. Thank goodness, this wind has given us some. You'll think me a nervous old fool, but I've been half-afraid of some kind of mass landing. Parachutes, maybe? Don't laugh at me, Daphne.'

'I'm not. Far from it. Father's torturers, you mean? But don't you think it's probably a more domestic affair? Suppose Niko was one of the men Hermione fell for? And Andros found out? No,' she dwindled to a halt. 'It doesn't make sense. Why would Niko kill Hermione?'

'And it would not account for Chris Maitland being poisoned. Besides,' she stood up, 'I trust Andos absolutely. There have to be some absolutes.'

'Jacob doesn't. Trust him.' She nearly added: 'And nor do I.'

'Jacob Braun's a stranger. He wouldn't understand. Besides, how do we know we can trust *him*, Daphne? I like him very much, but what do we know about him? It would have been horribly clever to drop poison in the ouzo and drink just enough to make himself very ill indeed.'

'I don't believe it.' She was surprised at her own vehemence, and it got her a thoughtful look from Sophia.

'No? What do you remember about him on Kos, Daphne? We must consider all the possibilities.'

'Yes. I met him twice. First at the Asklepion. He asked to look at my guide book, told me about recognising the labels, invited me to dinner. I had to stand him up because of Chris hitting me. Then I ran into him outside the Museum and he bought me a Coke. Oh!'

'Yes?' Sophia leaned forward to hear better against the increased howling of the wind.

'I thought he was going to walk me home, but, suddenly, he was in a great hurry, as if he was meeting someone. But who would Jacob have known to meet on Kos?'

'We'd better ask him,' said Sophia. 'When he wakes.' She looked down at him, felt his pulse. 'He's so deep in sleep it's near unconsciousness. You'd better stay with him. Let me know as soon as he wakes. I think I'll postpone my meeting of the elders until he can speak at it.'

13

Jacob slept on. The wind howled outside. Daphne moved her chair a little nearer to the bed and wished she had done first aid. I'll get Sophia to teach me, she thought. And, strangely, felt herself shivering. With cold? With fear? Too much was happening, too fast. Hermione ... Niko ... Chris. Two deaths that might have been dismissed as accidents, one that could only be murder. A murderer panicking?

What was that? She looked up, startled by movement, not noise, and saw Andros standing in the entrance to the courtyard.

'Don't let me disturb him,' his voice was low, just audible against the howling wind. 'Sophia sent me to find out how he is. How soon she can hold her meeting.'

'I don't know. She said to let him sleep. He hasn't moved.' Don't be alone with Andros in dark corridors, Jacob had said. She could hardly be more alone than here, with a half-conscious man for company, and the strong wind at work outside. Something in her wanted to make a dash for it, out to the guards. But that would be to leave Jacob, helpless, alone with Andros. Was she crazy? Imagining things? Anyway, no chance of flight. Andros was squarely between her and the cloister. Sophia had sent him. Hold on to that. There must be some absolutes, Sophia had said. And that Andros was one of hers.

He moved a little nearer, looming over her. 'I've been wanting a chance to talk to you, Kyria Daphne. There are things we should discuss, you and I.'

'Oh?' If Sophia had sent him with a question, surely she would expect him back with the answer? 'Shouldn't you let the Kyria know?'

'About the meeting? Time enough for that. I told her I had other things to see to. Niko's a great loss. Do you realise I am now the only person who knows the secret channel? It's a grave responsibility.'

'I should think so.' Was it also, in some curious way, a threat? 'But I gather the question's academic for a few days.'

'Academic?' For a moment the phrase baffled him, and she had a cold feeling that this made him angry. 'Oh – you mean the wind? Yes, we're cut off here for the moment. Time to settle various things.'

'The murders?' She was beginning to be very much afraid.

'Nothing to settle there. It's too clear, surely; a late lesson to the Kyria against inviting strangers. Obviously Braun and Maitland were in it together. My poor sister: I don't know what she spotted, we probably never will. She and Niko . . . I had hoped they would marry in the end. Of course he would try to avenge her. Unless Braun confesses, I don't suppose we will ever know whether he or Maitland killed him. Braun probably, since now he's killed Maitland. Ingenious to poison himself, too. And mad of the Kyria to risk leaving you to guard him. I came as soon as I could.' A quick glance at Jacob, motionless on the bed. 'He looks harmless enough, but poison's a dirty weapon. Kyria Daphne,' he leaned nearer to her and she would not let herself recoil from the powerful smell of garlic, and raki, and man. 'It is about your cousin we have to talk, about the Kyria. She really is your cousin?'

'Why, yes. That's why she invited me here.'

'And your father's, too. Our mysterious guest. So he has first claim.'

'Claim?'

'To Temi. We are a law-abiding race, we Greeks. We were the first law-givers, after all. We recognise the claim of blood. But in your father's case, he is too old, a broken man. It would be to let weakness succeed weakness.'

'You call the Kyria weak?' Anger battled with fear.

'Shall we say she has not been very wise? I warned her how it would be; that it was opening the door to everything we had feared, but she would not listen. Now, she must pay the price.'

'What do you mean?'

'You can't think we haven't discussed it all, we Temiotes? It's our island, our life that she is playing games with. We'd planned to be good to her, let her have her day out . . . We could still do that if you would help us, Kyria Daphne.'

'How?'

'One of two ways. The choice is yours.'

'Thank you.'

He inclined his head gravely, quite missing the irony of her tone. 'We respect you, Kyria Daphne. It is not everyone comes out unscathed from the Tholos. And we wish to respect the Kyria's wishes, so far as is possible. So — Temi is to be ruled by a man and a woman, as it was when the Kyrie David was alive. That was a man. No problems then. But since she has been alone, the Kyria has grown strange . . . self-willed, giving way to instinct instead of reason. Just like a woman. It's time for her to go. Would your mother take her back to live with her?'

'My mother?' The thought was fantastic.

'No? Your father then, perhaps. But that's not important; it's the succession that matters. We had thought, in line with her wishes, that Anastasia and I, or Zoe and I . . . But you would be better, Kyria Daphne. Everyone would accept you.'

'As what?'

'My partner. My wife, if you like.' Nothing changed in his grave, cool regard.

'And the alternative?'

'Obvious, surely? That you renounce all claim to Temi, and leave as soon as the channel is passable.'

'I'd need time to think.'

'There is no time. You must see that.' He stood there, stocky, menacing. 'I think you have given me your answer, Kyria Daphne. If you are not with us, you are against us.'

'But who is "us"? How do I know you speak for all the island?' She did not dare to tell him that she knew he did not speak for the women.

180

'Insolence!' She thought for a moment that he would strike her. And the fact that he withheld his hand was somehow even more frightening. An unmarked body? Another 'accident'? She shrank back and knew it was convincing.

'If I said yes?' Her voice trembled genuinely enough. 'What would it imply? And how could you trust me?'

'You'd give me proof.' Had he expected the weak woman to waver? 'Double proof.'

'Yes?' She tried to make it sound eager, willing.

He put out a deliberate hand, pulled the tunic from her shoulder, took hard hold of her left breast. 'Two easy things. You help me dispose of the murderer in there, and then . . .' His hand, vicious on her nipple, finished the sentence.

First throwing Jacob's body out of bed to make room? She swallowed hysterical laughter. No time for that. If she did not convince him that she had given in, he would kill both her and Jacob. Maybe would anyway? Would no one come? No reason why they should, not at this time of day. She was on her own, with no time, not even time to think. And no hope that the guards in the cloister would hear a scream against the roar of the wind. No hope at all?

She had one strength; his conviction of her weakness. She drooped against his savage hand, looked up at him, trembling. And that was real enough. 'How?' she asked. 'How would we get rid of him? Sophia would be bound to suspect, and then what would happen to our claim?'

The clever, casual 'our' convinced him. 'No problem.' He picked up a cushion, handed it to her. 'An accidental smothering. You'll do it.' It was hardly even a command. Sure of her now, he turned away for a quick glance towards the cloister. She seized the moment to look at Jacob, still as ever on the bed, but now, she knew, instinctively, beyond doubt, awake, listening, waiting. Understanding? Yes, she was sure of that, too.

Weapons? The cushion; the fact that Andros thought her negligible, Jacob helpless. And a water carafe on the table by the bed.

181

'Hurry!' Andros pushed her roughly forward.

'How?' she whispered, aware of coiled tension in Jacob.

'Idiot!' As Andros took his eyes off Jacob to spit it at her, she screamed, threw the cushion in his face, and went for his eyes. Jacob, coming up off the bed in one movement, had him round the middle; they rolled savagely on the floor, all three of them, punching, jabbing, kicking. Jacob must be weak as a child. What hope for them? Not much, unless she stopped behaving like a savage and used her head. Inevitably, Andros was concentrating on Jacob. She managed to disengage herself, reached for the carafe, seized her chance as Andros got his hands round Jacob's throat.

She hit as hard as she could, horribly hoping that the bottle would break on Andros' head, but it did not, and though he was shaken he was not stunned. She raised the bottle to hit him again and her hand was caught and held from behind.

'Stop it. All of you.' Sophia's voice, ice cold. And then, to the guards behind her. 'Tie their hands.'

'All of them?'

'Of course. Bring them to the lecture room. The elders are waiting there. We will finish this thing here and now. It's lucky I came myself or I would never have believed this. Are you badly hurt, Andros?'

'It's nothing!' He had staggered to his feet, held out his hands for the guards to tie. 'If they hadn't taken me by surprise . . . Forgive me for failing you, Kyria.'

'But, Sophia –' Daphne began.

'No.' Implacable. 'Not now. Later, you shall have your chance to speak. In front of the elders. It shall not be said that I listened to you alone, favoured my own kin. I saw you with my own eyes! Trying to kill him. How shall I bear it? I had such hopes of you.' She turned solicitously to Andros. 'I wouldn't believe you, old friend. I'm paid for it now.'

'Hush.' Jacob put a restraining hand on Daphne's. 'Not now.' He too held out his hands to be tied.

'But you can hardly walk.'

'I'll manage.' He looked from her to Andros, who was

making a business of being helped by Sophia and the guard who had tied him.

'Hurry up, you two,' said the other guard, Petros. 'Don't imagine you can make a bolt for it.' He sounded nervous, and Daphne could hardly blame him. 'There's guards all over now.'

'I'm glad to hear it,' said Jacob. 'Don't fret, Daphne. At least we're alive, thanks to you. Lord!' His words were torn from him as they emerged into the windswept cloister. Their balance impaired by their tied hands, they were hard put to it to keep on their feet as they struggled up to the entrance of the treatment area, and Daphne would never have believed she could be so glad to get into its sheltered and shadowy corridors. 'Where are we going?' she asked their guide.

'To the lecture room.' Sophia turned back to answer her. 'And I want no more talk. See to it, Petros.'

'Yes, Kyria.' But he sounded more anxious than ever and Daphne could only be sorry for him.

'Don't worry,' she said. 'We won't.' And got an approving look from Jacob.

Daphne had never been in the lecture room before and was glad when they entered it that the drastic experience in the Tholos had left her proof against claustrophobia. No natural light here. The big room had been carved out of the rock close to the entrance to the Tholos, but the air was pure enough, and a far-off murmur of wind suggested that there must be ventilators somewhere leading to the surface. Otherwise it was intensely quiet. The elders of the village were seated in a loose semi-circle around a central dais, Zoe, the village head man and the Papa in the centre. Three chairs on the dais. Anastasia alone there.

Sophia, entering first, had given swift orders to one of the guards on duty and he was placing three chairs below and to the left of the dais. Andros protested as he was led to one of them and Sophia turned back on her way to join Anastasia on the dais, where the third chair must be for Andros. 'I'm sorry,' she told him. 'We must clear this up publicly before you can join us.'

'Charming,' said Jacob quietly to Daphne. 'Judge and jury.' And then, to Petros. 'Would you move our chairs a bit? I don't much fancy being so close to Andros.'

'Very good, kyrie.' As Petros moved their chairs, Daphne wondered if he was not wavering towards their side. It was the first moment of hope she had had. Glances at the seated group of elders showed her that the Papa looked immensely pleased with himself, the head man frightened, Anastasia and Zoe anxious, and the other elders grave and preoccupied. Inevitable to suspect the strangers, be glad to have them found guilty. She had been hoping more than she had quite realised that her father would be present, but neither he, Mark nor her mother were there and she supposed this was logical enough at a meeting of the elders of Temi. But on the other hand . . .

Jacob must have been thinking along the same lines. He stood up as Sophia reached the central seat on the dais. 'Kyria!' She turned angrily to face him, but he went on quietly. 'This looks more like a trial than a meeting. May we not therefore reasonably ask that our fellow guests on the island also be present?'

'I second that.' Anastasia rose from her chair beside Sophia. 'This is no ordinary island meeting. We need every scrap of evidence we can get. I move that our guests be present as non-voting participants.'

A quick show of hands settled this almost unanimously, but Daphne noticed that it was only the hands of a few men that had opposed it. Quickly counting, she saw that the group of elders was composed of equal numbers of men and women – if you counted Andros. For the moment, with him out of action, the women were in the majority. If he had noticed this too, he seemed content to do nothing about it, presumably biding his time.

'He's very sure of himself,' she turned under the cover of a buzz of general talk to say this to Jacob.

'With the Kyria on his side,' Jacob agreed. 'Poor Sophia. Don't blame her, Daphne. Andros is her creation, remember, her child. Ah, here come the others.'

Three seats had been placed opposite where they were

sitting, and now Frances, Mark and Paul were being seated in them. They had been brought round the back of the dais so that there was no chance of their communicating with the three prisoners, but Mark fixed Daphne with an anxious, enquiring look. Frances was busy directing a furious monologue at Paul. Well, no wonder: she had not even known he was alive, still less here on the island. But there would be time for that later, Daphne hoped.

'Don't worry.' Once again Jacob had read her mind. 'Truth will out. That really is a truth universally acknowledged.'

Was it his certainty, or the unexpected quotation from Miss Austen? Anyway, she suddenly felt much better, and, catching Zoe's anxious eye, smiled at her, sure at least that she was an ally.

The hall hushed as Sophia rose to her feet. 'My friends, we are here to enquire into three murders. I beg your absolute attention as I tell you what we know so far. When I have finished, and not till then, I shall ask for your comments and any additional information you may have. If you disagree with anything I say, or have the slightest detail to add, I urge you to tell us. Let it never be said that justice was not done absolutely here on Temi.' Her grave, sad gaze rested on Daphne for a moment. 'Nor that personal considerations were allowed to sway our judgement.'

Daphne met her eyes steadily, but her heart sank. Sophia's very liking for her was against her now. It was Sophia who looked away at last, as she began a succinct and lucid account of what had happened on Temi since Hermione's death. It was being taken down verbatim, Daphne was glad to see, by the girl who acted as Sophia's secretary, and also taped. Justice was indeed to be seen and heard to be done. But how easy, what a relief to everyone, if it should turn out that the strangers were guilty. Hardly knowing she did so, Daphne reached out tied hands towards Jacob's. She received a quick, reassuring touch, and a warning look. They must not seem to be in collusion. It was not a cheering thought.

Sophia had almost finished. 'I left the Kyria Daphne

sitting with Mr. Braun,' she said. 'It never for a moment struck me . . . It was Andros who suggested this might be foolish. I couldn't believe . . . I sent him to make sure all was well. When he didn't return I went myself, taking the two guards from the guests' circle with me. I found Andros on the ground, defending himself as best he could. My cousin had a bottle raised to hit him. I could see her face. She meant to kill. That is all.' She sounded sad, defeated, old.

The Papa rose. 'You have given us the facts of this sad case most scrupulously, Kyria, and we all thank you from our hearts for your fairness. Surely the conclusions to be drawn are as obvious as they are painful? Three of the guests you invited came here, saw Temi and coveted it. Poor Hermione must have heard them plotting together and been killed for it, by either Braun or Maitland. It hardly matters which. Niko threatened them too, and was killed. Then our three criminals fell out among themselves. I can add one piece of information here. Mr. Maitland was overheard making urgent love to the Kyria Daphne, doubtless with an eye to the succession. Perhaps she told Mr. Braun; perhaps he was aware of it. At all events he decided the island would not be big enough for the three of them, and contrived to poison Maitland, taking enough himself, he hoped, to divert suspicion. It is just possible, I suppose, that the Kyria Daphne knew nothing of this, though it must be faced that it was she who contrived to find them in time to save Mr. Braun. And we have the Kyria's reluctantly given evidence that she joined in attacking Andros, would probably have killed him if the Kyria had not intervened. I propose, my friends, that the guilty couple be imprisoned until they can be handed over to the police on Kos, and that our friend Andros be allowed to assume his proper place among us.'

As easy as that? It could not be happening. And yet his argument made an appalling, deceptive sense. It left out so much. But where to begin? Once again, a buzz of talk had broken out and under cover of it Jacob whispered: 'Wait. Better not from us.'

She knew he was right and sat there quiet, sweating. Surely someone must see a hole somewhere in the brilliant, fallacious argument. She looked across the hall and caught her father's eye. But he shook his head, just perceptibly, then turned to Mark who was speaking to him eagerly, urgently. And once again that faint but definite shake of the head. This was no time for any of the strangers to speak.

And now, at last, Anastasia stood up, and Daphne remembered her offer of help that day at the village – how unimaginably long ago it seemed. The hall stilled to hear her. 'This is a sad and serious business,' she began, 'and we must all thank the Kyria for her scrupulous fairness when it concerns someone so close to her as the Kyria Daphne, but should we not also ask ourselves whether just because she is trying to be fair, she is not in fact going too far in the other direction? She is hard on the Kyria Daphne because she loves her. And our Kyria is no fool. I only met the Kyria Daphne once, but from that meeting and from what I have heard of her from Zoe and others I find it very hard indeed to believe that she could be involved in the kind of conspiracy my good friend the Papa suggests. I think this needs very careful weighing indeed. It is true that either Mr. Braun or Mr. Maitland could have got back to the Village Door and killed Hermione, but remember, my friends, that was their first full day on the island. How could she, already, have become a threat to them?'

'That is easily answered.' Once again, the Papa rose ponderously to his feet. 'The Kyria Daphne had been here for more than a week, insinuating herself into our Kyria's good graces, perfecting her plans while she awaited the arrival of her accomplices. I have just learned, with amazement, that the Kyria's mystery patient is in fact the Kyria Daphne's father. What part does he play in this plot?'

'A sinister one.' Andros stood, raising his tied hands for emphasis. 'Let me speak! My sister – my dear Hermione – was sent by the Kyria to take the secret guest for his treatment. What did she learn that roused her suspicions? We will probably never know. But the conspirators must

187

have recognised the threat she posed, and killed her. My poor Hermione. It hardly matters which one of them did it. It is done: my sister is dead, and my friend Niko. I ask justice for their deaths.'

'But not blind justice.' Anastasia broke in. 'There is something I must say. I had hoped, even now, not to have to, but I can see that all the arguments go back to Hermione's death. What I know may have bearing; it may not. Forgive me, Andros. Hermione came to me, a while ago, in great distress. She was pregnant. She was in despair. She would not kill the child, but hoped I would help her to kill herself. I almost wish, now, that I had. But you must see,' her accusing gaze swept the audience, 'that it could have been the father who killed her, someone who was on this island six weeks ago. In that case, the Kyria's friends are completely out of it.'

'She did not tell you the man's name?' Andros stood still, white-faced.

'No. She cried, and would not. And she would not let me tell the Kyria either. She still hoped, I think, in her heart that the father would relent. "He'll take me away," she said. "Before it is too late." And so he may have, but not the way she meant. We need to know who it was. Someone must have seen something, someone with her, here on this small island. So, think hard. Hermione was my good friend, she demands a vengeance.'

'And so do I,' said Andros. 'My name dishonoured.'

'Your sister killed.' Sophia stared at him with white contempt. 'It is all my fault.' She said it quite quietly, but something in her look and tone got her absolute attention. 'It was there so plain for me to see, and I would not. Because you were my son, my adopted child. I loved you, Andros, trusted you. And all the time . . . Poor Hermione. There was something your foster parents said to me, all those years ago. A warning they gave. I never understood. I suppose I didn't want to; but I remember it now. You! Always. Dominating her; slandering her; telling me false tales of her promiscuity; getting her pregnant at last, by accident, when she was growing older. And killing her, when her pregnancy threatened you. We never asked for your alibi, Andros, did we? Her own brother. My dear friend. And, if you killed her, what else have you done? If a sister, why not a friend? And, if Niko, then Mr. Maitland? Daphne, Mr. Braun, I am ashamed. I should have let you speak sooner: give your version of that scene. No, Andros, you will be silent now. Petros, see that he is.'

Daphne met Jacob's eyes for one of their moments of swift communication, then she spoke. 'It was about the succession, I am afraid. He came – Andros – said you'd sent him to see how Jacob was. Mr. Braun. Then – he stayed; said he wanted to talk to me. I was afraid . . . Jacob was so fast asleep. Andros said the islanders had decided it was time for you to retire, Sophia. They wanted to send you away. He suggested you go to my mother. They had thought that he and Zoe or he and Anastasia should succeed, he said, now they had decided it would be better if he and I did. I was to commit myself, prove myself his ally by helping him kill Mr. Braun. But he was conscious, listening . . . We attacked Andros together. That's what you saw, Sophia, and it's no wonder you misunderstood. We were desperate: fighting for our lives.'

'Lies,' shouted Andros. 'Filthy lies! I went there with the Kyria's message; they attacked me, quite unprovoked. As to the other slander, the story about me and my dear sister, what can I say? What must I say? That because our Kyria has been like a mother to me, the mother I lost so young, I have hesitated to admit, even to myself, that her mind was going. Now, my friends, the time has come; we must face it together. She is becoming senile; imagining horrors. An old woman who has been too powerful for too long. We have all known this, I think, in our hearts, and kept quiet because we loved her. We cannot afford to do so any longer. Men of Temi, it is my word against hers. I challenge her to come up to the Lady and repeat her allegations there. When she fails to do so, we will know it is time to choose her successor.'

Hubbub in the hall. Daphne, who had been concentrated on Andros, turned to see why Sophia did not control it and saw with horrified surprise that she was crying. She forgot all about the guards, about Petros behind her. One high, easy step and she was on the dais, her tied hands holding Sophia's as she turned to face the crowd. 'Silence!' She got it, absolute. But how to use it? To give Sophia time? 'Andros speaks of the succession,' she said. 'But the murders must come first. Hermione is dead, and Niko, and Mr. Maitland. I can see no way that their deaths can stem from her pregnancy. You are sure about that?' she asked Anastasia.

'Yes, kyria, quite sure.' Anastasia's quick, firm answer helped to establish Daphne's hold over the crowd.

'And this tale of promiscuity that Andros told my cousin; who can confirm that?' Her questioning gaze travelled among the men in the circle. There was some shuffling, a few whispers; nobody spoke. 'Anastasia, had you heard this story?'

'No. And I find it hard to believe. In our tiny community, how could we not have known? Hermione and Andros lived right on the village street, by the church. They keep – they kept very much to themselves. But there's no way we'd not have known. And there's more to it. Pregnancy is no disgrace, here on Temi. We welcome children. It puzzled me that Hermione minded so much. Now, I understand. Pregnancy is one thing: incest another. No wonder our Kyria is not herself. With your permission, Kyria Daphne, I move that this meeting adjourn, to meet again, perhaps in an hour's time, in the Temple of the Lady. Andros has the right to be heard there.'

'I agree.' Daphne raised her voice against an assenting murmur from the crowd. 'But we must not forget the murders. I move that we three suspects remain under guard for the time being.' A shout of approval from the crowd endorsed this, and she was free at last to turn back to Sophia, aware as she did so that Petros had left Jacob and Andros in charge of two other guards and come rather sheepishly up on to the dais to join her.

'Thanks!' She smiled at him. 'Keep close.' And then: 'Dear Sophia; don't mind so much.'

'I must. My fault. All of it. They were my children, he

and Hermione, and I let myself love him best. I let him fool me, all these years, almost helped him to, it seems to me now. Well: he's right about one thing. I'm for the dark, Daphne. I've always feared old age. Fought it. The dwindling, the slow decay. Now it's begun. I lost control: of them, of myself. So, he's right there, too. It's high time we discussed the succession. And it's going to be a battle, Daphne.'

'It most certainly is.' Daphne smiled at her. 'See! You're better already. Of course it's going to be a battle, and we are going to fight it, you and I, and win.'

14

'I thank God for you, Kyria Daphne.' Zoe joined them on the dais. 'Anastasia and the head man are arranging for the move up to the temple. Forgive me, but perhaps better you and the Kyria do not talk any more?'

'Much better. Thank you, Zoe. Dear Sophia.' Kissing her, she saw the girl who acted as her secretary hovering close by. 'Look after her?'

'I will, Kyria.' Was there a new note in the girl's voice?

'You see!' Zoe smiled as she bent to untie Daphne's hands. 'It's beginning already. She called you Kyria. But we've a long way to go yet. It's the men who are going to be the problem. Did you hear how Andros appealed to them, back there? We women have had our doubts about Andros for quite a while. Some worrying stories have leaked back from Kos. But not this about poor Hermione. No one dreamed of that. Of course he killed her. He knew what the Kyria would do when she found out. The end of all his chances for Temi. And he still means to fight for it. I wonder whether he can really face the Lady and lie. No one ever has. If he can, I am afraid the men will back him. I hope you're ready to fight for Temi, Kyria Daphne.'

'It's horrible. This violence; this talk of fighting. Against everything Temi stands for.'

'Yes.' Zoe faced it with her. 'But there comes a time when one must stand up for what one believes in. We're counting on you, Kyria.'

'You really think I can do it?'

Zoe smiled at her. 'Anastasia says you are stronger than you know. You've proved it. Quick and strong. You saved the Kyria's life; now Mr. Braun's. And — more important; at the meeting just now. You took over, and they let you.' She looked around, but the hall was full of eagerly talking groups and there was little chance of being over-heard. 'We women want a woman, of course, but there's no chance of Anastasia or me being accepted. It's too soon. Another generation: our children, maybe, will take over from yours, if you've managed things right. But, now, we don't want to stand. Temi is a heavy burden. Could you find someone to share it with you? That would help. It's true that it was better when the Kyrie David was alive. A woman, with a man behind her, working together, support-ing each other.' She paused, looked unhappy. 'Forgive me, not the Kyrie Mark?'

'I know.' Daphne met her eyes squarely. 'I seem to have learned that myself, here on Temi. I don't quite know how.' Did Zoe know she had let Mark push her into bed? Probably.

'No matter how.' Zoe's look held almost more under-standing than she could bear. 'You've learned it. And you've faced both the Lady and the Tholos. You must be on very good terms with yourself. That's why we want you. Who is good to herself, is good for others. We need your strength, Kyria Daphne. Things are not going to be easy, here, after all this.'

'You can say that again.' Mark joined them. 'It's going to be quite a job, Daphne love, but we'll manage, don't doubt it for a moment. Come on, it's time to get going. I can't wait to see this Lady who seems to put the fear of God into everyone.' He took her arm as if he owned her. 'I like your father, Daphne. That's quite a guy. Why on earth didn't you tell me about him? As for Braun, what the hell was he doing playing possum all that time while Andros was bullying you? Scared for his skin, I suppose. It would figure; they do tend to take good care of themselves.'

She pulled her arm free. 'I didn't exactly hear you speak-ing up in my defence.'

'I've got some sense, love. Much better let the natives sort it out for themselves, which they were bound to do. Your old lady's not stupid, just a bit past it.'

'I hope I'm half the person she is, when I'm her age.' His

casual dismissal of Sophia had severed her last tie to him. She turned away: 'Come on, Zoe, let's go.'

'Daphne, I must talk to you.' Jacob caught up with Zoe and Daphne outside the great gates of the Tholos area. 'There's something I have to tell you, before . . .'

'Everything comes out.' She managed a smile. 'Don't worry. I know, Jacob. You told me, right from the start. Sophia knows, too. About your recognising her labels; picking me up on purpose. It's to her you need to explain.'

'But that's not the half of it. Oh, hell!' The oath, rare for him, acknowledged the appearance of Frances, hurrying to catch up.

'Monstrous!' Frances was really angry this time. 'You knew Paul was here, Daphne, and didn't choose to tell me? My own husband.'

'Ex husband,' said Daphne. 'How many years, mother?'

'Abandoned! Bringing you up by the sweat of my brow. While he jaunted about the world with this great invention of his. Making a mint, I've no doubt. Did he ever offer to share it? To help out with you? Not likely! And now he thinks he can walk back and take you over again, cool as you please. I count on you to tell him where he gets off, Daph.'

'There's a murder investigation going on right now.' Daphne was glad to see the upper doors looming ahead. 'And father has been tortured almost out of his mind for his invention. Would you have wanted to share that?'

Sophia, Anastasia and the other elders had reached the huge doors now and they swung open on to light and the far-off roar of the wind. Emerging in her turn, Daphne was relieved to find that the valley of the temples was sheltered from the main blast of the meltemi. 'Yes.' Zoe confirmed this. 'I'm sure it was one of the reasons this place became so sacred. That and the Tholos. You'll have understood by now how exhausting the wind is when it comes. How glad one is of shelter.'

'I'll say. But, Zoe,' Daphne had remembered something. 'What about the channel? Andros told me he was the only person who knew it now Niko's dead.'

'That's what he thinks,' said Zoe. 'Anastasia and I thought of that, a while ago. We both managed several trips to Kos and took careful, surreptitious notes. It might take us some time; we'd have to go dead slow; but we could do it.'

'And so could I,' said Jacob Braun. 'I worked at it, too, on the way here. A secret's always a challenge, isn't it? And I have the kind of memory that rises to that.'

'That's good.' Zoe gave him a quick, considering look. 'You're full of surprises, Kyrie Braun.'

'I don't want to be.' He spoke to Daphne. 'I want to explain . . .'

'No time.' Sophia had mounted the plinth of the great statue of the Lady and was waiting while the group of elders settled on the steps below. Andros had found himself a perch on a fallen pillar a little to one side, his two guards below him, and was waiting, like Sophia, for the moment to speak.

The murmur of voices stilled, and Daphne was aware again of the muted roar of the wind from outside this sheltered valley. Here was peace, she thought, meeting the eyes of the Lady, peace and the place of reason. Which must be fought for. How strange. She met Sophia's eyes now, and exchanged a smile with her, relieved to see that she had herself well in hand again.

'My friends.' Sophia's clear voice rose at last above the distant bass of the wind. 'We have come here to give Andros his right to speak in front of the Lady. Do you still declare yourself innocent of your sister's death, Andros?'

He threw back his head and spoke even louder than she had. 'I have a terrible story to tell,' he began. 'One that affects us all nearly; one of treason and treachery. All of them the result of your weak rule, Kyria Sophia. Niko's treason; Niko's treachery. Yes, I confess it; I killed my friend Niko when I understood at last what he was trying to do to our island, to Temi. He was seduced, on Kos, by a woman who told him she knew all about Temi — God knows how, through the Kyria Daphne perhaps. She told him she had great plans for our island as a place of inter-

195

national tourism. She had hired Mr. Maitland to do the designs; those who helped her would win places on the board of directors. The Kyria Sophia would be sent packing, but otherwise she promised there would be no change in the traditions, the atmosphere of Temi. That would be part of its quality for tourism, she said. My friends,' he turned away from Sophia and the statue to address the elders direct. 'I confess it to you. I listened, at first, to find out the full extent of this plot against everything we hold dear. Then, I was tempted. She spoke, Niko said, this woman, of a new life, here on Temi. Of true equality, of luxury for all, not just for the guests in the sanctuary. All of us earning; all of us sharing. And real democracy again – an end to the petticoat tyranny we have endured.'

'Face the Lady, Andros.' Sophia's implacable voice interrupted him. 'This is no time for political speeches. You are here to tell us of Hermione, of the murders. Are they part of the profits to be shared?'

'Niko betrayed me. Would have betrayed us all.' He threw back his head to meet the statue's eyes. 'In my rage, I killed him. Men of Temi, you will understand me. I had to do it to save us all, our way of life, which he threatened by his treachery. Let his blood be the sacrifice for our new beginning. I tell you –' Now he was speaking to the elders again. 'I killed him as a soldier would a wartime enemy. As I killed the enemies of Greece when I was a boy. He was my friend, but I saw that he was trying to exploit the project for his own ends. That was bad enough, but when I realised what he had done to my sister, to Hermione: then, in my wrath, I killed him. Who among you would not have done the same?'

'You are not facing the Lady,' said Sophia. 'And you are not making sense, Andros. Are you trying to tell us that it was Niko who planned all this? Niko, who everyone knows was merely your shadow. You know – we all know – that if Niko had loved Hermione, he could have married her, with our blessing. Niko loved only you, and, by your own admission, you killed him. Now, you will tell us about this woman, and her plans for Temi.'

'No need. I will do so.' A black-clad figure had emerged from behind the statue. 'Nobody move!' Light gleamed on the gun she held pressed against Sophia's side. 'Or I kill your precious Kyria.' And then: 'A fine unconvincing tale, Andros! Were you thinking of double crossing me, too? You certainly took long enough getting them all up here. And where are the others?'

'Dead.'

'Fool!' As she pushed the concealing chador aside to speak more clearly, Daphne saw a wisp of purple hair. Pam Slaughter. She stood for a moment, surveying the horror-struck group of elders, then made her decision. 'Down on your faces, all of you. Or I kill your Kyria. Not you, Andros. This is your last chance. You will tie them up for me.' The gun, jabbing into Sophia's ribs, underlined the threat.

Tie us, then kill us, one by one? The certainty struck cold in Daphne's heart. But, with Sophia's life at stake, how could they not obey?

'Quick!' The order was sharp, close to hysteria. Which made her doubly dangerous. The elders shuffled their feet, looking sideways at each other, then, slowly, heavily, the Papa went down, first to his hands and knees, then on to his face. The head man and one or two other men began to follow suit. Jacob reached out, touched Daphne's hand quickly, telling her something. What? Think: Sophia. She had stood, so far, still as the statue. What would I do, if I were standing there? And, instantly, cold with horror, Daphne knew, and waited with Jacob for the moment to come.

'Down!' A scream now, the gun prodding Sophia's side. Most of the elders were on their faces. Pam's attention shifted for an instant from Sophia to Daphne: 'Down, you, if you want . . .'

'No!' Sophia turned, swift and supple, to grapple for the gun. It barked once as Daphne and Jacob rushed forward to grab Pam's ankles and bring them down from the plinth together. Chaos. Screams. Some of them her own? Pam Slaughter fought like a wild animal, like a mad woman for a few moments, then suddenly collapsed.

It was over. Daphne struggled to her feet. Zoe was bending over Sophia, tears streaming down her cheeks. Paul and two of the guards were binding Andros with the belts of their tunics.

'Best tie the woman, too,' said Jacob. 'She's probably faking.' And then, 'What of the Kyria, Zoe?'

'It's bad,' said Zoe.

'It's enough. Nothing to be done. I'm the doctor. Trust me for that.' Sophia's voice was a thread. 'Do you mind blood, Jacob? Lift me so I can speak to my friends.'

Pam was safely tied. Jacob bent to lift Sophia gently, and Daphne saw the great red stain on the side of her tunic. 'Should I?' His eyes met hers with the question.

'Yes, Jacob,' Sophia's wisp of a voice was firm. 'Let me finish what I have begun.'

'She has the right.' Daphne swallowed tears, turned to the horrified group of elders: 'Come closer. The Kyria wants to speak to you. I am afraid they may be her last words. She gave her life for us all. For Temi. Listen to her.'

Many of the women and some men were crying as they closed in around the base of the statue. 'Quiet now.' Jacob raised a hand and they were silent, leaving only the distant howl of the wind.

'My dear friends.' Sophia's voice was just audible, a painful whisper. 'I have loved you all. Now it is time to say goodbye. To make my will. Do not grieve for me. I have feared old age lately. The long dwindling . . . Now I am spared it. Now I can go in peace. But only if I know that what I have done here on Temi is safe, will last . . . I leave that to you, my good friends. You have seen how it can be threatened. Can I trust you to preserve it? For my sake. For the world's. My own rights in Temi, I leave, before you all, to my dear niece, Daphne Vernon. You must think about the succession . . .' As her voice dwindled a little buzz of talk broke out. The stain on her tunic was spreading. She moved a little in Jacob's arms and Daphne raised a hand for silence and got it, absolute. 'Greek can be so savage to Greek,' Sophia went on a little more strongly. 'I had thought, lately, an outsider . . . Two . . .

198

A woman and a man ... Best? Poor Andros, I had so hoped ...' The words came harder, more slowly now, and the group of elders leaned close, to hear. 'Daphne perhaps? And – I had been wondering ...' She smiled up at Jacob, whispered: 'Maybe Jacob Braun?' Her head fell back against his arm.

'She's gone.' As he bent to look, Daphne wondered if he had taken in her amazing last words. Zoe, weeping uncontrollably, leaned forward to close the staring eyes.

'I protest!' Mark shouted from the back of the shocked crowd. 'I am husband to Kyria Daphne. It is my right –'

'We are not talking of rights.' Anastasia interrupted him coldly. 'We are talking of the great lady we have lost. She gave her life for us, for Temi. We must not be unworthy of her. For tonight, we mourn her. Tomorrow will be time enough to talk of the succession.'

Jacob had laid Sophia's body down gently on the base of the statue. Now he turned to face Anastasia. 'Maybe we can clear up the murders here and now,' he said. 'The woman is recovering. Put her and Andros face to face, and they may talk.' Sophia's blood on his tunic gave him, Daphne thought, an absolute authority.

He proved right. Confronted with Andros, Pam Slaughter broke into a low, vicious stream of obscenities. 'Maitland warned me,' she said at last. 'Back on Kos. Said you and Niko had plans of your own for Temi. What did you do to Maitland? And Niko? I thought he was your friend. You wanted Temi all to yourself, did you, and killed them both? I should have listened to Maitland; he said you would never bring my friends, as you promised.' She looked angrily up at the sky. 'If it had not been for this wind, they would have come to me by parachute. You thought you'd leave me up here to starve, did you? To go mad, by myself with that horrible statue! Then you'd have "found" me, blamed me for everything. Climbed to power over my dead body.'

Andros spat in her face. 'And you! You told me you were bringing tourism to Temi; to make us all rich. And all the time you were planning some filthy take-over, to make it a guerrilla base, or worse. Ah – you didn't think I'd find that out. But your friends aren't as single-minded as you. They got impatient, waiting on Kos, for the summons, found our ouzo too tempting, got drunk and talked. They're in no case to come to you now. A mad plan from start to finish; I should never have let myself be fooled – and by a woman!'

'I would have been all powerful.' She turned suddenly to Daphne. 'Absolute ruler. Properly armed, we'd have dominated this end of the Mediterranean. Named our own terms. And you, milk-and-water miss, what plans have you for Temi?'

'That's for the Temiotes to say.' How very strange. The elders seemed to be waiting for her to speak. She caught Anastasia's eye, looked a question and got a quick, decisive nod. 'Help me, Jacob.' Standing where Sophia had stood, at the knees of the great statue, she looked down for a moment at Sophia's body, so still, so small. There would be time for that. Now, she had a duty to Sophia. 'My friends.' No need to ask for silence. 'You heard what my cousin said. There is no way that it can be legally binding, I would think, but I feel it binding on me. I am at your disposal, if you want me. If not, I will leave as soon as the wind drops and the channel is passable. For now, I suggest that Anastasia and the head man take charge. Surely the first thing to be done is for the prisoners to be locked up safely and my cousin's body . . .' She stopped, choked by tears.

'Perfect.' Jacob helped her down from the plinth. 'Just right. Daphne, we have to talk – hell!'

'Nice work, Daph.' Mark had pushed forward to join them. 'First step to a neat take-over, I'd say. But don't you think it's about time you named me Prince Consort? The sooner the old lady's little misunderstanding is cleared up, the better, surely? The city fathers are talking about a meeting of the whole island tomorrow and they need to know what's what before they get voting.' He reached out a careless, proprietorial arm to pull her to him.

'No, Mark.' She took a step back into the shelter of the statue. 'I told you. It's over between us. Please . . .'

'Over, is it? What makes you so sure?' She had forgotten how ugly he looked when crossed. 'What'll you do if you find you're carrying my child?'

'Bear it, I hope.' Surprisingly, it was Jacob who answered. 'In every sense of the word.' He turned away, leaving both Mark and Daphne momentarily silenced, to greet Paul Vernon. 'Sir! I've been badly wanting to talk to you. I represent . . .'

'In a moment.' Paul took both Daphne's hands. 'Don't mind too much, Daphne. She was a great lady. And her one fear was a slow dying. She told me so just the other day. I'm glad you're going to do as she wishes.'

'If they want me.'

'They'll want you. The head man is a nonentity, Sophia told me, and the Papa scuppered himself when he went down first on his face. I've been watching it all, remember. The women want you, and the men know they are better off independent as they were under Sophia. There will be problems, obviously. Foreigners aren't very popular as landowners in Greece these days. Of course the ideal answer would be some kind of international status for Temi. Now Greece is a member of the Common Market, it should be possible to achieve it. I might even be able to help . . . Yes?' He turned at last to Jacob.

'That's what I was trying to say, sir. I've been looking for you for a long time. I represent a group of international businessmen who have heard about the work you are doing, want to back you. No – it's all right – I know something of what you have been through. You can trust my bosses; they honestly want to help you use your discovery for good. I'm sure, if you were to decide to settle here on Temi, with your daughter, they would help you get international standing for the island. They're – quite powerful. I'm sorry, Daphne. I did try to tell you.'

'Yes, you did.' She was proud of her own level voice. 'I suppose it was one of your bosses you were in such a hurry to meet that day on Kos?' How could she bear the fool she had been?

'Yes. He'll be a great help, when we can get in touch.

With everything. He carries a lot of weight with the Greek Government. Daphne –'

'I wish to God I understood what was going on!' Frances' petulant interruption gave Daphne a chance to fight the seething rage that must not show. 'Will someone kindly explain. What has all this to do with Hermione's death?'

'Everything.' Jacob answered her. 'It was not just because she was pregnant, I am sure, that she was a threat to Andros. I imagine that he deluded himself that when he achieved a take-over here on Temi he would be able to get away with the pregnancy. That may even have been partly why he joined the plot in the first place. No doubt he was fond of her, in his fashion. But she must have got an idea, somehow, of what he was planning. Perhaps he was careless, took her too much for granted . . .'

'I remember now,' said Paul. 'The day she took me to the Tholos, she was terribly unhappy. I could feel it. Something was weighing on her mind. I'm afraid the Tholos probably helped her to make it up, decide she must tell Sophia.'

'There was more to it than that.' Daphne was glad to plunge into this rational discussion. Later, there would be time to face how Jacob had fooled her. Too much time. 'Sophia nearly drowned in the pool,' she went on. 'I thought she had fainted. That's what she said. But Hermione helped rescue her; she was terribly upset. Do you think she may have suspected Andros? Thought he had given Sophia something?'

'He may have done so, come to that,' said Jacob. 'Sophia's death would have smoothed his way to the succession. But whether he did or not, thinking he had must have settled things for Hermione. Decided her to speak. And he killed her before she could. Which panicked the other two. Started everything. I think it was each man for himself after that. With the woman immobilised up here. I take it Andros had got himself keys to all the doors, but I'm sure he didn't give them to the others.'

'No.' Daphne remembered something. 'Sophia and I met Chris Maitland outside the Valley Door the other day. He said he'd been revisiting the scene of Hermione's death, but he must really have been trying to get to Pam Slaughter, to tell her what was going on. Maybe to try to back out.'

'Pam Slaughter?' asked Jacob. 'She is the woman who sat next to you on the plane, isn't she?'

'Yes. It's hard to believe. But she did keep turning up, back on Kos. She was at Tingaki the day Chris ran me down.'

'Putting the finger on you?'

'I suppose so. Poor Chris, I don't suppose he had any idea of what he was getting into.'

'Don't waste too much sympathy on him,' said Jacob. 'He was in it for everything he could get. He just reckoned without Andros, who outplayed him all along the line. And very nearly got away with it. What a gamble, to get us all up here in the hope that the woman – Pam Slaughter, you say? – would create a diversion for him. It nearly worked, too. It was touch and go back there. If Sophia hadn't acted . . . She saved us all, Daphne. She must have died very happy.'

'But she's dead.' Looking up, she saw that while they had been talking the prisoners had been taken away and a little procession of elders had formed up behind Sophia's body, carried by two guards on an improvised stretcher. 'I ought to go with her –'

'No,' said Jacob. 'For tonight, she's theirs, Daphne. Besides, they need to talk it out among themselves. And besides again, you are coming up to the sacred grove to talk to me. Please? I'm sure your father will look after Frances. I expect they have things to talk about, too.' His smile was both amused and apologetic.

'I'll say,' said Frances. 'Come on, Paul. Mark, you'd better come, too. No one ever shifted Daphne once she got that look on her face. I wish you joy of her, Jacob.'

'Thanks! And you, sir?' He turned to Paul.

Surprisingly, almost shockingly, Paul laughed. Then, 'No affair of mine,' he said. 'I lost the right years ago. But I hope you two are going to let me stay on your island.'

'What do you mean, "our island"?' Suddenly, shockingly, Daphne's hard control broke. 'Going a bit fast, aren't you? Nobody's even asked me, let alone Jacob. And, if they did, I'd like to know what makes you think I'd dream of going into any kind of partnership with someone who has been making a fool of me, laughing at me, pulling the wool over my eyes ever since we met? You have to be crazy!'

'Maybe so,' said her father. 'But just the same, I think you'd better go on up to the sacred grove and work out just how to put your apologies to the Temiotes at their meeting tomorrow, when I think the two of you are liable to be unanimously elected to run things together.'

'I'd rather be —' Daphne paused, remembering the reality of Sophia's death. 'Oh, very well.' She turned impatiently to Jacob. 'Let's get it over with.' She walked beside him in steaming silence up to the top where she had sat that first day with Sophia. She stumbled once and was ready to shrug off his steadying hand, but he left her to right herself.

'The wind's dropping, had you noticed?' He sat down at last, a little away from her. 'Petros told me it would. We'll be in touch again in two days. Everything needs to be settled by then. It doesn't give us much time.' The quiet around them was formidable, the distant view blurred before her eyes. 'Try to understand, Daphne.'

'I do; that's the trouble. You were hired to find my father. What I don't see is why you told me all those lies about why you wanted to get to Temi. All that talk about a golden age, and benevolent rule by women! A lot of blarney for passing on to Sophia, I suppose, while you got on with your male chauvinist plans. But why the hell not tell me you were looking for my father? I'd have helped you.'

'No lies, Daphne. And no male chauvinism, either. Everything I said about Temi was absolutely true. But, don't you see, I didn't dare speak about your father. Everything we had heard suggested he was in great danger. And what did I know about you?'

'Nothing.'

'Exactly. You came on to that plane looking as if the furies were after you. I spotted your labels right away, wanted to speak to you, but that girl had you cornered.

No way I could get to you, but I watched you all through the flight. And saw someone else was, too.'

'There really was? I thought I'd imagined it.'

'Oh, no. He was there all right. You're going to have to take great care of your father, Daphne. I'm not sure the wisest thing wouldn't be to make a public announcement that he's cured, his secret public knowledge. I do hope you are going to make an end of the secrecy, here on Temi.'

'You speak as if I had already been elected.' Why was it so disconcerting that he seemed to be leaving himself entirely out of the picture?

'Well, your father's right, you're bound to be. I don't know what the legal position will be about Sophia's public bequest of the island; it depends on the terms on which she held it; but you are so obviously the best person . . . I can promise you that my group of employers will back you to the limit, and that will count for a great deal.'

'But what about you?' Nothing was going as she had expected.

'Me? I don't know. What they pay me for finding your father might even see me through my doctorate.'

'But Sophia named you, too. Everyone seems to think –' She stopped, blushing furiously.

'Oh, that. Don't give it a second thought. Just people jumping to conclusions; nothing for us to worry about. Sophia was very near her end, poor darling, probably didn't know what she was saying. What we do know is that she sent for you, wanted you, and you have proved you can do it. Hang on to that. I don't need to tell you that Temi is richly worth working for, worth saving, do I? Only, Daphne, may I say one thing?'

'Of course you may.' Her heart pounded.

'Stick to your guns about Mark. You'll have your father; he'll stand by you, I'm sure.'

'Yes.' Dully. The future stretched before her, infinitely bleak. Had she really imagined it all, that instant communication between the two of them? Twice, they had read each other's minds, acted in unison. Now, they were poles apart.

Best get it over with. She stood up: 'I suppose I had better advertise.'

'Advertise?'

'Why not? Something like: "Wanted, partner to share in running of small island." I'd think I'd be snowed under with answers, wouldn't you? Specially if I said it was a small Greek island.'

'I don't understand you, Daphne.' He stood too, faced her, blue eyes puzzled. 'Back down there, you blew up at the idea of a partnership, and I don't blame you a bit, I've behaved like a fool. But at least I'm the fool you know. If you'd have me as a partner, let me help you keep Temi the place your wonderful cousin made it, I'd be proud to do it.'

'Would you really? Sophia did seem to think it was a job much better done by a man and a woman.'

'A woman and a man, you mean?' A hint of laughter in his voice now. Then, soberly: 'I talked a lot to Sophia. About what she wanted for Temi. The gentle civilisation; the example. And I'm sure she was right in thinking it needed a woman in charge; a real woman, not an imitation man. I agreed with all of that, it was just on the secrecy that I split with her, as I told you. If you take me on as partner, Daphne, I'd want a firm agreement about that. After all, an example's not much good unless it's publicly visible. And what we want the public to see is you in charge, with me as back-up. Personal assistant, something like that. Moral support. We could think of a name for it.'

'Could we? I couldn't do it alone, Jacob. Everyone keeps calling me strong but I'm not as strong as that. Besides, think of Sophia . . .' She choked down tears, went on. 'As to the secrecy, surely that's going to be settled for us? There's no way it's going to be possible to maintain it when we hand Andros and Pam Slaughter over to the police.'

'Exactly. That's why we must get everything settled, one way or another, at tomorrow's meeting. So — if they ask you, or us, we offer a partnership, right?'

'Right.' Dust and ashes. He was holding out his hand. 'A partnership, then.' Their hands met, spoke, clung. Was she in his arms, or he in hers? They drew apart at last breaking at the same moment into laughter that was close to tears.

'Couple of fools we nearly were.' He held her by the shoulders to look down at her lovingly.

'"Better the fool you know,"' she smiled back at him rather tremulously as she quoted his words. 'I really began to think I'd imagined it all. The instant understanding . . . Or that you were disgusted . . . You don't mind too much about Mark?'

'He's not my favourite person. But it's you, the you now, that I love. I suppose he has to have contributed something to that.'

'Thank you.' She put out a tentative hand to touch his cheek. 'I love you, too. I can't think why it took me so long to realise.'

'Mark,' he said. 'Standing in the way; trying to absorb you. Nearly succeeding, let's face it. Now, I've known all along, since that first day, when you looked so lost on the plane. It's made me behave like an idiot . . . I'd never been in love before: you're the first and only.' He laughed. 'Remember how I infuriated you that day at the Asklepion on Kos?'

'You noticed?'

'I notice everything about you. I was reading your mind, I think, long before you tuned in to mine. That's why I was so shaken when you turned on me, down there in the temple. Switched off, suddenly. We nearly lost each other, Daphne.'

'I know. Frightening.'

'You and your advertisement. Did you say it on purpose?'

'I don't know.'

'And it doesn't matter. We're together now; nothing can touch us. If the islanders decide they want us, fine, we've a future here and I won't be too proud to live on my rich wife.'

'That bothers you?'

'Maybe a little. Stupid. Temi's quite a proposition. We'll earn whatever we get.'

'Perhaps we won't get it. Then what?'

'Then, my darling, we will eke out a frugal living working for my consortium and looking after your father. And very nice, too. But I hope we get Temi. For Sophia's sake, among other reasons.'

'Dear Sophia.' These tears were less painful. 'Do you think she knew?'

'About us? I'm sure she did. Or she wouldn't have named me. Don't cry, my darling. She died splendidly. And lived well. We'll have a job to live up to her.' He held out his hand. 'We are supposed to be walking in the sacred grove, remember?'

She smiled at him. 'You asked me to, that first day on Kos, at the Asklepion.'

'So I did. And you ran away.'

She took the outstretched hand. 'I won't run now.'